PRAISE FOR *TERMINATED*

"Ray Daniel has nailed it. Nailed the story, nailed the writing, nailed the whole clever, original and quirky deal. An authentically riveting thriller, with wit and skill and a voice you can't forget. Terrific."

—HANK PHILLIPPI RYAN, ANTHONY, AGATHA, AND MACAVITY WINNING AUTHOR

"A smart, snappy, suspense-filled entertainment that knows just when to ratchet up the action, just when to turn the plot, just when to twist the knife. And more than that, it's filled with fascinating characters, snarky humor, and some sharp social observations, too. You'll read far into the night and come away with two things: a deep sense of satisfaction and sweaty palms from turning the pages so fast."

—WILLIAM MARTIN, *NEW YORK TIMES* BESTSELLING AUTHOR OF *BACK BAY* AND *THE LINCOLN LETTER*

"Ray Daniel delivers a fast moving and engaging story with fully-blown characters, biting wit, and sparkling dialog. *Terminated* is a terrific debut novel. There is a new kid in town who deserves a wide audience."

—GARY BRAVER, BESTSELLING AND AWARD-WINNING AUTHOR OF *TUNNEL VISION*

"Ray Daniel not only delivers a suspenseful, twisty, action-packed yarn, he's created an everyman hero named Tucker who will linger in the reader's conscious long after the final page is read. A terrific debut for a promising new series."

—STEVE ULFELDER, EDGAR-NOMINATED AUTHOR OF *WOLVERINE BROS. FREIGHT & STORAGE*

"Ray Daniel knows what he writes and has written a winner."

—MIKE COOPER, AWARD-WINNING AUTHOR OF *CLAWBACK*

TERMINATED

TERMINATED

A TUCKER MYSTERY

RAY DANIEL

MIDNIGHT INK
WOODBURY, MINNESOTA

FIRST EDITION
First Printing, 2014

Book design and format by Donna Burch-Brown
Cover images: iStockphoto.com/16410403/©franckreporter
            iStockphoto.com/13537814/©mblea041
Cover design by Ellen Lawson

Midnight Ink, an imprint of Llewellyn Worldwide Ltd.

This is a work of fiction. Names, characters, places, and incidents are either the product of the author's imagination or are used fictitiously, and any resemblance to actual persons living or dead, business establishments, events, or locales is entirely coincidental.

Library of Congress Cataloging-in-Publication Data
Daniel, Ray, 1962–
    Terminated : a Tucker mystery / Ray Daniel. — First edition.
        pages   cm
    ISBN 978-0-7387-4069-0
1. Software engineering—Fiction. 2. Murder—Investigation—Fiction. 3. Mystery fiction. I. Title.
    PS3604.A5255T47 2014
    813'.6—dc23
                                        2014008764

Midnight Ink
Llewellyn Worldwide Ltd.
2143 Wooddale Drive
Woodbury, MN 55125-2989
www.midnightinkbooks.com

Printed in the United States of America

For Jeff and Rachel.
You're the best!

ACKNOWLEDGMENTS

I would list everyone who has helped create *Terminated*, but the list would be longer than the novel. My friends, family, coworkers, and fellow writers have supported me in every way that it's possible to support an author. Thank you all!

When I told my wife Karen that I wanted to be a writer, she thought it was a great idea and continues to think it is a great idea regardless of the challenges. No matter how things went in the writing world, I knew I could come home to a big smile and someone who would say "I know you can do it." Thank you, Karen. I love you!

Thank you to my first writing group: D.C. Harrell, Kristin Janz, Joan Kosmachuk, and Christian Powers. They were the first people to meet Tucker and their insights, comments, and monthly deadline helped me launch my writing career.

Thank you to my second writing group: Sibylle Barrasso, Shelly Dickson Carr, Hans Copek, Judy Copek, Bob Long, Carol Lynn, Wynter Snow, and Paula Steffen for our weekly sessions. You helped Tucker and me find our voices.

Thank you to my agent Eric Ruben at the Ruben Agency and my editor Terri Bischoff at Midnight Ink. Your faith in my abilities and in the Tucker Mysteries mean the world to me.

Janet Rosen, thank you for helping me give Tucker his emotion and humanity.

Thank you Joseph Finder for taking the time to give me advice about my career and about writing. You've helped so many people in the Boston writing scene and I'm grateful to be one of them.

Clair Lamb, thank you for helping me get *Terminated* over the finish line. You are an outstanding editor.

Thanks to Gary Braver, Mike Cooper, William Martin, Tim McIntire, Daniel Palmer, and Steve Ulfelder for reading the early edition of *Terminated* and providing blush-worthy review comments.

Thank you Hallie Ephron for being the little editorial voice in my head that keeps me on the right path.

Hank Phillippi Ryan, I always feel good about where I've been and where I'm going after I talk to you. Thank you for your friendship and support.

Finally, thank you to the members of Mystery Writers of America of New England, Sisters in Crime of New England, and Grub Street. You all make Boston a wonderful place to write. I love Boston and I love writing with you.

SUNDAY

ONE

Morning sex is, in fact, everything it's cracked up to be. The languid sharing of pre-caffeine pleasure, the gentle moaning in a sunlit room, and the natural hormonal cycles of a healthy thirty-three-year-old male combine to create one of life's optimal experiences. Sadly, my chances at living the dream evaporated when my best friend told me that he had figured out how to catch my wife's killer.

I had been standing in the galley kitchen of my shotgun condominium in Boston's South End, sipping orange juice and rallying myself from a night of tequila and unexpected pleasure. I was thinking about Maggie and how she had murmured that I should get back to bed as soon as possible. I sipped my juice and felt my blood sugar rise.

Click and Clack, my hermit crabs, scuttled around on their pink sand. Hermit crabs were the perfect pets. They didn't poop on the rug, they listened well, and they added life to a bachelor apartment. I had wanted to get a pair when I was married, but Carol thought they were gross. She called them cockroaches in mobile homes, which was quite unkind.

Clack was wearing a new shell that I had picked up for him at Revere Beach. He had discarded his original shell, a fluorescent orange monstrosity that some sadist had covered with sparkles.

"You're looking good, my friend," I said to Clack and toasted him with orange juice.

I reached for my BlackBerry. It was locked, so I entered the password and opened the Twitter app. What should I tweet? Oh what a night was too obvious, and Back in the saddle again was too crass. I hit upon it:

It's a beautiful day in the neighborhood.

But then my stomach churned, and I added:

I hate tequila mornings.

I once had been a big Facebook guy, maintaining a group of friends who didn't mind the fact that I only communicated with them in the two or three minutes where I was waiting for software to compile.

I quit Facebook soon after Carol died. The constant messages of condolence and "How are you doing?" felt like an invasion. The barrage of Farmville requests, "Repost this if you care about..." messages, and pictures of cute kittens went from being annoying to painful. I switched to Twitter, where the conversations were short.

I had downed my orange juice and was heading back to bed when the door boomed behind me. It crossed my eyes. I turned and stumbled toward the living room looking for my pants. The door boomed again. I thought about Maggie trying to sleep and said, "Coming!" The booming stopped.

My pants were piled in front of the door, still inside out from when Maggie had torn them off. I righted them, pulled them on, and looked through the peephole, expecting to see a neighbor. Instead, I saw my best friend, Kevin.

I pulled the door open, took a step back, and swept my arm in a *come in* gesture. Then I belched and bolted to the john as my stomach roiled. I stood over the toilet, hands on knees, catching my breath.

Kevin and I had been roommates at MIT. We were an unlikely pair. I was a smart kid from Wellesley, and he was a smart kid from Revere. We worked great together. He put up with my late nights of drinking. I put up with his late nights of studying. We had both slept as late as possible.

Kevin closed the door and followed me. He stood in the small space where my bathroom and bedroom met kitty corner at the end of the apartment. "Good God, Tucker. What happened to you?"

"Tequila."

"You can't drink tequila."

"I can if I'm motivated."

"Sure you can."

Kevin dressed like a banker and exuded the wholesome energy of a guy who had run five miles before breakfast. His skin shone, his eyes were clear, and his spiky cropped hair was perfect. He crossed his arms and looked at me as if I were a puppy tangled in its own leash.

My stomach decided to keep its contents. I stood up and squeezed past Kevin to get back to the kitchenette. I popped open the carton of orange juice and poured myself another glass.

Kevin said, "I will never get used to you doing that."

"Doing what?"

"Drinking orange juice when you're hung over."

"What should I drink?"

"Pepsi. Nice, warm Pepsi."

"That's disgusting." My gut lurched again. I put my hand to my mouth and collected myself.

Kevin said, "You OK?"

"I'm fine. Now scoot. I have to go back to bed."

"Why?"

As if in answer, the door opened and Maggie peeked her head around the corner. She pulled it back when she saw Kevin and said, "Tucker, I need to get to the shower."

I remembered that Maggie's clothes were also in the living room. I took Kevin by the arm and led him to the door. I gave him a little push and said, "Sorry Kev, you've got to go now."

Kevin resisted my push. He said, "We need to talk."

I said, "Fine, we'll talk later. How about dinner?"

"No. We need to talk now. In my office."

"Why can't we talk here?"

"It's official business."

"FBI business?"

"Yeah," said Kevin, and he turned toward the front door.

Apparently Maggie needed more than the shower, because as soon as Kevin's back was turned, she made a naked dash across the two feet that separated the bedroom from the bathroom. She looked great, even at high speed.

I was getting peeved. I opened the door and pulled Kevin into the hallway.

"Can't you see what's going on here?" I asked.

"Of course," said Kevin. "I have excellent observation skills. I'm a trained investigator."

"Dude, you're in the cybercrimes division at the FBI. I don't think it makes you an investigator. You're a hacker with a badge."

"And you're a hacker with a girl," said Kevin.

"Exactly. And when was the last time that happened?"

Kevin closed my apartment door, and we stood on the little landing. He said, "I feel bad, Tucker, I really do. But this is about finding Carol's killer. I have a lead."

Carol and I had worked together at a security software company called MantaSoft. We were both programmers. I ran the project, called Rosetta, and she worked on it. It ended badly.

I said, "Tell me more about this lead."

"I will when we're in my office. I don't want to do this in a hallway."

My thoughts of Maggie and morning sex disappeared, burned off by memories of the impotent rage that had coursed through me when I had found my wife, dead in the kitchen. "You're not screwing with me, right, Kevin? This is real."

"It's a shot. I can't promise anything."

"OK," I said. "Wait for me downstairs. I'll need about ten minutes."

Kevin smiled. "You won't regret it." He turned and trotted down the stairs.

When I entered the apartment, Maggie was sitting in front of the galley kitchen, wearing a towel and sipping orange juice. She asked, "Is he gone?"

"Yup."

Maggie stood and dropped her towel to the floor. I could feel my eyes dilating. Her small breasts stood at attention. Drops of water glistened on her toned legs. She was the best-looking fifty-year-old woman I had ever seen. She walked toward me and pressed herself against my bare chest. Her short, spiky, salt-and-pepper hair tickled my nose. Her fingers ran down my spine as she kissed my nipple and asked, "Shall we go back to bed?"

I hugged her close, feeling the lats and trapezius muscles. If this was what my body would look like when I was in my fifties, I'd be ecstatic. I kissed her on the cheek and stepped back, disengaging myself.

"I'm sorry," I said. "I've got to go. Do you think we'll see each other again?"

Maggie held my face in her hands and said, "You can be sure of it, dear."

TWO

FBI HEADQUARTERS SITS IN a curved building across the street from Government Center, the plaza where Boston fans celebrate Patriot Super Bowl wins. We have duck-boat parades for the Red Sox, Celtics, and Bruins championships. I think all championship trophies should just be renamed "The Boston Cup."

Kevin and I rode up the elevator from the parking garage. We had said nothing on the drive over. I'd asked him about the clue, but he said to wait until we reached his office. Now I had nothing to think about but my hangover.

I said, "I shouldn't be upright. I think I'm gonna puke."

"It's your own fault."

"I could have slept this off. But you had to show up at the crack of dawn."

"Crack of dawn? It was 9:30."

"Exactly."

Kevin's office was a spare government-issue cave. I slumped into a guest chair made of chrome and fake leather. Kevin's desk was made of chrome and fake wood, and held a computer and a picture of his wife and kids. A basketball poster hung from the wall over a wire-mesh wastepaper basket with a little net and a Boston Celtics backboard. The trashcan was about five feet from Kevin's desk. Wads of paper were scattered on the floor around the basket.

I pointed at the wads. "That's just pathetic. I hope you investigate better than you shoot."

Kevin handed me a folder and said, "These are confidential, but they're definitely connected to Carol."

The folder contained pictures of a naked woman in what looked like a hotel room. She was lying on the bed, facing away from me. Duct tape bound her arms and wrists behind her back. More duct tape bound her knees and ankles. The gray tape looked like steel. The pictures gave me an unpleasant sexual jolt.

I closed the folder and said, "Thanks, but no thanks. I can download my own porn."

"That's not porn. Keep looking."

It sure looked like porn. The naked woman faced one way, then another. Closeup pictures, faraway pictures. All the pictures showed the same woman, the same bed, the same duct tape, and the woman lying in the same position. She wasn't moving.

I asked, "Is she dead?"

Kevin said, "Yes."

"Who is she?"

"You don't know?"

I found pictures of the woman's face. Her nose and mouth were covered with tape. She must have suffocated. My stomach rolled. This was sick. After the pictures of her head from the front and back with the tape on it, I came to a picture of her face with the tape removed.

"Holy shit. That's Alice Barton," I said. Alice was a nervous, mousy woman Carol had hired to help her manage the software code on our project. We were supposed to have a hiring freeze, but that didn't stop Carol. She had gone right to Jack Kennings, the CEO, and gotten her requisition approved. That was Carol's way; even the CEO couldn't resist her.

"Alice Barton," I repeated. "Do you know who killed her?"

"Someone at your old office says that maybe you did."

"Who?"

"I can't tell you. It's confidential."

"Someone accuses me of murder and you won't tell me who it was?"

"Well ... I can't."

"This is bullshit," I said. I was pissed off. The police had investigated me for months after Carol was murdered. I didn't want to go back under the microscope.

"It doesn't matter, anyway," said Kevin. "I know you didn't do it."

"How do you know that?"

"Because at the time of death, you were drinking tequila with your lady friend."

How did Kevin know that?

Sherlock Holmes claimed that we solve puzzles by deduction and come to the answer through a linear string of logic. That's crap. You really solve puzzles through a flash of insight. Then you work your way back through the logic so you can explain it to others. After years of debugging software, I was good at generating flashes of insight.

My programmer brain cranked on the Mystery of the Tequila Girl Alibi and came up with the answer. I remembered that I had tweeted last night while Maggie and I were eating dinner and doing shots.

Is it tequila then lime then salt, or the other way around?

"You read my tequila tweet," I said. "You saw that I was in my apartment."

"Yup. I keep telling you to turn off that location feature. It's creepy. The tweet had a map that pointed at your house. And it had a time stamp. So I know where you were at the time of the murder. By the way, who was that woman? I'll need it for my report."

"Maggie."

"And her last name?"

My brain kerchunked. She had never told me her last name.

"I don't know."

"Did she tell you her age?"

"What's that supposed to mean?"

"When she peeked at me from the bedroom, I saw a flash of gray."

I crossed my arms and said, "Your observation skills at work again?"

"It's my superpower."

"Oh, I see. You're Nosy Man, invader of privacy."

"You didn't answer my question."

"I don't know. Fifties, I guess?"

Kevin broke into a wide smile. "You, my friend, are cougar bait!"

"Har. Har."

"Where did you meet her? Water aerobics?"

"I met her at the Thinking Cup. She was having trouble with her computer. And she doesn't do water aerobics. She does yoga. She's in fantastic shape."

"How did she wind up in your bed?"

"Her computer was full of viruses. I offered to make her dinner and re-image her hard drive."

"Is that what they're calling it now?"

"Nice. She brought a bottle of Patrón, and one thing led to another."

"Like I said. Cougar bait."

I stood and started picking up Kevin's wads of paper and putting them into the basket. My brain sloshed each time I grabbed one of Kevin's missed shots. The hangover was winning. I dropped back into my chair and reached for the picture of Alice. She stared up at me from the crime photo. Her dead eyes were asymmetrical—one mostly closed, the other mostly open. Her lip was torn from the tape being pulled off. Or maybe she had torn it trying to breathe.

I closed the folder.

"Did your source say why I would kill Alice?"

"Revenge."

"Why would I want revenge against Alice Barton? I didn't know her."

Kevin picked up the folder. Fiddled with it in his hands. Opened it. Closed it. Looked at me. He said, "I'm just repeating what I heard."

"I understand that. What's the problem?"

"I don't believe it myself," said Kevin. His face flushed.

My stomach was starting to twitch. I'd never seen Kevin like this. "Now you're scaring me. What could be so terrible? Why would I kill Alice?"

Kevin took a deep breath. "Because she stole Carol from you. The person told me that Alice and Carol were lovers."

That was the final drop of poison in my already roiling tequila stomach. I stood up, rushed to Kevin's trashcan, and puked all over his Boston Celtics backboard.

THREE

I SAT ALONE IN Kevin's office as he dealt with his despoiled wastepaper basket. My stomach felt better, but I couldn't get my bearings. I was confused. Carol had been a lesbian?

"You didn't see that one coming, did you, baby?"

I moaned. Carol was sitting at Kevin's desk, wearing her funeral dress.

"Jesus, Carol, not now."

"It seems like as good a time as any."

Carol's legs slid beneath her dress as she crossed them. Whenever she did that, I thought about how those legs had felt under my hand, how my fingers had caressed the strong muscles. She looked as good as the day she died. Her black hair cascaded over her shoulders, and the plum dress draped across her breasts. They were part of a glorious body that I hadn't touched in the last six months of our marriage.

Carol had first appeared to me the week after her funeral. I had decided to sell the house and was looking at the place in the South End. I was checking out the bedroom when she arrived.

"Hello, baby," she said.

I jumped across the empty room.

"What the hell?" I stammered.

"So you're selling our place? How come?" Carol walked over to the window and looked out at the building next door. "This is awfully crowded. Don't you like our house?"

"You mean *your* house," I said.

"Oh, God, not this again."

"You wanted that house. I never liked it. There was too much grass and it was too big."

"It was big so we could have a family," she said. "I didn't want to raise kids in the city."

"Yeah, well, you weren't going to get a family by not sleeping with me."

The Realtor had come back into the room, and Carol vanished. The Realtor asked, "So what do you think?"

"I'll take it."

So I moved to a new place, but Carol kept showing up.

Part of me wanted her to leave me alone. Let me move on. But another part was happy to have her back. It was an uneasy relationship, just like when she had been alive. I didn't know what would get her out of my life, but I knew it had to happen.

"Is it true what Kevin said? Were you having sex with Alice?" I asked.

Carol smiled. "What do you think?"

"I think that if you were having sex with Alice, you could at least have offered me a three-way."

"Don't be gross."

"I'm just saying it would have been a good way to break the news."

14

"If I were having sex with Alice, it would have been your fault. You were enough to put any woman off the whole idea of a penis."

"I don't know about that. Maggie seemed satisfied."

"Don't you trust that woman."

Kevin opened the office door. I glanced at him, and when I looked back at Carol, she was gone. *I really do need to get to a shrink.*

Kevin said, "Were you talking to someone?"

I said, "Do you see someone?"

"No."

"Well, then, there you go. Where's your wastepaper basket?"

"I threw it away. You got orange juice pulp in the wire mesh."

"Sorry about that."

Another agent followed Kevin, filling the small office with his bulk.

Kevin said, "Tucker, this is Agent Miller."

Agent Miller shook my hand and said, "Kevin's told me a lot about you. Call me Bobby."

If you took a bowling ball, taught it to talk, and bought it a custom bowling-ball suit, you'd wind up with Agent Bobby Miller. His bald head reflected the buzzing overhead lights, and his massive chest filled my field of vision.

Bobby said, "Kevin wants me to show you something." He handed me a folder with his meaty hand. "Check these out."

Kevin said, "Unless you're gonna puke again. I'm out of wastepaper baskets."

I ignored Kevin and spread the new folder out on his desk. The folder was full of pictures like the ones of Alice, but with different women. In the top picture, a small blonde with big breasts was on a hotel bed, tied with duct tape and suffocated.

I said, "You've got more of these?"

Bobby said, "Yup."

I pointed to the top picture. "I don't know her."

"You wouldn't. Her name was Courtney Acres. She was a prostitute in San Francisco."

Under Courtney was another picture. Another blonde, big boobs, duct tape.

Bobby said, "Maria Scarborough. Prostitute in Orlando."

Next picture, a different blonde. Next one, another. Bobby had memorized the name and city for each one. I didn't know the women, but I knew the cities: Dallas, San Antonio, Reno. I had been to all of them. They had all hosted the biggest software conference in the security industry: SecureCon.

I asked, "Where is SecureCon this year?"

Bobby turned to Kevin and said, "You were right. He is smart."

Kevin said, "Wicked smaht."

Bobby said, "It's in Boston. All these women were killed by the same guy. We call him the Duct Tape Killer. Good old DTK."

"And you figure that he killed Alice Barton?"

"I'd bet you a dinner at Legal's."

"What's this got to do with me?"

Bobby said, "Nothing. You see that, Kevin? Tucker agrees with me."

Kevin said, "He doesn't agree with you. He doesn't have all the facts yet."

"What facts?" I asked.

Kevin ticked numbers off his fingers. He liked to do that, talk in outline form.

"Fact 1. DTK kills blond prostitutes on Thursday afternoons. This time he killed a brunette engineer on a Saturday night. It breaks the pattern."

Bobby said, "Maybe he just got bored."

"Fact 2. Someone told us that Tucker had killed Alice."

Bobby said, "But you said that was bullshit. You said that guy hated Tucker."

I said, "What guy?"

Bobby and Kevin said together, "Can't tell you."

"This is bullshit."

Bobby said, "Exactly."

"Fact 3," continued Kevin, "The brunette engineer who DTK killed on a Saturday worked with Tucker's wife, Carol."

Bobby said, "That doesn't count. There was no duct tape with his wife, her throat was fucking cut from ear to—"

Kevin and Bobby disappeared, telescoping away into background noise. I was standing in my kitchen again. Carol's corpse lay in the center of a giant bloody graph, the blood having run down the grooves of the kitchen tiles. I couldn't reach her without stepping…

A strong hand gripped my shoulder.

"Tucker, come on back, buddy." It was Kevin.

I said, "I'm OK." But my breath was still coming in shallow gasps.

Bobby picked up the folder and said, "Now you got me saying insensitive shit in front of your friend. I'm done with this. Listen, Mr. Cybercrime, stick to spam and porn, OK? This isn't your strong suit." Bobby shook my hand, "Good to meet you, Tucker." Then he left, slamming the door behind him.

I was still shaky. I stood. "I gotta go, Kevin. I need to get out of here."

Kevin said, "Just stick with me. Just a little longer. You need to know one more thing."

I remained standing. My breath had returned to normal, but the adrenaline in my system had turned to bile. "What could I possibly need to know?"

"Someone's going to sell Rosetta."

"Shit yeah, Kevin. MantaSoft is going to sell it. That's why they paid me to write it."

"I'm talking about the source code. Somebody is going to sell your source code."

Source code is the equivalent of a software manuscript. Once you have the source code, you can create your own versions of the product. You can pirate it, modify it, or hide viruses in it. You have complete control.

I said, "That sucks, Kevin, it really does. But MantaSoft is a security company. They won't lose the source code. On top of it, they fired me. Fuck 'em."

"I'm telling you it's all related. Carol, Alice, you getting fired. It's all related."

"How?"

"I don't know."

And then it struck me.

I said, "You want me to do your job."

Kevin was silent.

I continued, "This is just like in school. You still can't debug."

The world of top software engineers is broken into two camps: designers and debuggers. Designers, like Kevin, are organized architects who can build cathedrals out of information. You ask them for a program that can do email, and they'll give you one that can do email, but that can easily be expanded to do text messaging, Twitter, Facebook, and Google+. They have ordered, logical minds that resonate when they see an elegant solution. But those ordered, logical minds have a weakness: debugging.

Designers, like Kevin, make poor debuggers. They're like Han Solo in *The Empire Strikes Back*, futilely punching the disabled hyperdrive and shouting, "It isn't my fault!" They'll look at a bug a hundred times and tell themselves, "It shouldn't be doing that." On the other hand, I'll look at the same bug once and say, "You subtracted when you should have added." My mind branches into all the alternate realities of the code and jumps to the thing that breaks the software. I'd saved Kevin's ass before when his works of art just didn't work.

Now Kevin was trying to get me to do that for him with Alice's murder. He couldn't put the pieces together, and he wanted me to help.

I said, "This has nothing to do with Carol, does it?"

Kevin said, "Of course it does."

"You just wanted me to get all worked up so I could figure it out for you."

Kevin studied his shoes. "I need your help."

He looked pathetic. I wasn't happy to hear myself say, "What can I do?"

"So you'll help?"

"It depends," I said. "What do you need?"

"Like I said, it's damn strange that you were fired the same day that Carol was killed. And it's damn strange that the DTK killed someone on your project on a Saturday night. I think that you getting fired is a key here. I want you to find out why you were fired."

"And how do I do that?"

"You ask Nate Russo. He still works at MantaSoft."

That wasn't going to happen.

19

"I'm sorry, dude, but I'm done here. I'm not talking to Nate. I hate Nate. I'm going home." I headed for the door. At the door I stopped and said, "The guy was like a—forget it."

Kevin called after me, as I strode down the hall and out of his office, but I ignored him. I wasn't going to talk to that backstabbing son of a bitch Nate Russo.

FOUR

I STORMED UP TREMONT Street with Government Center on my left and Kevin's office building on my right. My cell phone rang. I looked at the caller ID: Kevin. I sent the call to voicemail. I was going home to enjoy my life as a bachelor.

First, I was going to get food. Later, I would go for a run. I liked to run a few miles along the Charles. It would serve the double duty of keeping me in shape and venting my spleen. That night, I would watch the Red Sox on my HDTV, with a beer in one hand and a slice of pizza in the other.

At Park Street Station, I considered how to get home. I could go underground and take the T, or walk through the Boston Common and Public Garden. But there was no good food on the T, while I could grab a snack if I stayed above ground. I decided to walk home.

The Common was full of people. I strolled through the park and circled the Frog Pond, a big, manmade puddle that cools the city kids in the summer and gives them a place to ice skate in the winter. Since it was a hot summer day, the pond acted as an oasis for young mothers who watched their charges run into the pond and waddle out with expanded diapers.

I walked past the pond and saw a trim redhead crouched in the path, hand-feeding a squirrel. I noted the redhead's legs as they stretched the material of her shorts. I hadn't noticed a woman in months, but my night with Maggie seemed to have changed that. I wondered if this was what healing felt like.

My BlackBerry chirped and I looked at the message. Speak of the Devil. Kevin's text message said, "Call me!" He would have to wait.

The redhead was having trouble getting the squirrel to eat. The animal kept approaching her and veering away, only to come back to look longingly at the peanut in the redhead's hand. She was holding the peanut between thumb and index finger and saying, "Here you go…"

I put words into the squirrel's mouth in a falsetto voice, "Oh God, I want that peanut so bad. But she's big and scary!"

The girl turned and said, "Tell me about it. He's a skittish little thing."

I said, "I think he's worried about the way you're holding the nut. Try resting it in your palm."

She turned her hand palm up and rested the peanut in the center of it. The squirrel approached her, stood on its hind legs, and reached over her fingers to take the morsel. Then it retreated a few feet, sat on its haunches, and ate.

The redhead stood up. She was tall and fit, with small breasts and green eyes that complemented her green sports bra. She said, "You know a lot about squirrels."

"I watch a ton of Animal Planet, but I learned about squirrels while growing up on the streets."

"The streets?"

"Back in the 'hood: Wellesley."

"I see." She smiled and put out her hand. "I'm Jeanette."

I reached out to shake, but was distracted by Carol. She had appeared behind Jeanette. Carol said, "Baby, you have the attention span of a pigeon."

I followed through with the handshake. "Hi, Jeanette. I'm Tucker."

Jeanette pushed a strand of red hair behind her ear and smiled.

At this point, I imagined myself asking Jeanette if she'd like to get coffee over at the Thinking Cup. But Carol wouldn't go away, and I felt inhibited.

The squirrel was bounding back toward us like he was collecting rent. I said, "It looks like your buddy wants another peanut."

Jeanette fished out a peanut as I turned and walked away. Carol fell into stride next to me. I pulled my Bluetooth headset out and snaked it into my ear. If you walk down the street talking to your invisible dead wife, people think you're crazy. However, if you put a Bluetooth headset in your ear, people think you're industrious, even if you are crazy.

I said, "You know, most widowers are allowed to move on with their lives."

Carol said, "You call this moving on?"

"It's a start."

"Don't you even care who killed me?"

"Of course I care. Why don't you tell me?"

"Because it doesn't work that way."

I didn't respond, and we walked together toward the Public Garden. We'd had this conversation before, and it didn't get any better with time.

Carol broke the silence. "Why were you wasting time with Red back there?"

"I wasn't wasting time."

"Oh please."

"What?"

"Kevin gave you a simple task. You should be calling Nate to find out why he fired you."

"I don't want to talk to Nate," I said. Then, "Why do you suppose he fired me?"

Carol's voice took on an edge. "I'm sure I don't know. I was being murdered. Do you ever think of anyone but yourself?"

"Oh for God's sake, not this again."

Carol raised her hands. "Look, I don't want to fight. What did Nate say when he let you go?"

"He said the company was making a change."

"So why didn't you ask him for more specifics?"

"What's the point? He was just going to lapse into that legal bullshit they use to keep you from suing them."

"It's been six months. He should be able to talk freely. Just call him."

"No."

"Fine. Don't call him. What do I care?"

I stopped walking and stood at the edge of the green lawn. A siren wailed as an ambulance trundled down Charles Street and into the maze of Beacon Hill millionaire brownstones. Perhaps it would go through to Mass General; perhaps it would stop at the house of some guy who thought his money would protect him. The ambulance that had pulled up to our house in Wellesley had not bothered with a siren.

Carol stopped walking and turned. I felt the sea breeze slide across the Common, and Carol's hair stirred in response. She said, "What is it?"

"When does this end?" I asked.

"What?"

"This thing we're doing. You popping up, me wearing a headset so I don't look like a lunatic. When does it end? When do we move on?"

Carol stepped toward me. My nose twitched as I strained for a whiff of her perfume. Instead I smelled the ocean. She looked back across the Common, toward the sea, up into the blue sky, then back to me. She said, "I don't know. It's no fun for me either."

"Why don't you just leave?"

"It's not that simple. Call Nate, baby. It's our best shot." I blinked, and she was gone.

Thank God.

I walked across the vast expanse of Boston Common. Originally people had grazed cows and hanged witches in this space. Now they just sunned themselves and threw Frisbees for their dogs. The Common ended at Charles Street. I bought an Italian ice from a vendor, and tweeted:

Just bought an Italian ice from a Pakistani.

The crosswalk at Charles Street was blocked by a knot of tourists who were waiting for the light to change, even though no cars were coming. *This is Boston, folks. You don't need no steenking light.* I stepped through the knot and crossed into the Boston Public Garden, my favorite place in the city.

Frederick Law Olmsted designed the Boston Public Garden before he designed Central Park. It was like every other comparison between Boston and New York. Boston was always first: first public school, first underground train station, first World Series winner, the list goes on and on. New York has had to make up for its embarrassing string of lateness by becoming the most powerful metropolis in the history of the world. It's pathetic.

I wound my way past the flowerbeds, sat next to the Swan Boat lagoon with my back against a tree, and admired the skyline. The John Hancock Tower was blue today, mirroring the perfect sky. In front of it, the red bricks of Back Bay combined with the green of the trees and the splashes of color from the flowers to produce a visual masterpiece. A Swan Boat made the turn around the small island in front of me and paddled across my view, propelled by a college girl in shorts. I dug into my Italian ice.

But I couldn't enjoy it. Kevin wanted to know why Nate had fired me, and so did I. It just made no sense. I had been running a software project for MantaSoft, and it had been going great. We were meeting schedules, people liked working for me, and the product was going to be huge.

It came without warning. One day Nate had called me into his office and fired me. *Sorry, Tucker. We've decided to make a change.* I was stunned. I had stumbled away from him, grabbed my car keys, and driven home.

That was when I found Carol. She was lying on the kitchen floor with her hand at her throat, as if she had been trying to stop the blood that covered the floor. Her legs were at an awkward angle. She must have been thrashing before she died. Her blue eyes were open, and I felt their accusation.

Kevin tells me it wasn't my fault, that there was nothing I could have done. He says that if I had been at home protecting my wife, instead of at work getting fired, I would just have been killed alongside her. Maybe he's right, but maybe I could have done something. Distracted the guy, disarmed him, or sacrificed myself so Carol could get away. Instead, I had stood in a kitchen doorway as the scene seared itself into my brain.

The next months were a blur. I barely remember the funeral, being investigated (Kevin says the husband is always the first suspect), and selling the house. Things happened, but the details were missing. I was just going through the motions of life, doing what had to be done. I had some money stashed away, so I worked out, wandered the city, attended the Sox, and became a hermit right in the middle of a town full of women, parties, and sports.

My Italian ice was sour. I might learn to like the single life, but I hadn't chosen it. Someone had chosen it for me when he broke into my house and slit my wife's throat. I'd tried to ignore that fact, but it gnawed at me and reminded me that I had been helpless in the face of a monster.

I put down the Italian ice and pulled out my cell phone. It was time to call Nate.

FIVE

My dad deserves credit for the way he died. He was on the fifth tee. They tell me that he had just lined up his shot, aiming slightly left and hoping his natural slice would bring him around a dogleg, when he collapsed. By the time his buddies reached him, he was dead, victim of an aneurysm. It was quick and it was painless, an excellent dismount from the apparatus of life.

Dad was an engineer. A real engineer, not a computer engineer. He designed missiles for the U.S. government. He had expected me to follow in his footsteps, to bend iron and mix explosives, to master the physical sciences and build useful machines. He thought software design was basket-weaving with a keyboard. My biggest regret was that he never saw me running the Rosetta project. I'm sure he would have been proud.

I met Nate at the MIT placement center a year after my dad died. I was interviewing for a job with MantaSoft. I came in at the end of the day, the worst possible interview slot. Nate was obviously tired, worn out after a day of dragging answers out of shy engineering students, but we hit it off immediately. His energy increased as we talked about my work at MIT and life as a college hire at MantaSoft. At the end of the interview, Nate asked me if I wanted to get some dinner. My job with MantaSoft was sealed.

For the past ten years, Nate had taken over for my father. He taught me things I could never learn from my mother: how to make a martini, wear a suit, and shake hands ("the webbing of your thumbs have to touch"). He advised me and groomed me. We went out for the beers I never had with my dad. We talked about office politics, the Red Sox, and the best way to make it through life.

He didn't believe in mixing work with romance. He suggested that I *not* start dating Carol, the attractive new girl at work. When I ignored his advice, he got me reservations at the best restaurants. Later, he congratulated me on our engagement and attended our wedding. Two years ago he promoted me to project leader on Rosetta, our secret wonder product.

Rosetta was a decryption system built into a corporate security manager. It would let companies decrypt all the files on their network. Employees would have no way to keep secrets from the all-powerful IT department. We were testing the first working version when Nate called me into his office and fired me.

My brain shut down. I blathered on about the schedule and the task list. I asked him when I could apply for my job again. I started to cry. Nate looked mournful through the meeting. His final kindness was to let me clean my desk without a security escort. I spent my last hour at MantaSoft wandering around the office, looking for Carol. I found her when I got home.

Nate's last act as my surrogate father was to attend Carol's funeral, a mournful bald head in the crowd. We hadn't talked then, and we hadn't talked since. The pain was too great. My finger hesitated over the *N* key on my BlackBerry. Nate was still on speed dial.

Bulling through my misgivings, I pressed the key and held it down. The BlackBerry told me it was connecting. I put my Bluetooth headset in my ear and listened. One ring, two rings, then Nate's voice. "Hi, you've reached Nate Russo. Please leave a message."

The two rings told me that Nate had gotten the call and had pressed ignore. He had shunted me to voicemail.

"Asshole," I said to myself. I put the phone in my pocket and headed for home. I crossed the bridge that spanned the Swan Boat lagoon. The captain I had seen before was paddling her boat under the bridge. I glanced at her, but with no heart in it. Nate had hung up on my call. It was just as well. The relationship was ruptured. Any attempt to put it back together would be awkward and confused. I continued over the bridge.

As I left the Public Garden, a shrill buzzing filled my head. I had left my headset in my ear, and I had a phone call. I looked at the caller ID. It was Nate.

Decision time. If I ignored him, I could stay safe in my little world where I was the victim and Nate had screwed me. If I answered it, I might find out that getting fired was my own damn fault. I might find out that I wasn't so smart, that Nate never really liked me, and that MantaSoft was doing fine in my absence. Then again, I might find out who killed Carol.

I pushed the button and said, "Hi, Nate."

"It's Nate," he said redundantly, obviously having rehearsed his opening line.

Then, nothing. I stood on the corner of Arlington and Boylston, next to an ice cream truck. A kid was tearing the wrapper off a red, white, and blue popsicle shaped like a rocket. A guy with no shirt and tiny yellow shorts ran past, his breath inaudible and his body glistening. A duck boat turned the corner. The headset was silent. Nate and I had said hello. What should we do now?

Nate broke the ice. "I'm glad you called."

"Yeah, well, I was thinking about you."

Another pause. Then he said, "I need help."

"You mean programming help?"

"No, it's way beyond programming. Something horrible has happened. Can you meet me at the Boylston Suites Hotel in an hour?"

"Well, I don't know. I've got a busy day," I lied.

"Tucker, please. Please help me."

Ten minutes ago, I would never have agreed to help Nate or anyone at MantaSoft. That had changed. The "please" made all the difference. Nate's gentleness, his politeness, and his desperation turned me around. I remembered our first dinner together, the weekly mentoring sessions, and even the time he took me fishing.

My feelings for the old man flooded back like water through a dam, but it was dirty water. Nate had stuck a shiv in my heart and broken off the handle. The piece was still floating in there. I wouldn't let Nate do that to me again. I'd be careful this time.

"Sure," I said. "I'll see you in an hour."

SIX

THE BOYLSTON SUITES HOTEL is a monument to Boston's lucky architectural history. The prosperity of the 1960s blew past Boston's dying textile industries. While other cities were making money and dropping down the architectural equivalents of bell-bottom pants, Boston was too broke to build.

The Northeast started making money again in the 1970s, around the time that those other cities were looking at themselves and crying, "My God! What have we done?" Boston's architects learned from the failure of the '60s and designed buildings like the Boylston Suites Hotel that enhanced the city rather than overpowered it.

The hotel shares the corner of Boylston and Hereford Streets with the oldest firehouse in Boston. It sits across Hereford Street from the firehouse and mimics the firehouse's old, brick facade and graceful arches. The convention center, whose granite and glass exterior makes no attempt to match its surroundings, sits across

Boylston Street. I was walking back and forth in front of the hotel, vacillating.

The most important rule of debugging is that there are no contradictions. You could tell that someone sucked at the job when they insisted, "There's no reason for it to be broken." If it had no reason to be broken, it wouldn't be broken.

The same was true of my relationship with Nate. There was no reason for it to be broken. There was no reason for the man who supposedly loved me like a son to fire me and destroy my life. Unless he didn't love me like a son, and in fact, didn't like me much at all. Then it would all make sense.

My condominium on Follen Street was only a few minutes' walk from the hotel, so I had gone home, showered off the tequila stink, shaved, and put on a collared polo shirt and chinos. I hadn't worn these clothes for months. They were my work clothes. I left my apartment and got back to the hotel by cutting through the Prudential Center shops.

It was all going well until I put my hand on the hotel's revolving door. As I touched it, my mind filled with images of a cold Nate, a where-the-hell-were-you Nate, a Nate who had rejected me once as an employee and was planning to finish the job as a surrogate father. I told myself it was ridiculous. *He* called *me*. Well, he called me after I called him. Still, that was something. I couldn't imagine that he would call me back and ask for my help simply to screw with me. I took my hand off the door and turned toward the street. I turned again and walked back toward the door.

Intellectually I knew that it must be OK, but as I approached the door again, I veered and walked down the street toward the firehouse. I turned down Hereford and walked toward the side door. Maybe I could sneak up on him. I changed direction again. Sneaking

33

in the side was stupid. Why walk in the side? If he saw me walk in the side, he'd think it was strange. I walked back to the front and touched the revolving door again.

"Oh for God's sake, baby, just shake the man's hand," said Carol, who had appeared over my shoulder. "It's Nate. He loves you."

"Loved," I corrected.

"Get through that door!" said Carol. Her vehemence propelled me. I pushed through the heavy revolving door. I stepped out into the lobby and considered going back into the street. It was too late. Nate was there. He saw me and waved. *Crap.*

My stomach clenched as adrenaline shot through me. Nate was standing in the middle of the hotel lobby. He reminded me of Santa, if Santa were thin, beardless, and wearing a suit. It was the eyes. He had those twinkling blue eyes from the Coca-Cola ads. They were eyes that said that he understood, and that he cared.

I avoided his eyes. I looked at the lobby instead. It was an oasis of green plants, little canals, and koi. Nate was on a bridge over a canal. He beckoned me to join him. I focused on taking the first step. Once I took it, it led to the other steps and I strode across the lobby in a blur. The only thing I could see was Nate's outstretched right hand.

I walked up to Nate, took his hand, and said, "Hello." That was all I got out before Nate pulled me toward him, trapping me in a hug. Nate was shorter than me, and his tight hug pushed his face into my shoulder.

I stood for a second, stunned, with my hands outstretched to either side of the little man. My defenses faltered and I returned the hug, crushing Nate into my chest.

Nate said, "I'm sorry."

I said, "For what?" *Firing me?*

"For not calling you months ago. I was afraid you'd hang up."

"I never would have hung up on you."

"Well, you would have been within your rights. It was horrible what happened, and I should have been there. How has it been?"

Well, I've been bumming around the city and playing video games. "I'm good," I said. "I've got my act together."

"I'm glad. I wanted—" Something over my shoulder distracted Nate. He said, "Are you up for a little work? Because I could sure use your help."

I said, "Sure, Nate."

"Excellent!" Nate put his hand on my shoulder and turned me to face somebody. "Jack!" he said. "How are you doing? You know Tucker, right?"

I was standing face to face with MantaSoft's CEO, Jack Kennings.

The CEO stuck out his hand. "Hello, Tucker."

SEVEN

Jack Kennings looked, talked, and (if you got close enough) smelled like a CEO. He was six feet two inches tall with light brown hair, an athletic country-club build, and chiseled features. He had crisp blue eyes, bleached white teeth, and could spit quotable one-liners that pleased every reporter within earshot. He wore a gray double-breasted suit. I had always been a little afraid of Jack.

Jack was a smart guy and a tough leader. He had an engineering degree and knew how to build technology. Carol told me she'd once seen him trying to debug our code. She thought it was cute. I had been in meetings with him. They were crisp, efficient, and tightly controlled. He got things done.

Jack asked, "What brings you two back together?"

Nate said, "Tucker's coming to work for me on a special project."

A flicker of concern flashed across Jack's features. He said, "I guess that hiring freeze isn't working."

"Oh, Tucker's not an employee. I'm bringing him on as a contractor to do technical due diligence on Bronte."

Bronte? What the hell is Bronte?

Jack said, "We have someone for that."

"We did," said Nate. "Alice Barton."

Jack said, "Oh, shit. You're right." He turned to me. "Do you know what happened to Alice?"

I'm not sure which twist in my mind caused me to lie. Perhaps it was the fact that Kevin had raised the notion of finding out who had killed Carol. Perhaps it was a simple distrust of the company that had expelled me. Perhaps I was just being an asshole. I said, "No."

Jack said, "She was killed last night. Murdered." He shook his head and said, "Hell of a thing. Still, Nate, don't you have anyone on your team who could handle this?"

Nate said, "No one who can get it done by Thursday and no one with Tucker's expertise and reputation."

There was a moment of silence. Jack stared into space, apparently lost in thought. Abruptly, he said, "Gentlemen, I have a meeting." He shook my hand and continued, "Welcome aboard, Tucker. I'll need your report by Thursday."

He was gone in a swirl of executive authority. I stood next to Nate in the lobby of the Boylston Suites Hotel. Next to me, a little kid was throwing fish food at the koi. I turned to Nate and said, "What the hell just happened?"

Nate said, "You've got a consulting job. Congratulations." He started walking toward the conference rooms in the back of the hotel.

"What am I doing?"

"You're my special assistant."

"Do I get paid?" I asked, crafty businessman that I am.

"Sure."

"What do I get paid?"

"What do you want?"

"I want to know why you fired me."

Nate stopped walking. He put his hand on my shoulder. "There's so much water under that bridge," he said.

"What's that supposed to mean?" I stepped out from under his hand so that it fell to his side.

"It's just that—well—the reasons are complicated."

"Are you dodging the question?" I asked.

"I just have trouble seeing what you'd gain from the discussion," Nate said.

"I think they call it *closure*."

"I doubt it would give you closure," said Nate. He crossed his arms. "It just doesn't seem relevant."

"Well, that's what I want. Take it or leave it. Do you want me to work on this Bronte thing or don't you?" I wasn't much of a negotiator. My engineering side thought that all that posturing and positioning were bullshit. Nate knew that, and he knew that if he didn't give me what I wanted, I would walk.

He took a deep breath. "OK. Meet me at Ciao Bella at six tonight. I'll buy you dinner and tell you what happened."

"Deal." We shook.

"Bronte Software is across the street at the convention, setting up their booth. Why don't you go check it out?"

"Tell me again why we care about Bronte?"

"Because Jack wants to buy them for fifty million dollars."

"Why does Jack want to buy them?"

"He says 'technology.'"

"They've got technology worth fifty million?"

"How should I know? That's your job now. Head over to the convention hall and pick up a badge and a show pass. See you tonight at six."

Nate left me standing in the large atrium of the Boylston Suites Hotel. A koi fish bobbed to the surface and looked at me. I put out my empty hands and said, "Sorry, pal, I got nuthin'." I headed out of the hotel and across the street to the convention hall.

EIGHT

I HAD GONE TO every SecureCon trade show for the past decade, and I had to admit that I enjoyed this orgy of marketing. MantaSoft brought its engineers to the show to make customers feel like technical partners in product development. We would give presentations, answer questions, and glad-hand the IT geeks who bought our software. I felt a familiar jolt of anticipation as I walked into the place.

"Tucker!" A shrill, happy voice called across the convention lobby. It was Shelly, the receptionist from the local MantaSoft office. I'd known Shelly for years. We'd sort of grown up together. We joined MantaSoft at the same time, went on double dates with our future spouses, and even got married within a few months of each other. Shelly had started having children immediately.

Today she was round and happy, apparently pregnant again. This would be her fourth.

I said, "Shelly!" and gave her a big hug around her belly. "When are you due?"

Shelly looked confused. "Due? What do you mean due?"

40

Uh oh.

I stammered, "Err—ah—due to—"

"Are you saying I'm fat?"

"No! No. I would never—"

Shelly laughed. "Ha! I'm just screwing with you." She chucked me on the arm. "Don't you know better than to guess that a woman's pregnant? I'm seven months along. Nate called and told me to get you some badges. Here's one for the show, and here's one for the office. Nate said that you were contracting with us. I think that's great. It'll be nice to have you around. I felt so bad for you when you left. Is everything OK now? What are you doing?"

I had let the waves of Shelly's chatter wash over me and didn't register the question. After a long silence, I realized it was my turn to talk. "Oh, I'm taking over for Alice Barton for a few days."

Shelly's eyes filled. She said, "Oh. Of course."

"So you heard."

"Yes. The police were here. They asked everyone about Alice. Of course, it was odd that she died and Carol died, given that they—" Shelly reddened.

"That they what?" I asked.

"Um. That they both did the same job on the same project."

"Is that all that they did together?"

Shelly reached up and gave me a peck on the cheek. She said, "I gotta go, hon. It's time to get the booth ready for the show."

She turned and scurried away, leaving me standing in the lobby. I considered chasing her, badgering her, getting her to give me an answer. But I knew that she'd just clam up, and then I'd be some jerk harassing a pregnant lady. I tweeted:

Why is the husband always the last to know?

NINE

I WALKED INTO THE trade show and remembered why the Sunday before the show opened was my favorite day. Workers rolled blue carpet over the bare concrete between the booths. The booths were set up in rows and columns with the carpet acting as streets and avenues.

By Sunday afternoon all the companies in the show had erected their booths. Colorful walls, bright signs, and flashing computer monitors promised the untold riches that would be saved by each security innovation. Some booths had little theaters where twenty people could sit and watch a pitch. The presenters were practicing in front of empty chairs. Others relied upon videos to attract attention. The technicians in these booths were checking sound levels.

I decided to check out the MantaSoft booth before moving on to Bronte. As it was every year, the booth was enormous, taking up an entire trade-show block. The black manta logo was suspended from the ceiling with the slogan "Revolutionary Security" underneath. As I got closer, I saw a replica of the Minuteman Statue from Lexington.

As usual, the logic of the marketing dweebs escaped me. The Minutemen were America's first militias. They were crazy guys with guns who didn't like the government. It seemed that MantaSoft was supposed to protect companies from people like the Minutemen. On the other hand, it was a cool way to acknowledge the show's location. Perhaps I was being too logical.

I was meandering around the empty booth when I saw a guy who was definitely not part of the Revolutionary Software theme. He was Roland Baker, a British asshole in a gray suit.

There are very few things I hate. I hate the New York Yankees. I hate tripe. I hate warm Coke and flat beer. I hate talk radio. I hate assholes who stand up at baseball games and wave their arms trying get the rest of the crowd to rise. I hate golf. Yet if you took all those things and wrapped them up in a big wad of hatred, I would hate the wad less than I hated Roland Baker.

The man was a scumbag who came to work at MantaSoft a year ago. I wasn't even sure who hired him, but somehow he got assigned to my project, Rosetta. He was the kind of guy who knew that he sounded smarter being negative than positive, so he would argue with every decision just for show. He'd ask generic questions like "What is your backup plan in case your current backup plan doesn't work?" He wore a suit to work in an engineering group. He never wrote code, but he was fantastic at ingratiating himself to Jack. The day Nate fired me, Roland became the lead on Rosetta. It was like seeing your puppy given to Cruella de Vil.

Roland didn't see me because he was yelling at a young woman half his size. The small, attractive woman was looking at Roland and nodding as he yelled at her. I decided to see if she needed rescuing and sauntered over. Roland was facing away from me, so I snuck up on him.

"Well, bloody well fix it!" said Roland in his Monty Python British accent. I despised that accent. Whenever I heard Roland talk, I expected to see a sixteen-ton weight fall on him.

She was about to respond when I tapped him on the shoulder. "Displaying the leadership skills that made you what you are today, eh, Roland?"

Roland whirled as if he'd heard a gunshot. "Tucker? What the hell are you doing here?"

"I was going to take my old job back. But seeing as you're doing it so well, I've decided to stay retired."

"You bloody well had better stay retired. Nate fired you for a reason."

"That remains to be seen."

"What does that mean?"

"Wouldn't you like to know?"

"Where did you get that badge? Does Jack know about this?"

The woman had been watching our exchange. She was a petite blonde with a curvy body wrapped in a T-shirt and jeans. Her conference badge said her name was Dana Parker. Dana edged out of my field of vision as I sparred with Roland.

I said, "Jack knows. I wouldn't worry if I were you. They haven't asked me to fix the mess you made of Rosetta."

Roland gave me a hard look. He said, "What mess? What have you heard?"

"Heard? I haven't heard anything, but you've been running this thing for over six months. It's got to be a mess by now."

"Sod off. If Nate didn't hire you to look after Rosetta, then what are you doing?"

"I'm doing market research for biteme.com. I'm sure you've heard their motto: Bite me."

Roland tilted his head, and I could his eyes shifting as he thought. "Market research? You're just a stupid code jockey. That's why you lost your job. You wouldn't recognize a market if you stepped in it."

"Ooh. We are a testy little Brit today. What's the matter, Roland? Code out of control?"

Instead of answering, Roland looked over my shoulder. The cute blonde was back and had one finger pointed up as she tried to get a word in. Roland looked at her and said, "What?"

"Are we done?" she asked.

"Yes. Now go and fix your code."

"Yes, sir." Dana turned to me and said, "It's a pleasure to meet you." She stuck out her hand and we shook. It was an odd, fishy handshake. When it was over, I was holding a slip of paper. I put the paper into my pocket before Roland could see it.

"Goodbye," Roland said to Dana. He turned back to me. "I don't know what you are bloody well doing here, but I will find out."

"You go, Sherlock."

I turned and left. I took Dana's note out of my pocket. It had been hastily scribbled on a MantaSoft business card. The card had the logo shaped like a black manta fish with the wings of a stingray and a whip-like tail. Dana's full name was next to the logo: Dana Parker. Her title was under the name: Principal Software Engineer.

That had been Carol's job.

I flipped the card over and saw purple ink on the back. She had written the note in a strong feminine hand. The loops and whirls said, "Newbury Street Starbucks at 3. Help!"

TEN

You can learn a lot about companies from the way they present themselves at a trade show. Bronte was no exception. Its blue booth was dominated by a large, cylindrical saltwater aquarium filled with sharks. The sharks were three to four feet long and swam in lazy counterclockwise circles. The slogan emblazoned across the tank was "Move or Die." Bronte was not a subtle company.

When I arrived at the booth, two engineers were standing in front of the tank debating shark species. I could tell they were engineers because neither one knew what he was talking about, but both were certain they were right.

"It's a leopard shark," said the first, who wore sandals and carried a man-purse.

"No, it's a nurse shark," said the second in a Red Sox cap, a green logo shirt, and jeans.

"No. It's a leopard shark. You can tell by the spots."

"What spots?"

"The spots behind the gills," said man-purse.

"Those aren't leopard shark spots," countered Sox cap.

"OK, Mr. Spot." He snorted at his own pun. "What kind of spots are they?"

"They're just spots. It's a nurse shark. Look at the teeth."

"Why would a nurse shark have teeth like that? Those belong to a leopard shark."

"I had all the Jacques Cousteau books growing up, and that is *not* a leopard shark."

"It's not my fault you didn't read them ..."

A fat geek stuffed into a Bronte T-shirt saved me before I threw myself into the tank. The T-shirt was white, with a bloody shark-shaped bite taken out of the side. The guy would have lost his kidney. The slogan "Move or D ..." was stenciled across the shirt, cut off by the shark bite. The kid in the shirt said, "Holy crap! Aren't you Tucker? *The* Tucker?"

I said, "I'm *a* Tucker."

"You wrote the Nappy Time virus!"

Ah yes, the virus. Some things you never live down. Bill Buckner had the '86 World Series, and I had the Nappy Time virus. The virus came from an experiment I had done in college. I had been messing around with making a computer go to sleep based on how rapidly the user typed the keys. The childish and cruel (but very funny) idea was that the machine would most likely go to sleep just before a deadline.

I was curious to see if the program could spread itself to other machines through the Internet, so I wrote a little bit of code that used the computer's network connection to copy the program to other machines. The rudimentary security of that age was no match for my programming, and the Nappy Time virus was born.

Once I had the virus, I wrote a program for Kevin that cataloged all the pictures on his computer by the percentage of skin tone in them. It was a porn filter turned on its head. Instead of blocking the porn, it found it. I hid the virus in the porn-finder and emailed the program to him. I never expected him to forward it to his friends.

Nobody could prove that I wrote the Nappy Time virus, but I did get credit for it in the hacker community. It had made me famous among the kind of people who would argue over leopard sharks and nurse sharks.

"I was never convicted of writing that virus."

The kid in the shirt smirked. "Yeah. Right. Convicted."

"OK. You got me. I'm Tucker. What's your name?"

"I'm Kurt Monroe."

"What do you do?"

"I'm the Director for Product Engineering."

Bingo.

"Think you could give me a demo? I'd love to see what you guys do."

"A demo? Sure I'd lo—" The kid's eyes got wide as he looked over my shoulder. He said, "Oh. Hello, Ms. Bronte. Do you know Aloysius Tucker?"

A familiar, but tight, voice said, "Oh yes. I know Tucker very well."

I spun and there, resplendent in a business suit that identified her as a Captain of Industry, was Ms. Bronte. Also known as Maggie.

ELEVEN

My brain locked as I struggled to place the drunk, naked, and passionate Maggie of last night with the sober, fashionable, and cold Maggie who stood before me. Seeing her with her arms crossed and her blue eyes boring into mine, I said the only thing that came to mind.

"Hi, Maggie!"

Kurt looked at me as if I had called Darth Vader "Ani." He stammered out, "I was just talking to Tuck—"

Maggie ignored Kurt and said, "My name is Margaret."

I said, "OK."

"Margaret Bronte," she continued.

"I was just—" Kurt started again.

Margaret turned on him. "Kurt, please go check on the servers. I will handle Mr. Tucker."

"But the servers are—"

Margaret's eyes flashed and Kurt was gone. Perhaps the force was strong in her after all.

When I saw Maggie, I was happy and surprised. Then I was confused and surprised. Now I was annoyed and surprised, but mostly annoyed. It was obvious that Maggie, now Margaret, had not simply lusted after my trim runner's body. She wanted something else, and I was going to find out what it was.

After Kurt had evaporated, I pointed at the "Bronte Software" sign and asked, "Is there a Mr. Bronte?"

Margaret said, "Absolutely not. This is my company." She grasped my shoulder and started to guide me toward the curtains at the back of her booth. Like all small companies, Bronte had been relegated to the edge of the show, where a blue curtain hung from a metal frame to make a wall. There was a gap in the curtain. Margaret parted it and urged me through.

I walked past the curtain, and the show disappeared. We were standing on a bare concrete floor twenty yards wide that ran across the back of the hall. The gray concrete shone, reflecting the overhead lights. We were alone. Now I could get some answers.

Margaret got in my face. "What is the meaning of this?"

"What?"

"What do you mean stalking me to my booth? Calling me 'Maggie'? Embarrassing me in front of my employees?"

"I wasn't stalking you."

"So why are you here?"

I stammered, "Nate sent me here."

Margaret stepped back and said, "Nate? Nate Russo?"

"Yes."

"Why in the hell would you have anything to do with that old fossil?"

"He hired me."

Margaret cocked her head. "From what I heard, he fired you. And probably did more."

"More than what?"

"More than fire you from one job. I think he made you un-hireable."

"What do you mean?"

"Oh come on, Tucker, think! Are you working right now?"

"No."

"Doesn't that strike you as strange? You were the author of the Nappy Time virus."

"That was never proven."

She waved that off. "Whatever. It made your reputation in this industry. From what I hear, you were running the biggest project in MantaSoft. You should have been the hottest hire on the market."

I couldn't argue with that.

"And here it is six months later and you haven't got a job."

"I haven't looked."

"Then why isn't your phone ringing off the hook? Why aren't people climbing over each other to hire you? To get you back into the game?"

I had never thought of that. I said, "I don't know."

Margaret continued. "So you never heard the rumors about your breakdown. How you stormed into Nate's office, called him a thief, demanded more money, and had to be escorted out?"

"What?"

"It's called a whisper campaign. Someone makes a few calls, drops a few rumors. In a small industry like this it can be done in a day. Perhaps you should give some thought to where it started before you go running back to Nate."

"But what about—"

Margaret looked at her Rolex and said, "I have a meeting, dear. Let's talk again tomorrow."

She slipped through the curtains and was gone, and I was left back at my original question.

Why did Nate fire me?

I looked at my watch and pulled Dana's note from my pocket. *Help!* It seemed that I had a real, live damsel-in-distress, and I wasn't going to waste the chance to be a hero.

TWELVE

Like all great American cities, Boston is littered with Starbucks. They sit proudly on corners, squat mischievously under hotels, and tuck themselves into unused nooks and crannies across the landscape. Dana was smart to have specified the Newbury Street Starbucks. That narrowed the choice to two.

I assumed that Dana meant the Starbucks closest to the convention center, so I wandered down Hereford Street and took a left at Newbury. It was a beautiful day. Small knots of college girls ricocheted around the street, pointing, laughing, and ducking into stores. A guy played a drum solo on a set of overturned buckets. A big black guy in a red shirt and a baseball cap worked the sidewalk, greeting people in a loud happy voice and counting a wad of bills. I couldn't tell if he was a high-end panhandler, a drug dealer, or a parking valet.

I peeked through the big Starbucks windows to get a look at Dana before our meeting. She was sitting at one of the tables, sipping from a large green drink and staring at her laptop. She was wearing a T-shirt and jeans and no makeup. A strand of blond hair had come loose from her ponytail. She kept blowing at it as she stared. Her body exuded a lean athleticism and her eyes spoke of intelligence. She didn't wear a ring.

It wasn't clear what Maggie, now Margaret, wanted with me last night. But it was clear that she had awakened a part of me that had gone dormant when I lost Carol. I had been living in an odd, faded world where women had stopped registering on my senses. When I went running on the Charles, I'd notice the fractal nature of trees, the reflected spire of the Museum of Science, and the rigging on the sailboats. It just occurred to me now that I hadn't noticed the women. They must have been there.

Yesterday, Margaret Bronte had sat near me in the Thinking Cup on Tremont Street and asked for my help with her computer. I had said, sure, I'd take a look. I found a machine that was riddled with viruses, saddled with a bloated registry, and running more malware than software. I told her that I'd have to re-image her hard drive to fix it, and somehow this turned into her coming over my house and me cooking her dinner. The tequila was her idea. Come to think of it, so was the sex.

Regardless of Margaret's motives, she had accomplished one thing. She reminded me that women existed, and that they were good. I was reminded of it again as I looked through the Starbucks window and saw a sexy blond nerd blowing at a strand of hair. I needed a plan.

I'm not a fan of Starbucks coffee. It's too burned. But I am a fan of ice cream. A J.P. Licks ice cream store stood next to the Starbucks, so I ducked inside and bought two chocolate ice cream cones. I asked for small, so they were only the size of baseballs. I took the cones and walked into the Starbucks. Dana looked up and cocked her head when she saw the ice cream.

"I hope you like chocolate," I said, licking one of the cones.

Dana smiled and sat back in her chair. I tried to keep my eyes on hers and off the T-shirt that stretched across her chest. I failed. The shirt had the phrase "Math Is Hard" printed across Dana's breasts. If Dana saw my wandering eyes, she ignored them.

"I do like chocolate. How did you know?"

"You seemed like a chocolate kind of person." I handed her the unlicked cone. "Plus, you said you needed help. I think chocolate ice cream helps most things."

"Thank you," said Dana, catching a melted drop of ice cream on her tongue. She cleaned up the cone and looked at her enormous laptop. It covered the table. Several windows were open, all of them filled with computer code. "I really do need your help."

"So why the note? Why not just ask?"

"I didn't think Roland would like it. He can be sensitive."

"And moronic." I pulled up a chair and sat. "I'm here to serve. What's up?"

"Did you write this source code?" She pointed at the laptop.

"Maybe. Let me take a look." I glanced at the code. Despite its complexity, or perhaps because of it, I immediately knew that it was mine.

Other programmers have trouble when they try to use my code. They don't see the world the same way as me. Code that looks clear to me looks like rubbish to them. I understood why Dana jumped on the chance to have me help her.

Computers are simpletons. You tell them what they do, and they do it. The problem is that they can't figure anything out on their own. You have to tell them what to do in all situations by writing *source code*, text files full of instructions. For example, if I were teaching a baseball computer to play shortstop, I'd say, "If you get a ground ball, and nobody is on base, throw the ball to first." Simple.

Now, what if there is a runner on base? This is where the complexity comes in. You need to handle every possible situation as efficiently as possible. In the case of baseball, when you combine all the ways runners could be on base with the possible number of outs, you get twenty-four combinations. If you don't want to write separate code for all twenty-four cases, you need to figure out an algorithm for what you want the computer to do. You use that algorithm to create other algorithms. Soon the complexity is beyond what average programmers can understand.

Great computer programmers are literally ten times more productive than average ones because they can keep all this in their heads. I am a great programmer, thanks to genetics or too many video games. If Dana were average, she'd be in trouble trying to change my software code.

I got up and looked over Dana's shoulder while she explained what she had done to my handiwork. She started by showing me how she had modified the code. She smelled faintly of vanilla. I think it was her shampoo.

I stood behind Dana and put my hand on the back of her chair. I could feel the warmth from her body on my thumb. She was talking about the work she had done, throwing around words like *objects* and *methods*. Her commentary formed a pleasant background noise as I looked at the line of her neck and finished eating my ice cream cone.

Then she said something that caught my attention.

"What did you just say?" I asked.

"The bug happens here when they try to use this function," said Dana, pointing to a piece of code.

"Well, that's a simple problem. Nobody should be using that function."

"Why not?"

"I didn't write it that way. That was just for me to use. Nobody else should even know about it. It's based on something I wrote in college."

Dana turned and smiled at me. "Do you mean like the Nappy Time virus?"

"Exactly like the Nappy Time virus, only more powerful."

The smile fled. Dana said, "What?"

"Your cone's about to drip on you."

Dana looked at her ice cream, said, "Damn," and licked the thing into submission. When she got it cleaned up, she walked over to the trash and threw it away.

I asked, "Why did you do that?"

"I need to keep my figure."

I thought she was keeping her figure just fine, but I'd learned from experience that mentioning a woman's figure always ended in pain. So I just nodded.

Dana sat in front of her computer. She said, "We were talking about the Nappy Time virus. Is that what this code is?"

"Yeah," I said. "But more powerful. It's much faster."

"You put virus code into Rosetta?" Dana looked alarmed. It was an odd reaction and I became suspicious. This shouldn't have been a surprise to her.

I said, "Do you know what Rosetta does?"

"Of course I know. It decrypts files so employees can't hide information."

"Sure. It does that, but do you know how?" Dana looked at her laptop and poked at the keys randomly. I continued, "Well, do you?"

"I don't know cryptography, if that's what you mean."

"No, that's not what I mean." I felt bad. She looked miserable. I leaned in close so nobody could overhear. Her vanilla scent distracted me. I composed myself and said, "Rosetta takes over all the machines in a company's network to do the decryption. While people are home, their computers are still working."

She said, "OK, but what's that got to do with the virus?"

"It uses the virus code to take over the machines. That way the IT geeks don't need to run around installing software." I leaned in closer and whispered in Dana's ear, "It's the secret to Rosetta."

Dana sat back and rubbed her ear. "That tickles," she said.

"Sorry."

"Well, even if nobody was supposed to use your routine, we're using it now. That's why Roland wants it fixed."

"I'll say it again. Roland's an idiot. I knew he'd screw up this project."

"What do you think I should do?"

"I don't think you can do what needs to be done."

Dana bristled. "Are you saying I'm not a good programmer?"

It was pretty obvious that Dana wasn't a good programmer. But I wasn't going to say that. Instead, I said, "Someone needs to tell Roland to fuck himself. I'm not certain you can do that and keep your job." I sat down opposite Dana.

Dana laughed. "No. You're right."

"So you need to make it work."

"Yup."

"I'm not certain it can work. It'll take me a day to think about it. Then I'd need to explain it to you." I looked into Dana's eyes and trailed my fingers along the top of her laptop. "How about dinner tomorrow?"

"You mean you'll have the answer by dinner tomorrow?"

"I mean I'd like to take you out to dinner tomorrow."

"You mean like a date or meeting?"

I said, "It's a meeting that turns itself into a date. Kind of like a Transformer."

Dana thought for a moment and pursed her lips. Then she said, "No."

I said, "No?"

"No. Really, no."

"Why?"

"I've heard you like older women."

Dana Parker was definitely not the sweet kid that I took her for. In fact, I didn't think I liked her very much anymore. How did she know about me at all, let alone hear that I'd had been with Maggie? There's only one pers—*Son of a bitch!*

I asked, "Do you know Agent Kevin Murphy over at the FBI?"

"I do. He visited today because of Alice. We talked about the project, and your name came up."

I was going to kill him.

THIRTEEN

"This is a clear violation of Man Law!" I shouted into my cell phone as I walked down Newbury Street. Next to me a street drummer tattooed a rhythm for the shoppers.

"What?" asked Kevin. "I can't hear you."

"That's because there's some asshole banging on a bucket. Hold on." I ran across Newbury Street to get away from the noise. "You told Dana Parker I liked older women? I don't appreci—"

Kevin interrupted. "Wait. Dana Parker? Why are you talking to Dana Parker? You said you were going home."

"I was talking to Dana Parker because she wanted help with my code, and I was asking her out because she's cute, and she turned me down because you told her I was into older women."

"How did you wind up helping her with her code?"

"Roland Baker was yelling at her in the convention center and I went over to give him shit. Don't change the subject. I would have thought that you'd approve of Dana. She's my age and everything."

I had stopped stalking around and was standing on Gloucester Street in front of a cigar bar.

"Roland Baker? You're talking to Roland Baker? How did you wind up talking to Roland? I wanted you to talk to Nate."

"I did talk to Nate. He asked me to look into Bronte, so I went over to the trade show to check out their booth. And you haven't apologized for talking behind my back."

Kevin said, "Look, I'm sorry. It's a long…" he paused and said, "You went over to the Bronte booth? The Bronte people didn't see you, did they?"

"Just Maggie. I mean Margaret."

"Oh my Christ! You were talking to Margaret Bronte herself?"

"Actually I slept with Margaret Bronte herself. It turns out that Maggie's last name is Bronte. She was pissed to see me at her booth."

"It just keeps getting worse. This is bad, Tucker. It's really bad."

I stared at the giant cigar hanging in front of the bar. "What are you talking about?"

"This is why I was texting you. This thing is deeper than you getting fired. I think these people killed Carol. Didn't you get my text?"

"Yeah, I got it."

"Then why didn't you call me?"

Because Jeanette had great legs? No, the real reason was that I was having a tantrum. This whole deal with Nate, Roland, and MantaSoft had knocked me off balance. My emotions were getting churned into my gray matter, and that wasn't a good for logical problem solving.

I took a deep breath and blew it out.

Kevin said, "Tucker. Can you hear me?"

I said, "Yeah."

61

"We've got to get together and talk."

I was feeling calmer. I said, "I'll swing by your office."

"No. You shouldn't be seen around my office anymore."

"Fine, where do you want to meet?"

"Halfway to Hell. See you there."

Halfway to Hell. Great. I folded my phone and started walking.

FOURTEEN

Smoots are a unit of measure. They are defined by the height of one Oliver Smoot, who went to MIT and was essentially dragged across the Harvard Bridge by upperclassmen who used him as a ruler. The Harvard Bridge crosses the Charles River and carries Mass Ave into Cambridge. Harvard lobbied to have the bridge named after Harvard because of Harvard's long legacy in education. MIT lobbied to have the bridge named after Harvard because the bridge was structurally unsound. It collapsed shortly afterward.

The bridge is 364.4 smoots long, plus or minus an ear. I was 100 smoots across and making good time. Adrenaline and anger are nature's steroids. Where did Kevin get the balls to tell me that I had fucked up? How could I have fucked up? I just took a job with Nate. On top of that, he burned me with Dana. I was seriously considering tossing him into the river. Given how well they've cleaned it up, I didn't even think he'd dissolve.

The bridge carried a four-lane road and two large sidewalks. The Smoot marks are on the upriver sidewalk. I reached the spot, at

Smoot 182.2, labeled "Halfway to Hell," leaned against the railing, and looked downstream toward the Museum of Science. Kevin was nowhere to be seen. Tweeted:

A prompt man is a lonely man.

Ten minutes passed. The sun was warm, and the Charles shimmered as sailboats cut across it. A blond girl in a tight black top and small black shorts ran toward Boston. I glanced at her face. It glowed with exercise and health. Wisps of hair were plastered to her cheeks. I was glad to be noticing women again. She passed me and I watched her butt as she ran down the sidewalk.

Dana's voice echoed in my head. "Heard you like older women." What was that supposed to mean? If Maggie—Margaret—wanted to seduce me, what was wrong with that? It was consensual, fun, and, it turns out, healing. I hadn't had sex in over a year: six months since Carol had died, and at least six before that. I was a faithful husband, even as my marriage spiraled down into a long bout of cold shoulders on hot summer nights.

I don't know when Carol and I stopped having sex. For a while, it seemed we didn't have the time. Then it seemed she didn't have the energy. Finally, it seemed that every time we felt close, one of us would say something cruel and drive the other away.

It's not that I stopped trying. Carol was beautiful and, even when we were fighting, I wanted her. But something had snapped in our relationship, and sex wasn't an option. It got to the point where she wouldn't let me touch her.

Despite our problems, we never had separate bedrooms. This led to a long string of nights where I'd lay in bed and watch her undress. Her blouse would fly into the laundry bag, and her bra into the hamper. She'd take off her pants and walk over to her dresser wearing nothing but panties. She'd pick out a little cotton top, put it on, and come to bed. Then she'd prop a pillow between us, turn her back on me, and start snoring.

I think that's why I started working late. If I came home late enough, she'd be in bed and I could avoid the striptease. Even then, I'd have trouble sleeping next to a woman I knew to be beautiful, but who had become untouchable. During all of this I stayed faithful—though now I hear she might not have been faithful to me.

I wondered if we were on the way to a divorce. A wall had formed between us, and I couldn't figure out how to climb it. I had hoped to pull us back together after Rosetta shipped, but she was dead and I was alone in a big house in the suburbs. Nothing was resolved.

I moved to the city. As I see now, there were women everywhere, but I didn't notice them. The whole prospect of being with a woman just highlighted how much I had failed Carol, both in the bedroom and in saving her life. Margaret had reminded me that I had a lot to offer, even with my failings.

Now, standing on Smoot 182.2, I watched the girl with the nice butt run toward the city. There was no traffic on the bridge going toward Boston, and she was silhouetted against the skyline. I sighed. Maybe I shouldn't have slept with Margaret. Maybe that was a little whorish. Still, she hadn't taken off her bra and then propped a pillow between us, and it had been a long time.

I looked left to the MIT side of the bridge and saw Kevin striding toward me. He was about twenty smoots away, ignoring me and talking on his cell phone. I turned my head and looked toward Boston. *What the hell is going on?* There was still no traffic on the bridge. I crossed my arms, waiting for Kevin to reach me with the answers.

A moment passed, but Kevin didn't show up. I looked back to him. He was ten smoots away, and strolling. He closed his phone and started to take off his jacket. He winked at me and I saw his plan. We didn't know each other. He'd fling the jacket over his shoulder, stand next to me, and say, "Quite a view, eh?" To anyone else, I would look like a guy being picked up by another guy. A normal day in the city.

There was some honking coming from Cambridge. Some asshole had stopped his black car in the middle of the road, blocking both lanes. The honking got the black car moving, and it sped down the bridge.

Kevin had the jacket off. He threw it over his shoulder. As he started to put his phone into his pocket, his stomach exploded into a red mist. I heard a rattling burst of sound. Another rattle, and Kevin's chest exploded.

He looked at me, surprised, and stumbled. The black car rocketed past, its rear window closing.

Kevin took another step and dropped to a knee. His phone clattered to the sidewalk.

I ran to him. He twisted as he lost control of his legs and fell onto his back. I knelt beside him. Blood poured as if from a bucket. It bubbled and churned in his chest as he gasped.

He looked into my eyes. I grabbed his bloody hand and he squeezed it. Then he was gone. His blood ran across the sidewalk and covered Smoot 182.2.

FIFTEEN

AGENT BOBBY MILLER'S HEAD gleamed in the sunlight as we stood on the bridge. He was saying something in an urgent staccato, but his words rattled around in my head without meaning. I was looking over his shoulder to where they were loading Kevin into a body bag.

They had found me sitting against the fence on the Halfway to Hell marker, watching Kevin, waiting for him to move. Kevin's dead eyes stared up into the sun, not wincing or blinking. I had no idea how I had gotten against the fence, just as I hadn't noticed the circle of people form around Kevin and me.

Here I was again. The sole survivor. First Carol, now Kevin. They tried to lift Kevin into the bag and his shoulder slipped out of the EMT's hand. His head cracked on the sidewalk. He didn't flinch. I said, "I'm sorry, dude. I'm so sorry." I realized now, too late, that the situation was like nothing I had imagined. I had no idea what was going on.

There are different kinds of software bugs. Most are simple mistakes where the programmer compared two numbers improperly, or forgot to clean up something in the computer memory. Others are massive miscalculations that can destroy a project. These are architecture errors.

An architecture error meant that you had completely misunderstood the situation before you had started writing your code. It was like learning that your twenty-page midterm paper on World War I was actually supposed to be about World War II. When I was a project lead, I hated to hear about architectural errors because they meant that we were well and truly fucked. They meant that we had no idea what was going on. Kevin being killed in front of me told me that I had an architecture error. I had been working based on the assumption that this was a sim ...

"Hey, Tucker. Tucker, are you with me?" the agent asked.

I blinked and looked at Kevin. "They're taking him away."

"I know, man, I know. Look, let's get you home. We can talk in my car."

"No," I said, "I can walk."

"You can't walk. Look at yourself. You look like one of the living fucking dead. I'll give you a ride home."

I looked down at my clothes. The polo shirt and chinos were covered in blood. I even had blood in my socks. I said, "OK, Agent Miller, thanks."

He said, "Call me Bobby. I hate that Agent Miller crap. Wait here."

Bobby walked over to a police van and pulled out a bundle. He walked back to me and tossed me the bundle, saying, "Put this on. It will keep the blood off my seats."

It was a jumpsuit like the forensic guys were wearing. I put it on. It was too big, and I had to bunch the legs up at my ankles.

Bobby and I got into his Honda Accord and we headed down Mass Ave. He had been smart to get me away from the bridge. My mind was starting to clear, though there were still flashes of red reappearing before my eyes and bursts of gunfire echoing in my ears.

Bobby said, "Kevin didn't tell you anything?"

I said, "No. Just that I had screwed things up and that it was dangerous. He was pissed off that I'd gotten a job with Nate to look at Bronte. Do you know what he was talking about?"

"Me? No. As far as I knew, Kevin was just chasing a porn ring."

"What's wrong with porn?"

"Apparently the girls weren't actors. It was pretty dark shit."

"What does that have to do with Carol or with Rosetta?"

"None of this makes any sense to me. I thought Kevin was nuts."

"It seems he proved you wrong." I looked out the window at Symphony Hall.

"By getting himself killed."

"I think it was my fault. I shouldn't have gone to work for Nate."

"It's not your fault. Shit happens."

I said, "You think it's a coincidence? He gets shot just as I get a job?"

"Yeah. I can't see how they connect. I can't even see how his investigation connects. All Kevin and I did was walk around and talk to people at MantaSoft about Alice Barton. We got your name and Kevin said he would handle it."

"So you know about my alibi."

"Hell, yeah. You were being cougared. God bless, man, God bless."

I decided not to mention who the cougar was. I decided not to do anything until I had some idea of what was going on. Rule one of holes: When you're in one, stop digging.

I asked Bobby, "Were you there when someone talked about my wife?"

He shot his eyes at me, then back to the road. He said, "Yeah."

"Did you hear the part about her being a lesbian?"

"Yeah."

"Who said that?"

"Can't tell you." Bobby parked in front of a hydrant at the end of Follen Street and we got out.

"Thanks for the ride," I said.

"C'mon," said Bobby, "I'll walk you up to your place."

"There's no need."

"You got me thinking. You talk to Kevin, Kevin gets killed. Maybe you're next. I want to make sure nobody's up there waiting for you. I'd feel like a dumb fuck if I dropped you off and then had to drive all the way back here for a crime scene. Besides, we have more to talk about."

We climbed the three narrow flights to my apartment, Bobby in front. Five steps up, reach a landing, five more steps, reach an apartment, five more, landing, five more, apartment, five more, landing, five more, my place.

Bobby was huffing and puffing. "Jesus, do you live on the roof?"

"Just under it. It's only one more flight. It's got a patio."

We reached my apartment. I unlocked the door and Bobby opened it, gun in hand. I watched from the doorway as Bobby looked one way, then started to walk toward the other. He peeked into my office, opposite the kitchenette. It was an excellent hiding place. Empty. He looked in the bathroom and bedroom.

"All clear," he said, holstering his gun and walking back to the front door.

I walked. "Thanks." I started to strip off the jumpsuit, but noticed my fingernails. They had dried blood under them. My hands were covered in red-brown stains. I needed to wash my hands before I touched anything. Bobby followed me to the bathroom sink.

Bobby said, "We gotta talk. About what happened on the bridge."

"You know what happened."

"No," said Bobby, opening a notebook. "I know that we found Kevin dead on the bridge with you next to him. I know that you mumbled something about a car and I let it go because you were in shock. But you look like you're feeling better now and I need more."

"What more?"

Kevin's chest exploding flashed across my mind as I washed my hands. There was more under the fingernails. I found a brush and started scrubbing. I said, "I don't know what to tell you. Kevin was sauntering toward me with his jacket over his shoulder and then …"

"'Sauntering'? Why do you say 'sauntering'?"

"Because he was casual, like we didn't know each other. There was this little, I don't know, mechanical burping sound and …" My vision filled with Kevin's chest exploding as my brain rewound and reran the killing. The video in my head was slowing down with each repeat.

I continued. "I remember a button popping off his shirt and flying off the bridge. Then there was that sound again and there was more …" A shuddering gasp took hold of me.

Bobby put his hand on my shoulder. He squeezed and said, "You're doing great." It reminded me of Kevin doing the same thing. My breathing slowed.

I said, "He looked so surprised. And hurt. Like his feelings were hurt. He went to his knees and I grabbed him. That's when the black car drove by."

"What kind of car."

"I don't know. A big car. Black."

I watched the video in my mind again. "I saw a gun pull into the car as it went. There wasn't any smoke coming off it. How could there not be smoke?"

We were silent. The video kept restarting, replaying. Saunter-ing ... bullets ... black car. I kept groping for something I could have done to make things come out different. I caused this. I knew it. I'd gotten Kevin killed because I didn't know what was going on.

Bobby said, "Did you see the license plate?"

"No."

More silence. I finished scrubbing and started to pull off the jumpsuit. Kevin's blood covered my shirt. I pulled off the shirt and showed it to Bobby. "You need this?"

Bobby shook his head. I grabbed a facecloth and scrubbed blood off my neck. I looked deeply into the mirror. My hair was flecked with blood. I'd never be clean. I asked, "What do we do now?"

Bobby said, "We? We don't do anything. You just sit tight until we catch someone, then we'll need you at the trial."

I walked past Bobby into the kitchenette and pulled a white plastic garbage bag out from under the sink. I stuffed the jumpsuit and the shirt into the bag.

I said, "Sit tight? What do you mean 'sit tight'?"

Bobby had followed me to the kitchenette. He sat on one of the tall chairs and said, "You know. Just live your life."

I leaned on the counter. "Live my life? What's that mean?"

"Do what you were doing before any of this happened."

"I was helping Kevin before any of this happened."

"Well, you're not helping me. Just walk away."

Walk away? The thought of quitting stirred something deep in my mind. It was a feral thing that had been born when I found Carol on the kitchen floor. I had locked it away, afraid of what it wanted me to do. I got distracted from it when the cops accused me of Carol's murder. Then I had moved to the city and had forgotten about it. Now the thing emitted a low growl.

I said, "Walk away? That's bullshit."

"What?"

"Carol was murdered and I walked away. I was at work when some guy slit her throat. I should have been home protecting her."

Bobby said, "Fuck that. Guy like that would have killed you too."

"Maybe."

"Not maybe. Definitely."

"I'm not walking away."

Bobby took a deep breath. He looked at Click and Clack the hermit crabs, tapped on their tank. They ignored him.

Bobby said, "He saved your life, you know."

I asked, "Who? Kevin?"

"Yeah."

"How?"

"You told me that he pretended he didn't know you, that he threw his coat over his shoulder like he was just enjoying the day."

"Yeah."

Bobby said, "Well, it worked. The guy with the machine gun didn't know you were together, so he let you live. Kevin saved your life."

"I suppose."

"So don't fucking waste the gift. Quit working on this thing at MantaSoft and go back to your life."

"Don't you get it? I have no life. My wife is dead, my best friend is dead. I'm the last one left standing. Waste the gift? The only gift Kevin gave me is the chance to catch the bastard who did this to him. I've got to earn the gift."

Bobby said, "Earn it how? By getting yourself killed? There's better ways to handle survivor's guilt."

"Kevin told me that the key to solving Carol's murder would be knowing why Nate fired me. I'll bet that's the key to Kevin's too. This isn't the time for me to quit. It's time for me to get serious."

Bobby's face and bald head started to turn red. A vein pulsed along his right temple. He said, "Look, I get the whole 'Avenge me' thing, but you just saw Kevin get blown away by a fucking machine gun. From your description, it was a Heckler & Koch. That motherfucker fires fifteen rounds a second. How are you going to fight that? With your good looks?"

"I'm not quitting."

"Yes! You fucking are!" Bobby slammed his hand on the kitchen counter. The sound ricocheted through my head like a gunshot. I winced.

"I'm not quitting. I'm going to help."

"Who are you going to help?"

"You."

"I don't need your help."

This wasn't working. I decided to take a different approach.

"Listen to me," I said. "Rosetta is a distributed decryption system that harnesses a legion of zombie computers to create a massively networked supercomputer. It can decrypt a message based on a 2048-bit key in ten hours using a simulated quantum computer algorithm, and it can decrypt a 1024-bit encoded message in three hours."

Bobby stared at me. I continued, "Now, if you can tell me what I just said, then you're right. You don't need me."

Bobby put his hands on his hips, looked at Click and Clack, and swore to himself, "Goddamn, motherfucker, shit!" He stalked around my apartment, muttering. He looked back at me and said, "You're probably going to get killed."

I said, "I need this to end, one way or the other."

More stalking, more muttering, then silence. Bobby returned and said, "Well, if you're going to walk into the lion's den, you should know where the lions are."

I asked, "What's that supposed to mean?"

"It means you should know your enemies. The guy who told us that Carol was a lesbian was this British guy named Roland Baker."

"Damn it! I hate that guy."

"Yeah, well, he hates you too. So watch out for him," Bobby said, reaching into his shirt pocket for his business card. He gave me the card. "You run into any trouble at all, you call me." He paused and shook his head. "Now comes the tough part."

"What?"

"I have to call Kevin's wife, Charlene."

My breath tightened. I said, "Yeah. Me too."

We shook hands, and Bobby left me standing in my apartment. Now that he was gone, I wasn't feeling so brave. My plan to catch Carol's killer had rested entirely on finding out why Nate fired me. I'd counted on Kevin to tell me what Nate's answer meant. Now I wouldn't know.

I looked at the clock. I was having dinner with Nate in an hour. I needed a shower. I needed to get rid of these bloody pants. I emptied my pockets. Key, wallet, BlackBerry … and cell phone. I never carried a cell phone. I used a BlackBerry.

I examined the phone and realized that it was Kevin's. He was holding it when he died, and dropped it when he got shot. I must have picked it up on the bridge and stuffed it in my pocket.

I held the phone in my open palm, feeling its weird energy. It was the last thing Kevin touched before he died. The person on the other end of that call was the last person to hear his voice.

I pictured the scene, Kevin talking on the phone. He had looked happy and relaxed. He had been talking to a friend.

If Kevin had been talking to a friend, that person's name would be in the phone's address book. I clicked through the keypad menus and found the list of phone calls. The last call *had* been to someone in Kevin's address book. Someone close enough to Kevin to have her name recorded.

Why would Kevin have been talking to Dana Parker?

SIXTEEN

A FAT WOMAN WALKED a fawn pug down Newbury Street. I watched from my table as they stopped at the base of a maple tree that grew from a square patch of dirt in the concrete. The two of them formed an obstacle that parted the crowd like a boulder in a river. The pug sniffed at the base of the tree and expelled an enormous physics-defying dump. Its dump expelled, the pug stood on the patch of dirt under the tree and scratched backwards as if to say, "Take care of that." The woman said something inaudible to the pug and picked up the mess with an inverted plastic bag. She continued down the street with the pug's leash in one hand and a clear plastic bag of crap in the other. I tweeted:

Sidewalk cafes are overrated.

Nate and I sat in front of Ciao Bella. I drank a glass of Caol Ila Scotch. Nate drank Pellegrino water. I told him about Kevin. He expressed condolences. He asked how I was. I said, "Fine."

I wasn't fine. A hole had been blown in my mind. I stared at my Scotch as my brain rewired itself around the fact of Kevin's absence from my life. Nate's voice was a muffled buzzing across the table from me. I willed myself to focus on him.

"There was nothing you could have done," Nate said.

I slurped some Scotch and said, "We seem to be saying that a lot lately. There was nothing we could have done about Carol, or Alice, and now Kevin."

Nate frowned and sipped his water. "Something is spinning out of control," he said. "I only wish I knew what it was."

"Well, not to be self-centered, but I think it all started when you fired me."

Nate glanced at me, then away. He said, "I'm glad you're not being self-centered."

I let his comment hang in the air.

He sipped his water and asked, "Did you get a chance to look at Bronte's booth?"

Nate was ignoring the elephant at the table. Eventually, I was going to find out why I was fired, but I played along for now.

"Yeah, I visited the booth. Nasty sharks."

"Figuratively?"

"Literally. Big aquarium full of them."

"Other than the sharks," said Nate, "did you learn anything about their business?"

All I had learned so far was that Margaret Bronte liked it when you kissed the line of her jaw just above the neck, and that she had skilled fingers. I decided not to share any of this with Nate.

"I met Margaret Bronte. She seems like quite a lady. She asked about you."

"What did she ask?"

"She asked why I was hanging around with 'that fossil.' Her words, not mine."

"And what would your words be?" asked Nate.

I considered responses: *That backstabbing fossil? That enigmatic fossil? That curious fossil?* None of these options seemed helpful. I let the question go. I said, "She couldn't understand why you'd fire me. She thinks I'm brilliant. I agreed with her."

My Scotch was empty. I tinkled the glass toward our server. She nodded and looked at Nate, who gestured for another Pellegrino water.

I said, "Man, you are putting those away."

"The water? It's healthy. You should try some."

I shook my head. "I'm not drinking to get hydrated."

"I suppose not. Look, fossil jokes aside, Margaret's right. You are a brilliant programmer. That's not in question."

I said, "The question is: 'Why did you fire me?'"

"Yes, yes, we'll get to that. But I have to ask, if you're so brilliant, why didn't she try to hire you? Did she ever call you?"

I peered at Nate. This didn't add up. If he'd started the rumors, he wouldn't have asked that question. Unless he was taunting me. And Margaret herself said I was brilliant. Why hadn't she tried to hire me? Maybe last night was her first step.

"Margaret didn't call me. Nobody called me. Apparently, there were rumors about me."

"What kind of rumors?"

Nate seemed honestly surprised.

"The bad kind. According to Margaret, they say I went off the deep end and had to be escorted out of MantaSoft."

Nate said, "Well, that's ridiculous. We both know that's not true. I assume she didn't mention that she was in talks that would pay her fifty million dollars."

"It didn't come up."

"She doesn't want anything to screw up that deal. I think her 'fossil' comments were intended to drive a wedge between us."

"That's funny, because I would have thought that you firing me would have driven a wedge between us."

Nate frowned and said, "I have to hit the head." He got up and went inside to the restaurant. Served him right, drinking all that water. I sipped my Scotch and watched shoppers mill around on the sidewalk. I felt better when I watched people. I watched them carry their bags, drag their kids, and struggle to parallel park. I watched couples looking for a place to eat, arguing about directions, and walking quietly hand in hand. I watched people live, and as long as I watched them, I could keep the image of Kevin's exploding chest out of my head.

My mind returned to Nate. To my surprise, I wanted to trust him. I wanted to think of him as my father again. I wanted to use him as my rock and my sounding board.

I didn't really want to know why he fired me. I just wanted a friend. Bobby Miller was right. I should just let this drop. I could quit when Nate got back, and we'd never need to have this uncomfortable conversation.

Carol appeared in Nate's chair. She said, "Screw your courage to the sticking place, baby."

I said, "Thank you, Lady Macbeth." She disappeared as Nate sat in the chair.

Nate said, "OK. What do you want to know?"

Screw your courage to the sticking place. I said, "Before he died, Kevin told me that knowing why you fired me would be the key to figuring out who killed Carol."

"That's ridiculous."

"Doesn't matter," I said. "I want to know why."

Nate said, "It's like this—"

The server interrupted us, asking for our order. While I looked at the menu, Nate chose a bottle of wine. The menu was a dizzying assortment of Italian terms. The categories were incomprehensible: *zuppe, antipasti, insalate,* and something called *secondi piatti.* I gave up on the menu.

"What kind of wine did you get?" I asked.

"I got us the *Vino Nobile di Montepulciano.* It's from Avignonesi, Italy and—"

"Red or white?"

"Ah. It's red."

"Thanks. I'll have a steak."

Nate ordered the *filetto di manzo e gamberi,* and I got another Scotch.

Nate said, "You are drinking too much."

I said, "I put my liver on an extensive strength and conditioning program this year. It's paying off." Unfortunately, the Scotch was not having the effect I wanted. I wanted to forget Kevin on that bridge, but still remembered the pink mist, the burping sound of the machine gun, and the sheet-covered body. Waking up naked next to Margaret seemed to have happened in another life.

Nate said, "I fired you for two rea—"

The server arrived with the wine. She started her rendition of wine-presentation theater. She showed Nate the bottle. He nodded. She started on the cork. The delay was maddening. She took the cork out and handed it to Nate, who examined it and handed it to me.

I tossed it into a sidewalk trashcan using excellent foul-shot form. *Swish!* The server and Nate looked at me, then at each other. He made a "please continue" gesture. She poured a little wine into the glass. Nate sniffed it, sipped it, and said, "That's fine." The server poured the wine.

Nate said, "What were we talking about?"

"Stop fucking with me," I said. "You said there were two reasons you fired me."

Nate stuck up his index finger and said, "First, Jack told me to replace you with Roland."

"What? Roland was just some asshole. I don't think he ever wrote a line of code."

"It made no sense to me either, but Jack can be impulsive. He and Roland flew cross-country together. Roland must have impressed Jack, and apparently he had some ideas on the project."

"I can just see that conversation." I slipped into a British accent. "Here's what you do, Jack. Fire that bloody idiot Tucker and put me in charge. I'll get Rosetta out the door toot sweet."

"I don't think the British use the phrase *toot sweet*."

I drank some Scotch and said, "Roland's an idiot."

"He's an idiot with amazing political skill."

"The project wasn't even late. I can't believe you just caved."

"I didn't 'just cave.' Jack pushed me for weeks before I gave in. Jack even told me that he'd fire me and then replace you himself. I told him I was OK with that. I've had a good career. Something else pushed me over the edge. It was the real reason."

Our dinner arrived. My steak looked like a piece of dead cow that had been grilled to perfection. As for Nate, it turned out that *filetto di manzo e gamberi* was just steak with an Italian accent. We settled in front of our meals and cut into our steaks. I was right. Done to perfection, but I wasn't hungry.

I said, "You were saying about the second thing?"

Nate chewed and thought. I could see him considering his words.

"It was Carol," he said.

"What was Carol? She was doing a great job. OK, she was a little sloppy there at the end, but she was training Alice."

"It had nothing to do with her performance." Nate cut into his steak and chewed, then sipped his wine. I started drinking the wine myself. I couldn't remember whether it was a bad idea to drink wine on top of Scotch. The poem was either "Wine after whiskey, mighty risky" or "Whiskey then wine, you'll be fine." It didn't matter. I was drinking it anyway.

I said, "Well, then, what was it about Carol?"

"Carol asked me to fire you."

"What?" I blurted. A couple next to us looked at me. Maybe I was getting loud. I whispered, "Why would she do that?"

Nate continued, "She was lonely. She broke down in my office. She said that your job was destroying your marriage, that she was desperate to get you out of MantaSoft." Nate sipped his wine. "She said she'd do whatever it took to get you back."

I stared into my Scotch, turning it in my hand and watching the ice cubes click over each other. A duck boat drove by. The guy in the boat said something about "shopping district," and the people in the boat laughed and waved and quacked at pedestrians. My jaw clenched, and I loosened it by drinking my Scotch, forcing it past the lump in my throat. Nate was silent.

I said, "You fired me because my wife cried in your office?"

"No. I fired you because I wanted to save your marriage."

"You had no right," I hissed. The couple in the next table looked at me again. I ignored them.

"I had every right. I was your boss. I could fire you if I wanted to."

"You had no right to take my personal life into account. My personal life was my business. If Carol was unhappy, that was my business. I was doing the best work of my life. You had no right to take that all away because I might have trouble at home."

"I didn't want your marriage on my head."

"It wasn't your concern!"

"Of course it was." Nate sipped his wine. "Look, I've had a very successful career. I built that career on people like you—people with an insatiable desire to prove themselves. I find these neurotic people and let them create miracles. It works great, except for the family problems."

I tried to say something, but Nate overrode me. "Do you have any idea how many families I've ruined? I watched people lose touch with their kids, fall into affairs, and get divorced because they were addicted to their jobs. Jobs that I gave them and addictions that I supported with praise, money, and promotions. I built my career on their misery and told myself that it was none of my business. It was different with you."

Nate drank some wine and continued.

"Tucker, you were, you are, like a son to me. I wasn't going to add your marriage to all the other ones I'd destroyed. Jack wanted you fired anyway, and it had reached the point where it was going to happen whether or not I did it. I figured that firing you would give you a chance to reevaluate your life and maybe fix things with Carol. It didn't work out. Carol got killed that day, and after the funeral you dropped out of sight. I should have called you sooner. We should have had this talk before, but I've been avoiding the subject. I'm sorry."

Nate cut into his steak with renewed concentration.

My plate was full of uneaten meat. I pushed it away, aligning the knife and fork in the universal signal of "please take this." I went back to drinking Scotch. Nate sipped his wine.

I gazed at the tree where the pug had pooped and said, "Well, it pisses me off. I appreciate what you were trying to do, but you ruined me. I'll bet Carol and I could have worked it out without me being fired."

"You think so?"

"Things were getting better. We might have had some thawing there at the end. Carol was talking about going away for a couple of weeks and reconnecting. Carol and I hadn't … ah … connected … for months. She wanted to go back to the Cape for a vacation. Of course, I wouldn't have been able to go."

"Why not?"

"Work, of course."

"You wouldn't have had work. That was the point."

I stood up. I needed to get away from Nate. I tripped over the three-inch stone wall that surrounded the cafe.

Nate said, "Be careful." As I started to walk away, he called out, "Are you still working with me on this Bronte thing? I need you."

I said, "Ask me tomorrow." I turned up Fairfield toward home. I still hadn't called Charlene.

SEVENTEEN

IT HAD BEEN A long, long day. The four Scotches weren't making me feel any better, and my right foot seemed to have developed an extra toe that got caught on every sidewalk crack.

"Hi, baby." Carol was walking next to me on the street.

I said, "I don't want to talk to you."

"Did Nate upset you? Poor baby."

I fumbled my headset out of my pocket, stuck it in my ear, and hissed, "You got me fired!"

"I tried to save our marriage."

We had reached the corner of Boylston Street. I decided to take a left and walk along the street rather than cut through the Prudential Center. I didn't think this was a good conversation to have in a mall.

I said, "You couldn't give me one success in life? You couldn't let me see this one project through?"

Carol scoffed. "Oh, please. Success? What was success to you? Making a new virus? Since when—"

"It was my project. It was my chance to prove something."

"Prove what? What did you need to prove so badly?"

"I was going to prove to you and to everyone that I'm not just a fuck-up who accidentally brought down the Internet. I wanted to show I could do a real job."

"I didn't need you to prove anything except that you loved me."

"Why did I need to prove that? Of course I loved you. I married you."

"That's not proof! You treated me like crap. You just married me to show yourself that you were a stable guy. I felt so blessed to be part of your solution to low self-esteem."

I was struggling to keep my voice down and to avoid looking at Carol. It's one thing to walk down the street talking to yourself on a headset. It's another to look at somebody no one else can see.

I said, "Why don't you get lost? Walk toward the light, or whatever it is you people do to move on."

Carol slowed and I stole a glance at her. Her lip was jutting out. She sniffled and wiped at her nose with her hand. She stopped walking. I turned and looked at her.

She said, "You never gave a shit about us, did you?" Tears were streaming down her face. "You don't care that Nate tried to help. You just care that you were replaced by Roland."

"That's not true," I said. I closed my eyes to collect myself. When I opened them, Carol had disappeared.

I was panting, staring into the spot where she had been. It was a mess. It was all a mess. Maybe we could have fixed it. The vacation on the Cape might have been just the thing to tear down the wall. I'd never know because some psycho had murdered Carol before we had a chance. Probably the same one who had killed Kevin and made Charlene a widow.

The thought brought me up short. I walked on toward my house. I didn't want to talk to Charlene in the street.

EIGHTEEN

CLICK AND CLACK HAD mounted an assault on their feeding sponge and were rapidly shoveling bits of freeze-dried seaweed into their mouths. They ignored me as I entered the kitchenette craving sugar. I opened the freezer and pulled out a pint of Emack & Bolio's Chocolate Moose ice cream. I'd bought it as a dessert for last night, but Margaret and I never got to eat it.

I broke out an ice cream paddle and carved the ice cream into a bowl. Got a spoon and slid onto one of the tall chairs in front of the counter. The whole time I kept an eye on my silver BlackBerry as if it were going to bite me. For its part, the BlackBerry was silent, waiting. It knew that it would get its chance.

Click and Clack waved their claws, eating. I said to them, "I'll call her. Just let me finish my ice cream." I walked around my apartment, eating as I went. I stayed out of my office. I knew that if I got in front of my computer I'd surf the web until it was too late to call. When I finished the ice cream, I put the pint back in the freezer, washed my bowl and the paddle, dried them, and put them away.

Now there was nothing on the counter but the crabs, Kevin's cell phone, and my BlackBerry. It was time to make my move. I grabbed the BlackBerry and dropped into the living room sofa. I looked out the front window at the afternoon sun and pressed the *K* key. It used to call Kevin at home. Now it would just call Charlene.

"Hello," said an older male voice. Charlene's father, maybe?

"Hi," I said, "I'm calling for Charlene."

"Yeah. She's busy right now."

"It's Kevin's friend, Tucker. I was calling to ... "

I heard the phone get muffled against a chest, then indecipherable human voices, a low-pitched one and then a higher one. A woman's voice. Finally the mouthpiece came away from the chest and I heard Charlene say, "Let me talk to him."

The older guy said, "Are you sure?" and then Charlene was on the phone.

"What did you do?" she said.

"Charlene, I—" I started.

"What did you do, Tucker? What did you do to get my husband killed?"

My heart got tangled in my guts as my insides twisted.

"I didn't do—I don't know—I wasn't."

"Goddamn it, Tucker, he was in cybercrime! He was supposed to sit behind his computer and read emails. What did you *do*? How did you get him out on that bridge?"

"He wanted to meet me there."

"Why? What did you *do*?"

"I didn't do anything!" I shouted. I shook my head. I had just yelled at a widow.

I suck.

"Oh, you did something. He never got into trouble unless it was with you. You with your goddamn drinking and stupid hacks. How did you get him killed?"

"I don't know! OK? OK? I don't know how I got him killed."

"You admit it? You bastard! You got poor Kevin killed and you admit it. He was helping you, wasn't he? He was helping you with that whole thing about Carol."

What could I say? I said nothing. She was right.

"Say something!" I heard the phone move away from her mouth. "No! No! I want this bastard to know what he did."

I shouted into the phone, "I'll fix it! Charlene, I'll fix it!"

"How will you fix it? How can you fix anything?"

"I'll find out who did this. I swear it! I'll find out or I'll die trying!"

There was sobbing on the other end that diminished as the phone was taken away. There was a pause and then the male voice was back.

"I'm sorry," he said. "She's not herself. She doesn't really blame you."

I said, "When's the wake?"

"Don't know yet. Charlene's making the plans."

"When she feels better, tell her that I'll see her then, and that I'll deliver."

"Deliver what?"

I said, "I'm sorry for your loss," and broke the connection.

My face was wet. I hadn't noticed when the tears had started. I lay on the couch as a flood of sorrow threatened to break through my defenses. I needed to get outside my head. I looked around my apartment to find a focal point.

There was a sock on the floor. It was left over from last night with Margaret. Was it only last night? I started thinking back to before I had met her, to the sudden craving for a coffee that had driven me into the Thinking Cup. I got it in a mug. I hate drinking out of paper. It was so pedestrian. The forces of Scotch and exhaustion combined with thoughts of coffee shops to drag me into a fitful sleep.

But there was no relief. Kevin's chest exploded in my dreams, Carol thrashed on the kitchen floor, and I ran from room to room in our old house looking for the shadowy figure who had killed them both. Abruptly, I found myself standing in a silent office.

It was my old office at MantaSoft, but it had changed. The walls were covered in moss, and vines dripped down from the ceiling tiles. There was someone sitting at my desk typing on my computer. He looked up at me. It was Roland Baker. He laughed and I startled myself awake.

It was dark. I looked at my watch. It was past 10:00 p.m. I'd slept for three hours. Perfect. I rose, washed my face, drank some water, and headed out into the night. I was going to keep my promise to Charlene, and I knew what I had to do. It was time to find out what was so goddamn special about Roland Baker.

NINETEEN

THE NAP HAD LEFT me sober enough to drive but drunk enough to take reckless action. I needed to figure out what the hell Roland had been doing as team leader and how this could have gotten Kevin killed, and I figured the best way to do that was to visit my old office in Waltham.

Waltham is northwest of Boston, about ten miles out on a beltway road that we call Route 128, but that the rest of the country calls I-95. At one time, twenty years ago, Route 128 would be uttered in the same sentence as Silicon Valley, as in, "High-tech hotspots such as Route 128 and Silicon Valley."

That was a long time ago. The Massachusetts high-tech industry collapsed in the late '80s, and now most of our engineers work in remote offices of Silicon Valley companies. My office in Waltham had been one of these satellites. MantaSoft's headquarters was in Palo Alto, down the street from Stanford.

The Rosetta design team, my team, worked in an enormous silver office building with a clock above its front door. They shared the building with an assortment of dot-coms, insurance companies, and PR firms.

I drove a Mini Cooper Zipcar to Waltham. The clock on the front of the building said 11:30 as I pulled into the empty visitor's lot. I had worked enough late nights alone to know that the office would be empty. I used the key card Shelly had given me to enter the building and took the elevator to the third floor. MantaSoft sat at one end of the hallway. It was time to break into my old office.

I paused at the MantaSoft front door. The door was oak and guarded by a card key reader. The reader blinked at me with its red eye. I didn't want my name recorded in the MantaSoft security system as a late-night entry, so I ignored the front door and took a left, walking down the hallway toward the back door.

The back door is a great example of how too much security results in no security. MantaSoft's hyper-paranoid security guards had decided that we had to have a lock on the door to the hallway. This meant that if you went to the rest room, you needed your card key to reenter. Of course, people forgot their card keys and needed to bang on the door after making potty. This was embarrassing to the person with the small bladder and annoying to the guy who sat nearest the door, an engineer named Ducky Gillis.

Ducky solved the problem by replacing the backdoor's generic knob with a combination-lock knob. Now people could reenter without disturbing him. Ducky had never asked permission to implement this change. In his words, "Questions you know the answer to, you don't need to ask." Soon after his victory over corporate security, Ducky quit MantaSoft to become a chair maker in Vermont. He took the knowledge of how to change the combination with him.

The knob was large and silver and had five mechanical buttons the size of pencil erasers. I keyed in the combination: 406—Ted Williams's batting average in 1941. I turned the knob and entered. Once inside, I eased the door closed and listened. The office was dark and silent. The air conditioning was off for the night, and the building was stuffy. I was comforted by the familiar space even though I felt like an intruder.

Thirty engineers worked in Waltham. Two rows of cubes ran down the middle of the office, which curved away to my right. To my left was a kitchen with the coffee makers essential to technological advancement. The cubes didn't have access to the windows. These were reserved for the offices along the wall—symbols of power. I had lived in one of those offices, though Roland squatted there today.

I walked through the eerie space and glanced into the cubes. People's family photos looked skeletal as my night vision removed the details and colors. The unused computers whirred. I lingered by Carol's old cube, right outside my office. The nameplate on the cube read "Dana Parker." Dana's computer whirred with reams of computer code sitting on her screen. She hadn't locked the screen. Sloppy. I considered sending a sexy email to Jack Kennings in her name, the usual punishment for an unlocked screen. Instead, I got to work.

It was time to get into Roland's office. His door was closed, but I knew how to break in. There's always a lazy person who'll get you through a security system. In my case, his name was Frank. Frank had locked himself out of his office once and missed an important meeting. Now he never locked his door and so became the weak link into Roland's office.

Frank's office shared a wall with Roland's. Frank had a credenza full of family pictures next to that wall. I carefully removed these and stacked them in order. That way I could put them back in the right spots.

I stood on the credenza and looked at the ceiling tiles. People are naive. They think that because the walls in their house go all the way to the ceiling, the same must be true in the office. They think locking their doors makes their offices into secure little boxes. They're wrong. Years of security hacking had taught me to look beyond the intended behavior of objects and study their design instead. Yes. A wall is supposed to separate two offices, but when you look at its design, you'll see why it fails.

The visible ceiling in an office building is suspended from the floor above to make room for air conditioning ducts, Ethernet cables, power cords, and the other hidden entrails of office life. Once you push up a ceiling tile, a new world is available. I stood on Frank's credenza, held up one of his ceiling tiles, and looked over the wall. I slid the tile out of the way, reached over the wall, and got a finger under Roland's tile. I lifted it and slid it aside, tunneling into Roland's office from above. I jumped and pulled myself to the top of the wall. Swung my feet up and looked down into the room.

It was a mess. In just six months, Roland had converted my immaculate workspace into a shitstorm of discarded magazines and sheets of paper. He had the same type of credenza as Frank, except that his was covered in piles of manila folders, discarded newspapers, and other trash.

I thought about quitting right there. Instead, I said, "Screw it" and kept moving. I hung from the ceiling, kicked some paper out of the way, and dropped. Hitting the credenza in a sprawl, I crashed across it and spread Roland's papers across the floor in an even layer, landing on top of them. So much for stealth.

I lay on my back assessing the damage. I wiggled my fingers and toes, stretched and craned my neck, and looked up at the office door. It was ajar.

"Idiot," I said to myself. I had assumed the door was locked and hadn't even tried it. I stood up in the slippery pile of spilled paper, turned on the office light, and opened the door all the way. I looked around, listening for any sign that I wasn't alone. There was none. I got behind the desk and sat down in front of Roland's computer.

The keyboard was horrifying. In only six months Roland had managed to deposit a thin film of oily gunk on the home row of keys. The mouse also wore a light patch of oil over the left mouse button. I shuddered and went to work. It was time to hack into Roland's account. Fortunately, he was running Windows.

Pity the poor bastards at Microsoft. Every time they try to make their machine easier to use, they open another hacker doorway. Take the sticky-keys feature. You press the shift key five times at login, and *voilà* you get a handicapped-accessible software keyboard. Or consider the fact that if you crash a Windows machine, it generates a crash report to be sent to Microsoft. This report comes with a handy link that opens the Microsoft privacy statement in Notepad, and Notepad gives you access to a File Explorer that can rename your files. Software guys like me can put these features together to ... well ... hack your computers.

Roland's computer was under his desk. Its fan whined as it struggled to suck air through the pile of paper that had been stacked on and around it. I crawled under the desk to find the power button. Oreo wrappers and yellow bits of Twinkie covered the floor. My hand brushed a dead bug that had apparently starved to death trying to digest the yellow cake. The rug smelled like feet. I lay on my back like a mechanic and snaked my arm into the space behind the PC to power it down and then up. I climbed out from under the desk and brushed myself clean as best I could.

I waited for the computer to complain that it had crashed, offer to email a crash report, and let me open the privacy statement in Notepad. Once I was in Notepad, I replaced the sticky-key program with the cmd program … that black screen the IT guy uses to type commands into your computer. Then I rebooted the computer, pressed the shift key five times, and had a black command window come up, ready for my command.

I typed the command that erased Roland's password, logged in, and waited for the interminable Windows login sequence to complete.

I thrummed my fingers on the desk and looked out the window. It was late and Route 128 was quiet. I looked across the highway at the dark trees beyond. How many times had I seen this view? The trees were full of green leaves, but I'd seen them turn red and orange and go bare. I'd sat at this desk, working late, and watched silent snow layer the trees and fill the highway. I remembered the warm feeling of virtue in these moments—the alpha dog status of being the hardest working guy in the office.

I looked back from the window. Carol stood among Roland's wreckage, looking out the window over my shoulder.

"Reminiscing, baby?"

"Yeah."

"Are you remembering how I used to leave here at six every night?"

"I wasn't."

"Did you remember how I used to cook dinner? Do you remember the Moo Shu hamburger recipe I got from Rachael Ray?"

"The one with the scallions and hoisin sauce?"

"They were good hamburgers," she said.

"Yes."

"It's too bad you never ate them."

"That's not true. I had them for breakfast sometimes," I said, typing into Roland's computer. It started its slow login process. Roland's computer was a pig.

"I gave up cooking after six months of eating alone."

I turned to her. "Why do you always dwell on the bad times?"

Carol blinked at me. I had caught her off guard. She had nothing to say.

I continued. "We were having fun when I got this job. You even volunteered to sit in that cube near me."

Carol said, "I did it so we could leave together."

"I know. It was fun."

"What are you talking about? You never left. You got this office and this job and you were the boss and then you never left."

"It was just until the project was done."

"Was it my fault?"

"What?"

"Wasn't I a good wife?"

"Of course you were."

"Then why didn't you love me?"

I tried to formulate a response, but my throat was filling with a choking ball of regret. I opened my mouth to speak but closed it when the ball began to burn. I turned to look at Carol, but the lights in the main office turned on and I heard a voice.

"Turn that light off!" Roland barked. The light snapped off, leaving my office as the only lit place. I bolted from the chair, slipping and stumbling on the stacks of printer paper strewn across the floor. I stayed low and scrambled into the cube across from the office door. Dana's cube. It was pitch dark under her desk. I curled myself into the spot.

Roland ran into his office and surveyed the mess.

He called out, "It's good that you rang me."

Dana stepped into view as she spoke. "I didn't know what to do. I almost called the police."

Roland said, "That would have been a bad idea. You did well. Now go home."

"But I thought I'd—"

"No. Go home."

I was screwed. I had hidden under Dana's desk. Right next to her handbag. She'd practically have to ask me to hand it to her. With her cube five feet from Roland's office, I couldn't move without getting caught.

Dana stepped into the office, looked around at the mess and then up. She said, "It looks like he came through the ceiling."

Roland looked up and said, "Bloody hell!" and then, "I thought I told you to leave."

Dana ignored him. She asked, "Did he take anything?"

Roland said, "I don't think so." He looked at his computer screen. Roland rattled the mouse, clicked, and said, "He was logged into my computer as me!"

Dana came around and looked at the screen. She asked, "How did he get the password?"

I gauged the distances needed to make a run for it. Dana and Roland were looking at the computer screen, but I could see their faces, which meant I was in their peripheral vision.

I might have escaped if I could start at a dead run, but I'd gotten myself wedged under the desk and would have to crawl before I could stand. I'd be in their full view. I decided that there was nothing I could do. My only hope was that Dana would forget her handbag.

Roland forced the issue. He was standing in front of the computer. His face had gone blank and he was completely still except for his breathing, which had gotten deeper. He leaned on the desk and had moved the mouse when Dana pointed at the screen and said, "Did he get into your email?"

At the sound of her voice, Roland erupted, "I said *go home!*" He shoved Dana toward the office door. She was a foot smaller than him, no more than five two, and the shove knocked her off balance. She shrieked as she slipped on the strewn paper, caught herself, and stumbled out of the office.

Dana regained her composure and hustled toward the front door. I sighed. Her bag was safe with me. With her gone, Roland reached under his Manchester United warm-up jacket and produced a small, boxy gun. *Oh fuck!* I pulled myself farther under the desk, as Roland walked around his desk.

Quick, light footsteps halted him. Dana was coming back. Roland hid his gun behind the door as Dana said, "I forgot my bag." She turned into her cube, bent, reached under the desk, and looked straight into my face. We made eye contact. I handed her her bag. She straightened, holding her bag, and said to Roland, "Don't ever push me again."

Roland said, "I apologize. I'm very upset. Now please go."

Dana went out the front doors. Roland watched her leave. I heard the front doors close, and Roland emerged with his gun. He called out, "Whoever you are! You can't escape! I'm going to search all these cubes!" He stopped and listened.

Roland skipped over Dana's cube. Apparently he considered it searched. He started working his way down the row. I crawled out of my hiding space and got ready to sprint. I risked a peek and saw Roland turn the corner in the cube farm. I bolted down the hall and out the front door where Dana had left. I heard Roland shout, "Hey!" but by then I was gone. I ran down the hallways and then down the staircase. I didn't stop running until my shaking hands were turning the key in my Zipcar.

MONDAY

TWENTY

"A GUN," SAID BOBBY as he examined his scone.

"Yes, a gun. A big fucking gun," I said. I was trying to make a point.

It was nine in the morning, and Bobby and I were sitting on black metal chairs at a sidewalk table in front of Wired Puppy, a local coffee shop that was holding its own against Starbucks. Miller was wearing an oatmeal-colored summer suit, white shirt, and bright yellow tie. He looked like he was playing the sun in a kindergarten play. I was wearing bags under my eyes from a sleep-destroying cocktail of alcohol and adrenaline. A two-foot black, wrought-iron fence separated us from the commuters who hustled down the street as we breakfasted on exotic coffees and blueberry scones. Bobby was sipping his coffee through a tiny plastic hole in the lid. I, classier than that, had asked for my coffee in a mug.

"He had a gun. So?" said Bobby.

"So arrest him."

"You want me to arrest Roland Baker because you say that he pulled a gun when you broke into his office."

"It was actually my office."

"No, it was actually his office."

"Whatever. I want you to arrest him for carrying a gun."

"It seems to me that I should be arresting you for trespassing."

"You're missing the whole fucking point!" I gestured with my mug, sloshed some hot coffee on my hand, swore, put it down, and crossed my arms.

"Jesus, will you relax?"

I had wolfed my scone. Bobby's lay unmolested on his plate.

"I need another scone."

"Get it later. Drink your coffee and relax."

"You gonna eat that one?"

"Yes," Bobby said. He picked it up and took a bite out of it.

I splayed myself across my black wire chair and rubbed my eyes with my thumb and forefinger. I said, "Fine. I'm relaxed."

Bobby kept talking. "Good. Now shut up and listen. I'm not going to do anything about Roland and his fucking gun." Bobby started ticking points off on his meaty fingers. "First, I told you so. These guys aren't fucking around. Second, it's your word against his. And third, I don't give a shit because Kevin wasn't killed by a gun that could fit under a Manchester United sweatshirt."

"But Roland probably has something to do with Kevin getting killed."

"Yeah, he probably does. So why the fuck would I arrest him on a gun charge that he could beat without breaking a sweat?"

I straightened and put up my hands. "Fine. Fine. You're right."

"Of course I'm right."

"So you're the expert. What should I do now?"

"I told you what to do. Find a safe hole and crawl into it."

"I won't do that."

"Why not?"

"One of these bastards killed my wife. I want to know who it was."

"Let the local police handle it."

"They're done handling it. They decided it was me, realized they couldn't prove it, and gave up. Stupid donut munchers."

"Hey! Cut that shit out."

I had hit a nerve, but I didn't care. I was pissed off, and the image of Kevin on the Harvard Bridge kept crashing into the image of Carol on the kitchen floor. Something ugly was writhing in the back of my mind, and I was getting tired of controlling it.

I said, "All I get from all you people is that you can't do anything."

"We can do lots."

"Yeah? What have you done about Kevin?"

Miller stared at me, his jaw clenching and relaxing. He took a deep breath and blew it out. He leaned back in his chair and looked into his coffee. I waited, eyeing the uneaten portion of his scone. Finally Bobby looked up at me.

"All right, fuck it," he finally said.

"What's that mean?"

"You're obviously going to keep poking around doing stupid shit trying to figure this thing out. I might as well use you to get some information."

"Clearly I live to be used."

"Shut up and listen."

I shut up.

Bobby said, "You told me that Kevin was pissed that you got involved with this Bronte company."

"Yeah. He said I fucked things up by talking to Margaret Bronte."

"Why?"

"I don't know."

"Maybe you could find out," said Miller. He popped the rest of the scone into his mouth, scraped his chair back, and joined the commuters on the sidewalk. I went into the coffee shop with my mug, got a refill and another scone, and grabbed a seat in the subterranean back room that was Wired Puppy's seating area.

Bobby was right and I was stupid. I had spent the night crashing around Roland's office when I could have been doing research on the Internet. I hadn't even checked out Bronte's website. It was time to get smart.

I finished my breakfast and climbed out onto the hot, sunny sidewalk. The humidity had already started to rise, and it was going to be another scorcher. My choices for Internet research were to either walk all the way back home in the humidity, or risk assimilation. I decided to risk assimilation. Tweeted:

To the Apple Store!

TWENTY-ONE

THE APPLE STORE ON Boylston Street loomed over the sidewalk like a crystalline Borg cube. Fortunately, Apple hadn't recently released some minor modification to one of their products, so I didn't have to negotiate a rope line of groupies to get into the place. I love Apple products. They're solidly built, run a secure operating system, and look great. But I could never understand the hysteria, the long lines, or the desperate need to be the first person in the office to own the latest iPad. My silver BlackBerry was still doing the job.

The store had just opened and was still empty. Blue-shirted Apple geniuses loitered about the edges of the rectangular room, checking machines, poking at iPads, and chatting. I walked to the center of the cube and mounted the glass spiral staircase, climbing the wide white stairs on the outer edge of the spiral and executing a 180-degree turn. The staircase deposited me on the second floor.

I approached the floor-to-ceiling glass wall at the front of the store and watched commuters and tourists navigate Boylston

Street. A girl in a yellow sundress walked across the street carrying a coffee with a confident swaying stride. She deftly sidestepped a guy in a striped shirt who had come to a dead stop on the sidewalk and was looking up at the store. He caught me looking at the girl, dropped his eyes, and entered the store. I followed her down the street with my eyes and tweeted:

`Enjoying the view from the Apple Cube.`

It was time to get to work. Large iMacs lined the edge of the store floor. I positioned myself in front of one away from the window and opened the web browser. Navigated to evernote.com, logged in, and was ready to do my research.

A blue-shirted genius popped up next to me. "Trying out the new iMac?"

I said, "Yeah. Love this thing." I Googled "Jack Kennings Manta-Soft."

The kid said, "Do you have any questions I could answer?"

Google produced reams of data. Jack Kennings had quite an Internet footprint. The top of the screen showed an interview on YouTube. I copied its URL to Evernote. Next was a series of interviews. These were uninteresting.

I Googled "Jack Kennings resume." Got a lot of six-year-old articles about how Jack was taking over as CEO at MantaSoft. Our old CEO, the founder, had been kicked out in a dispute with the board. Jack was the replacement CEO. He was going to bring "professional management" to the company.

The kid in the blue shirt had been watching me. He said, "You know you can use Bento for storing those notes."

The kid was just doing his job, so I was patient. "Yeah," I said, "I know, but this way I can access my stuff at home."

The kid said, "You're looking for his résumé? Is this guy on LinkedIn?"

I stopped reading and turned to him, "Hey, good call, dude. I'll check it." I pointed over his shoulder. "You have another customer."

The guy who had disrupted the girl in the yellow sundress was standing across the room looking at iPads. The kid took off to help him.

LinkedIn told me that Jack had been CEO of two previous software security companies. Before that he had been a VP of Engineering at a startup, and before that a director. Jack's climb had been swift and uninterrupted. He lived in the Bay Area and had gone to Stanford for both his undergraduate engineering degree and his MBA. *Stanford*. There are those from MIT who would have held that against him, but I was much too open-minded for that. I settled for pitying him.

I Googled "Jack Kennings +children +wife" to look into Jack's personal life. The only hits were from the local newspaper. Jack had run a campaign to raise money for a playground, a school, a battered women's shelter, and a dog adoption center. He had served as president of the PTO and had won the Social Entrepreneur of the Year award from the Stanford Alumni. I found a picture of Jack and his wife at a charity dinner. He wore a tux and she sported a red dress. She came up to his armpit and had the hot, blond, busty look of a second wife. Jack had a silly grin on his face. He knew he was a lucky guy. I added all this to my notes.

Margaret was next. The Bronte website mirrored the shark theme in Margaret's booth. The website showed that Bronte had two security products, some sort of network sniffer that would look through your network and report suspicious employee activity. This was nothing new. MantaSoft had had this technology for a year. The site offered a few white papers that would provide useful information to a security ignoramus, but nothing that a pro wouldn't already know.

High-tech companies have a constant struggle between marketing and product development. In most startups, product development wins and you get interesting products with lousy marketing: a misspelling-laden website that rips off the tag line from some unrelated product. *Securesoft: When it absolutely, positively needs to be secure.*

Bronte was different. Here the marketing was strong, but the products were weak. The site was crisp and sharp, the *Move or Die* theme was woven throughout the text, and the graphics were original and arresting. Margaret clearly knew how to position her product, even if that product was boring and delivered outdated functionality.

The Management page had a single picture of Margaret. She wore a black suit that complemented her salt and pepper hair. She stood at an angle to the camera, arms crossed, blue eyes boring into me. Her bio said that she was the founder of Bronte Software. I knew that. It said that she had previously worked for IBM, Cisco, and 3M. There was nothing more.

I went to LinkedIn and found Margaret's obligatory CEO page. It said that she was CEO of Bronte Design, and that she had previously worked for IBM, Cisco, and 3M. Nothing new. While Jack had over 500 connections on LinkedIn and was only one link removed from me, Margaret had ten links, and no connections to me.

I looked over my shoulder. Striped Shirt was standing behind me. He had been looking over my shoulder. Some instinct made my stomach twitch, and I decided to leave. I closed the browser and looked around. The kid in the blue shirt was helping a heavy woman wearing red shorts and a blue T-shirt choose an iPhone.

Her midriff was bare, but it was less a fashion statement than a consequence of physics. Striped Shirt had moved away from me and was poking at an iPad on a table, but he didn't seem to be using it. Just poking it. It was time to go.

I took long strides toward the frosted-glass spiral staircase at the center of the store. Striped Shirt also slid toward the staircase. I sped up and took a step on the narrow inner stairs of the spiral when he made his move. He ran toward me and hit me with his shoulder, knocking my hand away from the banister. The steps in the inner edge were narrow. I crashed headlong down the sharp, glass stairs.

One thing about falling down a glass spiral staircase: it hurts like hell. I raised my hands to block the stairs and my palms were creased with pain as they hit the glass edges. I flipped and my elbow hit another edge, and in another spin my forehead cracked into the glass. I stopped falling when I was halfway down the stairs and Striped Shirt was standing over me. He reached down as if to help me up, and I instinctively reached for his hand.

Striped Shirt pulled me close. He smelled of cigarettes, coffee, and cologne. His face was soft, but his eyes bore into mine. He said, "Mind your own business, Mr. Tucker." He had an accent. Eastern European? He dropped my hand, and my head bounced back onto the glass stair. I didn't see him leave. I had blood in my eyes.

TWENTY-TWO

THE LONG RED LINE train rumbled through the station, tickling the stitches on my forehead with its rushing wake of air. The breeze felt good. The sky was hot and blue above me. I had started to sweat on the Charles/MGH train station platform, elevated above the cars passing below on Storrow Drive.

The train had just left the Longfellow Bridge. It had emerged from its tunnel in Cambridge, crossed the river, and would now plunge under the city of Boston on its way south to Braintree. I had just walked to the station from the emergency room at Mass General Hospital, where an Indian doctor had put a shot of Novocain and four stitches into my face above my right eyebrow.

A police officer had visited me in the emergency room, asking whether I had seen the guy who pushed me and whether I could give a description. I had given him a broad sketch of a guy with dark hair and a striped shirt, but said that it had all happened too fast for me to remember anything else. I'm not sure why I lied.

In my memory, the fall happened in slow motion. I could still feel the rough skin of his hand knocking my fingers away from the guardrail, and the hard knot of bone in his shoulder hitting me on the spine. I had stumbled forward onto the narrow inner steps of the spiral staircase. I missed the first step and had slipped off the second, pitched too far forward to stop myself from falling. I remembered every blow on the steps: hand ... elbow ... head ... shoulder ... back ... other hand. Each one of them created its own knot of pain.

I could also remember the guy who pushed me. He had a wide face and a soft mouth. Black hair, black eyes, a small scar on his right cheek. He was a little walleyed, with his left eye drifting away while his right locked onto my gaze. That same rough hand grabbed mine, as if to help, and pulled me up. I could remember his message: "Mind your own business, Mr. Tucker." I remember him dropping my hand and running out of the store.

I told the cop none of this. I couldn't see how he could help me. At best, I imagined that he would ask me to come to the station, sign papers, fill out a report, or do whatever it was they did with people who had been attacked. I'd given the cop just enough information to get him to leave, and then I'd walked to the train station.

The train stopped moving and the doors whooshed open. I stepped inside and habitually put my Bluetooth headset into my ear. Carol liked trains. She arrived just as the train pulled out of the station.

She peered at the stitches over my eye and said, "Oh, baby, that looks so painful."

I said, "Looks do not deceive."

Carol reached out and came within an inch of touching the wound, but I knew she wouldn't. She said, "Those people are animals."

114

"Which people?" I asked.

"The ones who killed me. The ones who did this."

"So I'm getting closer. Good."

Carol's eyes started to glisten. She said, "No, baby. It's not good. You need to stop now."

Carol disappeared as the train slowed and entered Park Street station. I stood. The doors whooshed open, and I emerged into the bottom tunnel in Park Street. The Green Line light-rail trolleys were on the floor above.

Normally I liked walking in the train stations. The station's subterranean climate was cool and dry, and the flow of people walking in the same direction filled me with energy. But today was different. As I climbed the stairs, a Hispanic kid in a Celtics T-shirt came bounding down the stairs. He raised his hand to strike me, to push me back down the staircase. I tightened my grip on the handrail and shrunk inward, anticipating the blow. Then he was running on down the stairs, probably trying to catch the train I had just left.

I stood on the stairs for a moment, and then ran up them to get to the platform. I emerged breathless, and people stared at me. I could feel them looking at my cut like I was the weak one in the herd, the one that could be culled out and taken down. I averted my gaze from them and leaned on a support column to wait for the train. My stitches hurt.

The pain was mild but unstoppable. I had never been in a fight before. Growing up in Wellesley, going to MIT, and working in high tech had never exposed me, not once, to a situation where someone could or would inflict pain upon me. Now that it had happened, I realized how little control I had over my life.

I had always believed that I controlled how much people could hurt me. They could mock me, insult me, fire me, and even kill my wife, and I had this notion that while I couldn't control them, I could control my response. I could decide whether I cared about the insult, or worried about being terminated. I could even, I thought, decide how much I'd let Carol's murder get into my head.

But I couldn't control this. I couldn't control a guy pushing me down a staircase. I couldn't control him shooting me with a machine gun. I couldn't control the physical pain that this guy could inflict upon me. The way he could tear my skin and make me bleed. I couldn't stop the blood with a good attitude.

The trolley rattled into the station. I looked behind me, expecting someone to push me in front of it. There was nobody. The doors folded open and I climbed into the car. There were five people spaced around the car, sitting in their chairs and staring into space. The guy closest to me was wearing white iPhone earbuds. He had them cranked up so much that I could hear the music as I sat in a forward-facing double seat. The train started up, and then Carol was sitting in the seat next to the window. Black tunnel streamed past the window next to her.

I said, into my Bluetooth headset, "I'm not stopping."

Carol turned to me and said, "They'll kill you, baby."

"I thought you wanted me to do this. I thought you were hurt that I didn't want to find out who killed you."

Carol said, "I wanted you to ask Nate why he fired you. Then I wanted you to tell Kevin and let him catch them."

"Well, that's not happening now."

"I know," said Carol. "That's why you have to quit. There is nobody to save you now."

The train screamed as it took the hard turn under Boylston Street so it could head into the Back Bay. I waited for the noise to stop and said, "I'm not quitting. I promised Charlene. Did you know she blamed me for Kevin getting killed?"

"That's nonsense, baby. You have to listen to me. You didn't get him killed."

"The hell I didn't," I said, "Charlene was right."

"Charlene is grieving. She's hurt and angry and scared. She doesn't know what she's saying. She can't expect you to do this."

The black tunnel rolled by through the window with periodic lights shining in. I said to Carol, "I'm scared."

"I know, baby. I know."

"But I'm not stopping."

"But they'll kill you. I know they will."

I thought about the life that I'd lead if I stopped now. I'd hole up in my condo and go through the motions of life, just as I had for the past six months. I'd let my world shrink to my condo, the grocery store, and a Twitter account.

I said, "They may kill me. But this is no way to live."

The train pulled into Copley Station and filled up. A woman with a small child stood next to me, looking around for a spot. I stood, gestured to the two empty seats, and said, "Please." I caught the doors just as they were closing. They popped open again. The conductor whined, "Please move away from the doors" as I hopped off the train and headed up the steps.

Back on the street, I followed Boylston toward the convention center. It was time to man up and take my life back. I wanted to stop them before they killed again.

TWENTY-THREE

THE SECURECON TRADE SHOW was a madhouse of carnival barkers. The lights were up, the demos were cranking, and the booth babes were waving. More than a hundred companies were represented at SecureCon, and they were all trying to snag IT geeks.

Every year, thousands of geeks pack up their things, kiss their loved ones goodbye, and fly to SecureCon to see demonstrations of the latest network security software. However, once they get here, they develop cold feet about meeting a salesperson. They walk through the trade show focusing on the blue carpet, carefully avoiding eye contact for fear of being hypnotized, sparrow versus python fashion, into buying expensive new software.

The software companies need to get eyes off the carpet and people into their booths. They use a variety of girls, gadgets, and gimmicks to attract attention. Once in the booth, most geeks are happy to watch a software demonstration and drink a free cappuccino. This bizarre dance turns the show floor into a zoo.

The booth nearest to the front door had a *Star Trek* Vulcan in a blue shirt standing on a box. The Vulcan would gather a crowd with a variety of mentalist mind tricks, then send them into the booth to see demos. At another booth, poker dealers did a booming business. IT geeks watched demos to get poker chips. Then they played Texas hold 'em, and the winners traded poker chips for T-shirts, toy helicopters, or iPods.

The show had its traditions. A small but persistent company hired the same Elvis impersonator every year. The guy would stand on stage, gyrate, and sing hacked Elvis songs such as "Hard Drive Hotel," "Don't be Phished," and "You Ain't Nuthin' but a Virus."

Another booth had women in bikinis standing under fake palm trees. No pitch, just the women. The male IT geeks swarmed around the booth and were drawn into the demonstrations. The female geeks rolled their eyes and went to listen to Elvis.

MantaSoft marketing had gone all out on the Bostonian theme of "Revolutionary Security." To complement the Minuteman Statue, they had forced all the booth personnel to wear eighteenth-century garb with breeches and triangle hats. In a nod to political correctness over historical accuracy, the women also wore long coats, breeches, and triangle hats. I thought this was a shame. I find women in bonnets quite fetching. I headed back to Margaret's aquarium.

The sharks had changed direction and were swimming clockwise today. Their tails moved in short strokes as they lived up to the booth's "Move or Die" slogan. I watched the sharks out of the corner of my eye as Kurt Monroe, still wearing his shark-bite T-shirt, gave me a demo of Bronte's software. The shirt was jammed into his chinos to make a gut-restricting sling that kept Kurt's sizable belly from introducing itself. I was bored. The software was as original as a *Gilligan's Island* episode. Kurt had obviously memorized his demo and was charging through it with gusto.

"Here's the dashboard. Bronte's unified..." My mind wandered as Kurt bombarded me with a blizzard of marketing fluff. The sharks drifted back into my vision. I wondered who fed them. I fiddled with Kurt's business card in my pants pocket, and it reminded me that he was talking. I refocused.

Kurt was blathering on and spitting marketing terms like "platform independent," "Web 2.0," "cutting-edge technology," blah, blah, blah. I grimaced to stifle a yawn. My mind drifted to memories of my night with Margaret and the feel of her skin against mine. The memory shifted into fantasy as I thought about Dana, but the fantasy faded into a question about her role in the office last night. She was on someone's side. I just wasn't sure whose.

"This is the fun part." Kurt interrupted my thoughts. He was still giving his demo. "This is the résumé-catcher. If some guy in your company is looking for a job, you'll know about it before his headhunter." Kurt snorted a laugh at his little joke.

I decided to see if he had any game. "Does the résumé-catcher use Bayesian filtering?" I asked.

"I'm sorry, come again?" he said.

"Bayesian filtering. Does it use Bayesian filtering to catch the résumés?"

Kurt started spouting from the marketing guide. "The software uses advanced pattern-recognition algorithms to—"

"Yeah, yeah, yeah. But what kind of pattern-recognition algorithms does it use?"

Beads of sweat formed on Kurt's forehead like dew on a windshield. "I think it looks for phrases. Like, it will find 'employment history,' and so it knows the email has a résumé."

"Phrases. Not individual words?"

"Yeah. I guess."

"So it's not so much Bayesian as something like CRM114?"

Kurt's eyes drifted longingly to his screen and his memorized script. Gears chunked away behind his pudgy cheeks as he tried to figure out how to get me back on his happy path. I let him sweat and said, "OK, try this one. What if the employee encrypts the résumé? Can you catch it then?"

Kurt's face brightened, and he started to answer. His eyes widened as he looked behind me. I felt a soft hand on my shoulder turning me away from Kurt. It was Margaret. "Kurt, I'll help Tucker."

"OK, Ms. Bronte."

Margaret steered me away with a little push. "Come with me."

I said, "OK, Ms. Bronte."

Margaret headed back through the curtain behind her booth and ushered me through the gap with a *right this way* gesture.

I walked past the curtain and the show disappeared. We were alone, standing on the shiny concrete floor behind the curtain.

"It's a pleasure to see you," said Margaret.

"Same here," I said. Margaret was wearing a black business suit with a blue blouse open at the throat. She had simple diamond stud earrings on silver settings that complemented her short salt-and-pepper hair.

Margaret stepped closer. I could feel her aura as she invaded the edge of my personal space. She was a tall woman and almost came up to my nose. She looked up at me and asked, "What do you think?"

My chest clunked. "What do I think about what?"

Margaret laughed and stepped a little closer. She put my hands on her hips, with my fingertips resting on the top of her ass. "What do you think of my software?"

I thought her software was banal and derivative. I thought that it offered nothing new or state of the art to the industry. I thought the user interface looked like something that had been put together as a college project.

I said, "It's very nice."

Margaret's perfume wafted around me. I stayed in place, quietly taking it in. The feeling in my chest moved downward through my gut. I reveled in the attention.

"Well, you know," she said, "your opinion means a lot to me."

She kissed me. Her tongue danced on the tips of my lips. I said the first thing that came into my head.

"That Kurt guy is an idiot."

Margaret leaned back, her brow knitted. "Why do you say that?"

The spell broke. My hands fell to my sides. "He couldn't tell the difference between Bayesian filtering and a zit on his ass. What a marketing dweeb."

Margaret crossed her arms and looked at me with deep blue eyes. "Did you get to talk much technology with Kurt?"

"Well, no, I had just started."

"I doubt you'll get the kind of information you want from him."

"Really? But he's your—what is it?" I took out Kurt's card and examined the title. "Director of Product Engineering."

Margaret stepped close and took the card out of my hand. "His skills are more in people management. I know a better way for you to get the information you need."

"What's that?"

"Talk to me. Alone. Tomorrow." She tapped the card on my chest where it left little pools of warmth. "Have fun at the show, dear." She turned and went back through the curtain. Her perfume lingered as I stood on the concrete and blinked.

TWENTY-FOUR

I LOOKED AT THE gap in the curtain that had just swallowed Margaret and thought about what to do next. I didn't want to follow her through the curtain. She could be standing right on the other side, and it would be awkward. I decided to walk behind the curtain and enter the show from another point.

"Baby, you are gonna be one fantastic gigolo." Carol was walking alongside me.

"You think?" I said.

"Of course. You're a sexy beast. What grandmother could keep her hands off you?"

"Now that's unkind. Margaret is not that old. She's a dynamo."

"And you're an idiot. Do you really think she likes sleeping with you?"

"It sure seemed that way."

"You are the only thing standing between her and fifty million dollars. She wants you out of the picture."

"What's she going to do? Get me alone and strangle me?"

"I wouldn't put it past her."

"Can't you just let me enjoy the attention?"

"Listen, baby, being dead is not fun. Please tell me you won't be alone with her."

"You're just jealous," I said as we turned the corner of the curtain.

Carol's hands balled into fists. Her voice jangled into the edge of shrill, "You are such a fucking moron! How am I supposed to help you? I'm not jealous of the Crypt Keeper back there. If anything, I'd be jealous of that one." Carol pointed, and I saw Dana standing on my side of the curtain talking on her cell phone. She was facing away from me in a T-shirt and jeans.

I turned back to say that Carol didn't need to worry about Dana, but Carol was gone.

Seeing Dana got me thinking about her name in Kevin's cell phone. What did she have to do with Kevin, and why was he talking to her just before he died? I padded up to Dana. I felt sneaky, but I wanted to hear her conversation.

"Thursday night?" Dana said. She had her phone crammed against her right ear. Her shoulders were hunched and she was looking down. She chewed on the thumbnail of her left hand.

I stopped walking and eavesdropped.

"No, I can't go. Someone might see me," she said, and paused. "Kevin's family, for example…"

Dana was oblivious. Her voice sounded odd and congested. If I had been a real investigator, I would have listened to the whole conversation. But I couldn't handle the guilt.

I tapped her on the shoulder. When she saw me, her eyes flew wide and she said, "Oh shit, I gotta go." She killed the call and put the phone in her pocket. Her tears glistened under her eyes.

I stared at her. She dabbed at her cheeks with her fingers and wiped the back of her hand across her nose. I wished that I had a handkerchief to offer.

"What do you want?" she sniffled.

I didn't know what I wanted anymore. Dana's tears had surprised me. She was crying over Kevin.

Oh, Kevin, seriously? I know Charlene is a handful...

She said "Well?" and wiped at her cheeks one last time. She crossed her arms across her breasts. Her cotton shirt read, "Real women don't date Yankees fans."

"Were you talking about Kevin Murphy?" I asked.

Dana took a deep breath and blew it out in a long, slow exhalation. Her eyes moved up and to the right. "Yes," she said.

"What about him?"

"His wake is Thursday night," Dana said.

Now why didn't I know that? Nobody had called to tell me about Kevin's wake. Why would someone tell her?

"How well did you know Kevin?" I asked. "I thought he just asked you some questions. Were you friends?"

Dana said, "I don't want to talk about it." The tears started again. They welled in her eyes and spilled down her cheeks. She let them spill without trying to wipe them.

I felt like a jerk. She was keeping a secret, but I didn't have the heart to badger her and I wanted her to stop crying. "Let's go outside," I said.

"Outside where?"

"Let's take a walk around the block. It will give you some time to pull yourself together. I'll buy a handkerchief to offer you and we'll talk. I was Kevin's friend, too."

TWENTY-FIVE

As soon as we got into the light, Dana stopped walking. She stood on the sidewalk, and I stopped as well. Dana looked into my face and reached out and touched my stitches with gentle fingers.

"Oh my God, Tucker," she said. "You didn't have this yesterday. What happened?"

"I tripped," I said.

"You need to be more careful."

"So I've been told."

Dana's sniffling had stopped. She developed a purpose to her step as we walked onto Boylston Street and took a left toward Mass Ave.

Boston delivers wildly different neighborhoods within a block of each other. While Newbury Street is a tree-lined shopper's paradise, Mass Ave is a gritty street with cars and students jostling for position.

A car cut in front of us as we started to cross Mass Ave. The driver yelled, "Watch where you're going, jerk!"

"Fuck you, asshole!" I yelled back.

Dana said, "So you grew up in Boston?"

"Yeah. How did you know?"

"Feminine intuition."

We crossed the street without further incident.

I said, "Let me guess. You're from the Midwest."

"Born and bred."

"A corn-fed beauty from Iowa?"

"Kansas."

"Where in Kansas?"

"Near Dodge City."

"Dodge City is in Kansas?"

Dana asked, "How could you not know that Dodge City is in Kansas?"

"I grew up in Boston."

We continued down Mass Ave, past a bum holding a sign. The sign said, "I need a beer and a woman from outer space." *Don't we all, pal.*

Dana grabbed my arm and looked around.

"Oh shit," she said.

"What?"

"I need to go to the bathroom." She turned and headed back toward the McDonald's on the corner of Belvidere Street.

I put my hand on her shoulder to stop her. "God no. You don't want to go there. Those stalls have their own ecosystem."

"I really have to go."

"Come on. I know a better place."

I led Dana down Mass Ave to the Mary Baker Eddy Library. The library's reflecting pool and curving glass lobby sprang out of the city like a vision. We entered the lobby, our heels echoing off of the wooden paneling. A large reception desk stood in the center of the lobby, staffed by a cute receptionist reading a textbook.

"Hi," I said. "We're just here for the bathrooms."

She smiled and gestured to the left rear corner of the lobby. The public bathrooms in the Mary Baker Eddy Library are a blessing to all mankind. The restroom lobby had a brown rug and wooden paneling. There was a couch on one wall under a mirror. The men's room was to the right and the women's room to the left. Dana hustled into the ladies' room, while I used the men's room just to experience the luxury. The room was clean and stylish, with black and white tile and oval mirrors.

While I worked the urinal, I thought about ways to get information from Dana, to gain her trust. She knew more about Kevin than she was letting on. I finished up, washed my hands, and walked back to the front desk, where I bought two tickets from the receptionist.

Dana emerged from the restroom looking energized and relieved.

"Thank you," she said. "I never realized Boston could have such a beautiful bathroom."

"It's the Athens of America, baby. You haven't seen anything yet." I gave Dana a ticket. "I thought we should take a little break."

Dana took the ticket between thumb and forefinger. She said, "What's this?"

"It's a ticket to something I'll bet they don't have in Kansas."

"This isn't a date. Right?"

I smiled and said, "Of course not. That would be silly. I assume a pretty girl like you is seeing someone. Right?"

Dana smiled. "Nice try, Casanova." The smile vanished. "I should be getting back. Roland will be looking for me."

"Roland can wait," I said and extended my palm toward the entrance. Dana took my lead and entered.

The Mary Baker Eddy Library contains one of Boston's hidden treasures: the Mapparium. We walked past the front desk into the Hall of Ideas, a large marble waiting area with columns and wood paneling. True to its name, the Hall was full of ideas. They swirled along the floor and bubbled out of a quiet fountain in the middle of the lobby.

The doors to the Mapparium were on one side of the room. The other had dark wooden paneling and screens. Letters spun on the floor, projected from somewhere overhead. The letters coalesced into words and sentences that ran along the marble floor toward a screen on the right wall. They crawled up the wall and displayed a quote:

> "The highest compact we can make with our fellow is
> —Let there be truth between us two forevermore."
> —RALPH WALDO EMERSON

Dana was entranced by the quote and absentmindedly touched my arm. I maintained my composure and said, "Did you see the fountain?"

She turned toward the quiet fountain that dominated the center of the hall. Gurgling water rose from the center of its flat, glass disk and ran over the sides. Letters also swirled out of the center. They splashed and played among the ripples and then formed themselves into words and another quote:

> "In the adjustment of the new order of things,
> we women demand an equal voice; we shall accept nothing less."
> —CARRIE CHAPMAN CATT

Dana watched the quote float to the edge of the disk and disappear over the edge, washed away by the silent water.

She laughed. "What did you think of that one?"

"Do I think women should have the vote? I don't know. I think it distracts them from butter churning," I said.

Dana said, "Smart ass," and punched me on the arm, hard. *That's gonna bruise.* She asked, "What were you doing in Roland's office last night?"

Before I could formulate an answer, a young woman walked into the lobby.

"Welcome to the Mary Baker Eddy Library and the Mapparium. We are now going to enter the Mapparium, but before we do…" She went on to tell us about forbidden photography. Then she led us and an older couple through heavy paneled doors and into the deep blue of the Mapparium. The five of us walked across a bridge that spanned the middle of the earth.

The Mapparium is a three-story glass globe of the world as it looked in 1934. Visitors stand inside the globe and look out at stained glass panels lit from behind. Most of the Mapparium panels are blue ocean. The countries are shades of red, orange, yellow, and green.

Dana spun, trying to gather the entire globe at once. We settled at the center of the world, resting our arms on the wooden railings. Dana's shoulder touched my arm as our host introduced us to the Mapparium and its history.

A multimedia show started, "Welcome, *Bienvenue, Saludos, Willkommen…*" We learned about the world in 1934 and the countries that had disappeared and reappeared since that time. I heard some of the show, but Dana's quiet breathing was distracting me. While she looked at the red Russia, I looked at her and was struck by the way the blue of the ocean offset her blond hair. When we looked down at Australia, I was looking at her ankle and the way she hooked one foot behind the other as she leaned. My eyes wandered the equator and then Dana's waist and hips. I could see how Kevin would be attracted to her, but I couldn't see Kevin actually going through with it. My mother once told me that only two people really know what goes on in a marriage.

The older couple left us alone after the show, so I showed Dana the acoustics of the globe. The shape of the glass caused tiny sounds to be focused and amplified across the room. I stood at one end of the bridge and she stood at the other.

I whispered "Hi, toots," and the sound bounced off the glass. It was amplified in her ears.

She smiled widely and her laughter cascaded around me like a fountain. She whispered, "This is so cool," and it boomed in my ears.

"I thought you'd like it."

"Tucker," she whispered.

"Yes?"

"What were you doing in Roland's office?"

I asked, "Were you sleeping with Kevin?"

Dana bared her teeth in disgust and shouted, "No!"

The sound nearly knocked me off the platform.

I said, "I'm tired of lies."

I turned and left Dana standing in the globe.

TWENTY-SIX

THE HUMIDITY HIT ME full in the face as I walked out of the library. I heard Dana call behind me, "Tucker, wait!"

I walked to the corner of Clearway, crossed, and waited in front of the Christian Science Reading Room with my arms folded.

Dana looked both ways and crossed after me. She said, "What's the matter?"

"I'm tired of being lied to and interrogated."

"You ask me if I'm fucking a married man, and you're the one being interrogated? I saved your ass last night, and you owe me an explanation."

Dana looked down Mass Ave and said, "Let's go back to work."

"This way," I said and started walking down the uneven bricks of Clearway Street.

"This isn't how we came," said Dana.

"No. It isn't. That's the whole point of a walk around the block. You walk on four different streets and it brings you back to where you started."

"Why are you being such a dick?" Dana was working to keep up with my angry pace.

"You told me that you heard that I like older women. Where did you hear that?"

"I don't see …"

"Where did you hear it?"

"From Kevin, OK? Kevin told me when he was interviewing me."

"That's bullshit. Kevin wouldn't have told you that. He wouldn't even tell me who accused me of murdering Alice because she was Carol's lesbian lover."

Dana darted her eyes at me.

"Oh, so you knew it too," I said. "Was I the only one in the dark?"

We reached the end of Clearway and turned left at I. M. Pei's Christian Science administration building. I took the corner and charged up Clearway along the park that would bring us back to the convention center. Dana kept up with me. I had another thought and stopped walking.

I asked, "Who called you about Kevin's wake? Why would you get invited to his wake? Nobody told me about the wake."

"Is that what this is about?"

"Who were you talking to when I surprised you?"

"It was Kevin's wife, OK? I was talking to Kevin's wife."

"Charlene? How do you know Charlene?"

"How did you know Kevin?"

"Went to school together."

Dana spread her hands. *There you go.*

"You went to BU with Charlene?"

"Yeah. So now you answer my question. Why did you break into my office and scare me half to death?'"

"I scared you?"

133

"I'm a small woman in a dark office at night. A guy comes in the back door and so I hide. The next thing I hear is ceiling tiles being moved, and then scraping, banging, and swearing. Of course I was scared. I peeked into Roland's office, and you're lying on the floor. What were you doing there?"

I felt better. I *knew* that door was closed. I started walking again and said, "It's a long story."

"They're always long stories. Try me."

"Well, what were you doing there?" I asked.

"I was working. I work there."

"You didn't need to be there. You told me that you're staying at the Boylston Suites. You could have worked from your hotel room, just like you worked from the Starbucks."

"Now who's being interrogated?"

We crossed the street to avoid one of Boston's ubiquitous construction sites. A cop directed traffic while talking on his cell phone, waving cars past the hole in the ground and laughing at a joke coming over the phone. I suppose it could have been worse; he could have been holding a cruller in his free hand.

We walked up the sidewalk next to the convention center. I wasn't looking forward to rejoining the madness of Margaret's sharks and MantaSoft's triangle hats. Then I saw a vision.

Bukowski Tavern, its red facade tucked into a parking garage, shone as a beacon of serenity. I took Dana by the hand and led her back across the street to the tavern.

"Let's go in here," I said, opening the door for Dana. She looked at me, her lips tightened with misgiving, then walked through the door.

Bukowski is a long, dark oasis of fine beer and tasty food. It was as if someone had built the parking garage around a diner. A wooden bar ran down one side of the diner, and tables and chairs down the other in front of round windows that looked out on cars rushing down the highway.

I sat at the bar and motioned Dana next to me. She climbed on to the stool as the bartender came over.

I said, "Black Label" and looked at Dana for her order. The beer menu dazzled her. They had beers from every corner of the beer universe. She was still taking in the place and deciding whether to bolt. The kid behind the bar said, "Ma'am?"

Dana said, "Give me what he's having."

The bartender said, "Two Black Labels." He fished around in the refrigerator, pulled out two cans, and popped them open for us. He offered glasses, but I waved them away. Black Label needs to be drunk from the can.

"Bottoms up," I said and took a swig.

Dana took a sip of hers, scrunched her face, and said, "This tastes like ass."

"Canadian ass, to be precise."

"Why are we here?" asked Dana, sniffing her beer.

I drank my beer. It didn't taste like ass. It tasted like summers at MIT and good times with Kevin. I said, "We're here because we still don't trust each other."

"And you think beer will help?"

"It can't hurt."

"Why do we need to trust each other?"

"Roland pulled a gun last night," I said and watched her reaction. "When?"

"After he shoved you but just before you came back for your purse. I couldn't believe he shoved you. He's a dick."

"No doubt," said Dana. "Why would he have a gun?"

135

"Because he's a bad man," I said.

"And I thought he was just a run-of-the-mill jerk."

"No," I said. "He's evil. Empirically evil. That's why we need to trust each other."

"Because Roland is dangerous?"

"You work for him, and I—I just hate the guy."

"Why do you hate him? Why not ignore him?"

"I think he knows who killed my wife."

"Carol?"

"Yeah."

Dana looked at the beer taps and sipped her can of Black Label. Clearly she was regretting her decision to follow my lead. I drank my beer and let her think.

She turned to me. "You know, Carol's death is the reason I'm working all these hours."

"What do you mean?"

"She was in charge of organizing the code."

"Yup. She was very good at it."

"I'll bet she was. It's a very complicated project. Since she's left, the files have gotten all messed up. The scripts don't work anymore, and the project is out of control. Roland wants me to fix it."

"You've got your work cut out for you," I said, "especially since you weren't here at the start."

"Fortunately, you were." Dana drank and looked at me over the can. She said, "Would you like to start trusting each other?"

"Yes."

"OK, here." Dana reached into her bag and pulled out her wallet. She pulled out her hotel room card key and handed it to me. The plastic card read "Boylston Suites" and had a picture of a Swan

Boat. I took the card and raised my eyebrows at Dana. *Planning a little afternoon delight?*

Dana rolled her eyes and said, "It's a suite. I've set the front room up as an office. I like to have meetings there. The back room has the bed and it's off limits." Dana leaned close and whispered in my ear, "I'm in room 804." She sat back and said, "Come by at noon tomorrow. I'll have my laptop set up. Help me fix the code."

I looked from the card key to Dana. She was sipping her beer again. Her T-shirt moved tightly across her chest as she breathed. It interfered with my thinking. I was sure I was being played, but I couldn't figure out how it was happening. I decided to go along with her.

"Noon tomorrow," I said.

Dana hopped off her bar stool.

"Thanks for the Black Label. I'd finish it, but I don't want to."

I raised my can to her. "See you later."

Dana turned and walked out. I followed her with my eyes. As she left, she turned back to wave goodbye and caught me glancing at her butt. I averted my gaze and took a deep interest in my beer can. She smiled and walked out.

When the door closed, the bartender, who had been watching her too, turned to me. "She's a cutie, dude."

"She is," I said, "but I still don't trust her."

"Tell me about it," he said, latching on to the universal phrase of commiseration.

I drank beer and thought about Dana and why I didn't trust her. Something was wrong.

I flipped open my cell phone and dialed a number that was hardwired into my fingers.

137

"U around?" I texted to Huey. Huey worked for me when I ran the Rosetta project. Now he worked for Roland. He'd never answer a phone call, but he'd answer a text every time.

"Ya," answered Huey immediately.

"Pong?" I texted.

"Ya"

"1hr"

"kk"

Huey was a man of few, abbreviated words. I slurped the rest of my Black Label, paid for the beers, and left to grab a Zipcar. I was going back to Waltham.

TWENTY-SEVEN

HUEY WAS TUCKED INTO an office far from the front door and next
to the kitchen. He was a huge guy, eclipsing the sun for small children who got too close to his gravity well. Despite his bulk, he had
a light touch with a Ping-Pong paddle. He was also a coding genius.

We were friends in a way that was easy when we worked together
but awkward now that we didn't. It turned out that the only thing
that I had in common with most of the people who worked in this
office was a project and a cafeteria. When those were gone, so was the
friendship.

I had always liked Huey. He was completely guileless. Anything
that popped into his head popped out of his mouth a second later.
He was genuinely honest and kind, though useless in front of management or customers. One time he told Nate that the software was
shit and that we should all be fired. That's why I came to visit him.
I wanted unfiltered information about Dana Parker.

I poked my head in his door and said, "Hueeeyyy!"

Huey twirled his office chair and lurched himself out of it. He reached for me with giant meaty man-arms.

"I heard they hired you back," he said. "Fuckin' A! It will be so good to get rid of Roland."

I was enveloped in a big, sweaty hug. I reached as far around Huey as I could to return the hug and then started to push on his massive chest. "Air, buddy. I need air."

"Oh, sorry," said Huey, releasing me.

"I'm afraid you're still stuck with Roland," I said.

"Well that sucks. What are you doing?"

"Some consulting for Nate. Have you ever heard of Bronte Software?"

"No."

"Me neither. That's why Nate hired me to look into them." I turned and headed for the break room. "Up for some pong?"

"You know it," said Huey.

He surged past me and turned into the kitchen. I heard the pop of his ever-present Diet Coke. We walked to the recreation room at the front of the office. Huey talked a lot once you got him playing Ping-Pong. The physical activity soothed him. We walked past Roland's office. The door was closed.

"Where's Roland?" I asked.

"I dunno," said Huey. "I think he's at the show in Boston."

"I heard you had some excitement last night. A break-in or something?"

"First I heard of it."

The Ping-Pong table was in a long conference room that had been converted into a frat house. A plasma TV hung on the wall behind one end of the table, and a dartboard hung on the wall behind me. A massage chair took up another corner. We had all pitched in for that chair but nobody used it. Moaning in shiatsu pleasure is frowned upon in a corporate setting.

Huey and I grabbed paddles. I let Huey have his favorite, the one with the black handle. I also let him have his favorite end of the table, the one away from the door. It was an instinct I got from leading programmers. I let them win on the quirks while I focused on the big stuff.

We fell into the habits we had developed from playing hundreds of games of Ping-Pong. Programming is a mentally taxing activity. Though it looked like we were just sitting in front of our screens typing, we were really manipulating mountains of abstract data in our heads. It was mentally exhausting, and after a while we needed to do something physical. Ping-Pong is a great way to shift mental focus. It ranks up there with coffee in the pantheon of engineering support systems.

We played and I kept it close. When we were tied at ten, I thought it was time to learn more about Dana. I had just hit a ball with topspin. The ball hit the net, but the topspin made it climb over. It dropped to the other side.

"Dude, that's so freaking cheap," Huey said.

"Only when I do it," I said. "When you do it, it's genius."

"Well," sniffed Huey, "when I do it, it's planned."

I asked, "What do you know about this Dana girl?"

Huey said, "What?"

"That Dana girl. Do you know her?"

"Yeah."

"Where did she come from?"

Huey ignored me and served. We played the point. It was a long volley and Huey had gotten into that zone where he returned all my shots. Finally he broke me and I hit one long.

141

"Damn!"

"That was a good volley," said Huey.

"So where did she come from?"

"Who?"

"Dana."

"I dunno. She just kind of showed up."

"When?"

Huey served again. Apparently, he didn't want to talk about Dana. His serve touched the white edge of the table and dropped to the ground. An ace. Huey was pleased with himself.

I took advantage of Huey's moment of glory and asked, "When did Dana show up?"

Huey served and we volleyed three times before he hit it long.

"Damn," he said.

"When?" I asked again.

"When what?"

"When did Dana join the team?"

"I dunno. A couple of weeks ago? I didn't notice her for a while," said Huey.

"How could you not notice her? She's gorgeous."

"We had a release coming up, and I was having trouble 'cause Carol didn't train Alice enough before … before … you know."

"I know."

Huey's serve sailed long and it was my turn to serve.

I asked, "What was the problem with Alice?"

"She was a screwed-up chick. Really flaky. She stopped coming to work, the code releases backed up."

I served low and fast. Huey popped it up and it hit a ceiling tile. He said, "Ceiling's in play!" but it did him no good. The ball landed softly on my side of the table, and I smashed it past him.

Huey threw me the ball and I served it. As I served, Huey snapped his fingers and the ball sailed past him.

"My point," I said.

"That's not fair," he said.

"Why?"

"I was going to answer your question. You can't distract me with questions and then serve."

"Pay attention, then," I smirked.

"Dana joined just after Alice got flaky. And you're right, she's gorgeous."

I served. Huey returned my serve and said, "There always seem to be gorgeous women in that job."

I returned his shot. "Yup."

"Dana, and before her Alice, and before her … Carol." Huey returned my shot. Carol's name distracted me and my shot went wide right.

"Crap."

"Sorry, man, did I distract you?"

"A little."

"Pay attention."

"Pay attention," I mimicked. I served the ball and said, "Have you worked with Dana?"

"Yup." Huey returned my shot.

"And?"

"She kind of sucks at her job." The ball tocked back and forth between us.

I said, "Maybe she didn't get trained before Alice got killed."

Huey, playing like a hippopotamus in a tutu, reached the ball and daintily dropped a shot in front of the net. I couldn't get it. His point. We stopped playing.

"First Carol, then Alice. I was so focused on the release that I never put it together," he said. "Dude, that is freaky, isn't it?"

"Yeah, freaky," I said. "How's she working out? Is Dana any good?"

Huey returned my shot and said, "They're going to have to fire her. She's lost."

"That's a shame," I said as I returned his shot, low and tight to the left. A killer.

Huey returned my shot effortlessly and said, "Did you sleep with her yet?"

The ball sailed past me.

I said, "What kind of a question is that?" I walked to the corner of the room and swiped the ball off the rug. I chucked the ball at Huey's head. He caught it and smiled.

He served and said, "I just asked because you slept with every-one else in that job."

I returned the serve and said, "I never slept with Alice."

Huey returned my shot and said, "Well, no. Not alone."

This time I missed the ball completely.

"What the fuck are you taking about?"

Huey looked startled. Social dynamics weren't natural to him. He had to think things through before he'd know he'd made a faux pas. I watched the realization dawn across his face.

He looked at his shoes and said, "My serve."

I tossed him the ball and said, "What do you mean, not alone?"

Huey ignored me. His serve curved at me, and I instinctively re-turned it to the center of the table. He swiped at it and the wicked spin curved the ball to my right and away from me. The ball hit the wall behind me and rolled back to Huey. He picked it up and started to serve.

"Stop serving, you asshole," I said.

"Jesus, Tucker, what's wrong with you?"

"What do you mean I slept with Alice 'but not alone'?"

"Are we going to play?" Huey asked.

"Not until you tell me what you meant." I put my paddle on the table.

Huey had a compulsive need to finish things. If he didn't get closure to this game, it would bother him all day.

"C'mon. Pick up your paddle."

I picked up my paddle and Huey served. My return sailed long. Huey picked up the ball. I couldn't focus on him. *Not alone?* I couldn't get the phrase out of my head.

Oblivious to my mood, Huey served again. I hit the ball and said, "Finish saying that thing about Alice and me."

Huey returned my shot poorly. It floated lazily up and landed in the middle of the table. I lined it up and smashed it ... into the net.

"*Fuck!*" I yelled. The Ping-Pong, the office, and Huey were all dragging up memories that I thought I had safely buried.

Huey was lost around strong emotions. He said, "Jesus. It's just a game. Calm down."

"Serve that fucking ball and tell me what you meant by 'not alone.'"

Huey looked at me and then broke eye contact, focusing on the ball. He served and said, "I thought you knew."

I missed the ball again.

"Fuck me! Fuck me! What the fuck did you think I knew?"

"Stop yelling at me. I shouldn't be the one to tell you."

The door burst open behind me, and Roland stood in the doorway. Dana stood behind him. Roland said to Dana, "Well, fancy this. I thought I heard some exceptionally loud whining."

I took a step toward Roland and said, "I am sick and goddamn tired of…"

Roland ignored me. He turned to Dana.

"Get rid of him," he said. He walked off down the hall and unlocked his office. I took a step to follow him, but Dana grabbed my arm.

"Tucker, no."

I shook my arm, but she held on. Roland's office door closed, and I turned on her.

"Get rid of me?" I said.

Dana crooked her finger in a *come with me* gesture and turned. She walked out into the hallway. I followed her.

When we got into the hallway, Dana turned and said, "Please just go home."

"Why?"

"I worry about you."

"I could say the same. The last two women who sat in your chair are dead."

"I know."

"That doesn't bother you?"

"Are we still on for tomorrow?"

"Yeah, but that doesn't answer my question."

"Let's talk tomorrow." She turned and walked through the office door, letting it lock behind her.

TWENTY-EIGHT

RUSH HOUR SEEMS TO start earlier each year. It was six o'clock by the time I got back to my apartment. I unlocked the front door, grabbed my mail, and jogged up the twisting staircase to my apartment. I always get one workout a day.

I reached my door. More steps led off to my right. The staircase continued on to the roof. Maybe I'd go up there and have a nice homemade dinner. I had some romaine lettuce and some chicken breast. I'd grill the chicken and put it on a Caesar salad.

I worked the key and opened the door. The coffee pot sat on the counter where I had talked to Kevin yesterday. The dirty carafe was a tangible reminder of his life.

Kevin is gone.

I put my mail on the counter, sighed, shook my head, and opened the first piece of mail. It was the telephone bill. I had to use the bathroom. I put down the bill and walked toward my bedroom.

A wire bit into my neck, choking off my air.

I was startled and jumped. The jump tightened the wire further. I scrabbled at the garrote, followed it, and felt strong hands in latex gloves. I tried to scream, but my lungs wouldn't fill. The guy had been hiding in my office opposite the kitchen. He pulled at me. I resisted and turned, grabbing his hands to release the pressure and lifting him off the floor over my shoulder.

I tried to punch behind me, but I couldn't reach him. Scratching at the latex-covered hands was useless. The rubber protected the skin. I tried to hit him with my elbows. I found nothing. My vision was narrowing, and my ears filled with a rushing sound. The kitchen was withdrawing down a long tunnel.

The coffee carafe was at the end of the tunnel. I pulled toward it, but the guy held me back. I punched again and missed.

The carafe was right there. Just out of reach. I stamped down with my foot, and my heel caught him on the instep. He grunted and moved his foot. I lunged forward, grabbing the carafe and shattering it on the granite countertop. Cold coffee and glass flew through the room.

I stabbed the handle into the latex-covered hands, cutting them with jagged remnants of glass. I heard a grunt and cut the hand again. It moved out of reach. That loosened the wire for an instant, and I was able to turn my shoulder and punch back with the glass, catching the guy in the face.

He screamed something in a foreign language and let go. I spun completely and slashed at him. He blocked my blow, and the glass cut his hand again. He was wearing a dark suit and had blood running down the right side of his face. It was the guy from the Apple Store. He reached under his jacket and pulled out a gun.

I pushed him into the living room and ran out the front door and up the stairs toward the roof. I didn't want to be below him on the staircase where he could shoot down at me. I burst out the roof door and into the little deck that turned the roof into a city porch.

The buildings on my block are connected. Their roofs run together to make a broad plaza with firewall hurdles. I vaulted the deck's fence, landing on the roof. I didn't know what to do. If I ran across the roofs, he'd shoot me. I had no wind. My throat burned.

A voice called, "Under here!" It was Carol. She was beneath the deck. I dove, rolled, and lay still. I couldn't see Carol, but I heard her whisper, "Shhh."

I lay on my back, looking up through the thin space between the slats. Quiet footsteps walked above me. I saw a shadow on the deck. Then muttering in that language: Russian?

It was dark in my hiding place. It smelled of mold and rat droppings. The footsteps moved back toward the door, then disappeared. An ambush?

I pulled out my BlackBerry. I pushed a key. The phone was locked. A dialog box asked, "Emergency Call?" I selected the option and the phone dialed 911. I didn't have to talk. The phone's GPS would do the rest.

"You're safe, baby, just stay here." Carol's voice was tight and quiet. My heart was pounding, and I still had trouble breathing. My throat felt swollen, and I closed my eyes for a second.

I must have passed out, because strong hands were pulling me out from under the deck. I pulled back, wishing that I hadn't dropped the carafe handle. I said, "Get the fuck away from me!"

The guy was wearing a blue uniform. He said, "Easy, pal. Easy." Blue uniforms were everywhere. Cops swarmed over the roof. I was safe.

TWENTY-NINE

Now that I'd been attacked, Special Agent Bobby Miller didn't want us to be seen together in the Back Bay. We drove west on the Mass Turnpike and got off in Newton, where Bobby brought me into a little bar called Buff's Pub.

Buff's Pub was a large, single rectangular room decorated in dark wood. It was the kind of place where everybody really did know your name; at least, they knew Bobby's name. The long wall behind the bar had three plasma screens hanging from it. The wall opposite the bar held wooden booths.

Bobby sat across from me in the wooden booth farthest from the window. In front of him was a pile of bones that would convince future archaeologists that the people of Boston survived on nothing but chicken wings.

I had three bones in front of me, and one wing left in the basket out of politeness. I wasn't all that hungry, although my BBC Ale was making me feel better. I focused on Bobby, who was helping me understand my current situation.

"You are a fucking moron," said Bobby.

"Thanks." I drank my beer. "That's really helpful."

"I told you to quit."

"I told you that I'm not quitting."

"Fucking moron." Bobby took the last wing.

"What do you want me to do?"

"I want you to move to Florida, maybe go overseas, until all this settles down."

I said, "Florida? They got cockroaches the size of Smart cars down there. I'm not going to Florida. And I'd hate it overseas. They think Americans are assholes."

Bobby said, "Maybe they just think you're an asshole."

"Funny."

We were silent. We watched the Red Sox play the Philadelphia Phillies on the HDTVs. The networks had billed this game as if it was the biggest rivalry since Rome and Carthage: *Phillies delenda est*. It was all bullshit. We had bigger fish to fry. The Yankees were in first place again. Fucking Yankees.

The only good thing about interleague baseball was watching the pitchers try to hit a baseball. They looked as overmatched as I felt facing a guy with a machine gun and a garrote.

I sipped my beer and asked Bobby, "What would you do?"

"I told you. Florida."

"Really? Some guy cuts your wife's throat. Then he machine-guns your best man, pushes you down a staircase, breaks into your place, and tries to kill you with piano wire. Would you really run away to Florida?"

Bobby looked into my eyes and raised his beer to his lips. He said, "No." He took a drink and asked, "He pushed you down a staircase?"

I pointed at my stitches. "The spiral staircase in the Apple Store."

151

"The glass one? Jesus, that must have hurt like a motherfucker."

"It did. So, would you run away?"

"No."

"What's that?" I put my hand to my ear.

"No. I wouldn't run away."

I drank my beer. "Me neither."

"You never told me Kevin was your best man," said Bobby.

"He was. Best man, best friend, everything. We hadn't seen each other for a couple of months because he had little kids. But that's normal with kids. Or so they tell me." I drained my beer and said, "And now Charlene blames me for Kevin. She says it's my fault."

Bobby said, "Hmm."

"What? Do you think it's my fault?"

"It depends. Did you call him?"

"No."

"Did you decide it would be smart to go after a bunch of murders?"

"No."

"Did you pick a meeting place in the middle of a fucking bridge?"

"No."

"Then it's not your fault. It's his fault. So get that right out of your fucking head." Bobby drank some beer. "And it's not his fault because he didn't shoot himself with a machine gun. It was some cocksucker that needs to be stopped."

I said, "Some Russian cocksucker."

"How do you know he's Russian?"

"He swore in Russian when I hit him in the face with my broken coffee pot. I guess I paid him back for my stitches."

"Good job on that, by the way. It'll be tough for him to hide those cuts. Much as I hate to admit it, you're probably my best chance to catch these people."

"What do you mean 'these people'?"

Bobby took a chicken bone off the plate and laid it on the table. He said, "First you've got the guy who just tried to kill you."

"OK. That's one bone."

He put down another chicken bone. "Then there's the guy who killed Alice. The Duct Tape Killer."

"That's not the same guy?"

"Fuck no. The guy who killed Kevin and tried to kill you had a motive. Serial killers don't have motives. They just want to get their rocks off."

"So that's two bones."

Bobby grabbed a handful of bones and scattered them on the table. He said, "You got a merger, you got a couple of murders, you got money flying around, and you got a serial killer. It's a fucking mess."

I looked at the bones. It was a fucking mess. There was no rhyme or reason to the pile. But I had seen messes like this before.

I picked up a bone and said, "There's one thing holding all this together."

Bobby looked at the pile and asked, "What?"

"I don't know. But I solve shit like this all the time. Whenever it looks like there's a random pile of bugs, they always come from one central problem. One single key with lots of locks."

Bobby took the bone out of my hand and pounded fists with me. He said, "Let's find the key. I've got a plan."

I said, "Good. So what do I do?"

"Just keep doing what you do best."

"What do I do best?"

"You stick your nose in the wrong places and piss people off. Keep trolling around like that until they come after you and expose themselves."

"So I'm bait?"

"No, not bait. You're an irritant. Like in an oyster."

"Great."

"They're gonna do some stupid shit if you tweak them. I guaran-fucking-tee it. Then we catch them," Bobby said, and drained his beer.

"What kind of stupid shit? Killing me?"

"Well, we'd have to prevent that."

"How?"

"I have someone you need to meet."

"A bodyguard?"

"You'll love her. Just don't piss her off. She owes me a favor."

I slid out of the booth and stood.

Bobby asked, "Where are you going?"

"It's time to go visit Charlene," I said. "I need to make things right with her."

Bobby shook his head and said, "Ho boy. I talked to Charlene. She hates you. I'm not sure a bodyguard will help."

"All the more reason to see her."

Bobby slid out of the booth and rose. He said, "I'll set up a meeting for you in Revere. Bring a hat and a cell phone."

"What for?"

"The hat is for identification. The cell phone is so I can check that Charlene didn't kill you."

THIRTY

I parked my Mini Cooper Zipcar at the end of Kevin's dead-end street, climbed out, and took a moment to admire the view. Kevin had bought a house in Revere so he could stay close to his family. He had bought this particular house in Revere because it stood on the edge of a bluff and offered a broad panorama.

I watched a Boeing 737 descend toward a landing at Logan Airport. The plane passed over Suffolk Downs, a horse track, and then over triple-decker houses in East Boston. Enormous gasoline tanks sprawled across the flat ground in front of me, before a hill in East Boston with a cross on it. Beyond the tanks and the cross was the city of Boston. I could see the Prudential Center and thought about my apartment near its base. I wished I were there.

Kevin's driveway had three cars in it. His close-knit family was not going to let Charlene, Nicky, and Mary go through this alone. I knocked on the front door, and Charlene's father, Lou Giovenese, answered. He was a broad man whose muscles had gone to fat. His combover was skewed, as if he'd been rubbing his bald head.

I put out my hand and said, "I'm so sorry, Mr. G." I had known the Gioveneses since college, yet I had never graduated to calling Mr. Giovene by his first name.

He took my hand and pulled me close, pulling me into him over his belly. He smelled of oregano. He said, "Ah, it's a hell of a thing, Tucker." He released me and said, "The world we live in, eh?"

"Yes, sir."

"But I don't have to tell you. With your wife? They're animals out there."

I nodded. Animals for sure.

"Come on in. Want something to eat? There's plenty of food."

I entered the small front hallway, a finished porch actually, and then stepped into the dining room of a house in mourning. Dead-quiet energy suffused the place. The kids were nowhere to be seen, probably upstairs in bed. Kevin's little house had three rooms on the first floor and three on the second. The living room was in the front of the house and the kitchen was in the back. The dining room was in the middle. Charlene's mother sat at the oval dining room table with Kevin's mom.

The pain in the house was slipping into my gut and twisting it. I wanted to get away, jump in my car, get home, and lose myself in mindless web surfing. Instead, I ignored my tightening chest, stepped forward, and took Kevin's mother's hand. It was light, and small, and she looked at me with bewildered, searching eyes.

"I'm so sorry."

She nodded and pulled me close. I kissed her cheek. She held me and said, "You're a good boy, Tucker." I let her hold me as long as she wanted. She loosened her grip and I rose.

Charlene's mother had stood, all five feet of her in a light-blue summer dress. She hugged me and said, "Come on. Have something to eat." She pulled me into the kitchen, sat at the kitchen table, and poured herself wine from a jug. She glanced at my stitches and pursed her lips. But she didn't say anything.

The kitchen was full of condolence casseroles. I had learned years ago to never turn down food from the Gioveneses. It only led to more offers and finally recriminations. I wasn't hungry, but I picked up a plate and scooped some lasagna onto it. I sat at the kitchen table across from Mrs. G. Smiled at her and took a forkful of lasagna. But I had no heart to eat lasagna. My stomach was too busy trying to digest itself.

Mrs. G. sat with me and said, "First you lose your wife. Now this. What are we? Cursed?"

I stabbed at the lasagna and stared into the plate.

"Are you OK, Tucker?"

I wasn't OK. I was drowning. I was sitting in a chair, sitting in my dead friend's kitchen, balancing a piece of lasagna on a fork, and drowning. My breath was coming shorter, and the sorrow was about to overwhelm me.

I looked at her and said, "I'm doing OK."

"Did they ever catch the guy?"

"No."

"Ah, what do we pay taxes for?" asked Mrs. Giovenese, waving her hand in the air.

Charlene said, "We pay taxes so people like my husband can get murdered trying to catch Carol's killer."

I jumped from the chair and spun. She had been standing right behind me. Charlene was tall. Taller than me. Taller than Kevin. Taller than almost any woman you'd meet. She was proud of her height, and unlike many tall women who tried to hide behind bad posture, Charlene had always thrown her shoulders back, worn high heels, and dared people to live up to her standards. I had never understood how Kevin had tamed her.

I said, "Charlene, I'm so sorry."

Charlene said, "What are you doing here?"

I said nothing.

"I asked you what you are doing here, but never mind. I can see for myself. You're sitting in my kitchen, eating my food, and breathing my air."

Mrs. Giovenese said, "Now, Charlene."

"You stay out of this, Ma. Do you know what Tucker did? He got Kevin killed. I told Kevin to stay in his office and chase the porn sites and spammers. But no. He had a big lead and was going to catch the guy who killed Carol." She turned to me. "You put him up to it, didn't you? What are you doing here?"

I was mute.

Charlene continued, "I asked you what you were doing here."

Mrs. Giovenese said, "He's paying his respects. He's doing the right thing."

I said, "When is the wake?"

"What?"

"The wake. When is the wake? And where is it? Just tell me and I can leave."

"Don't you get it, Tucker? I don't want you at the wake. I don't want you anywhere near me, or the kids, or my family. I never want to see you again."

"But I'll catch the guy, Charlene. I swear I will."

Charlene's voice became deadly quiet. "Do you think that matters to me? Get out."

"Huh?"

She opened the back door out of the kitchen, the one that led into the yard. She said, "Get out. Out. I want you out of my house."

Mrs. Giovenese put her hand to her mouth and said, "Charlene!"

"Out! Now!" shouted Charlene.

I walked past her, through the door, and into the back yard. The door slammed behind me. I stood in the short grass and then walked around the back of the house past the cars in the driveway. Mr. Giovenese was standing by my car.

"She doesn't mean it," he said as he passed me a card with the wake arrangement on it.

I sat in the car and watched Boston shimmering in the distance. I was waiting for my guts to relax and my hands to stop shaking. My phone rang.

"I got you your meeting with a bodyguard," said Bobby. "Get your ass down to Revere Beach."

"What's his name?"

"It's a woman."

"What's her name?"

"She'll tell you. She doesn't like me to give it out."

"OK." I hung up. That was strange, but what did I know of bodyguards?

I put the wake card in my pocket and started the car. There was only one way I was going to that wake: as the guy who caught Kevin's killer. I just needed the bodyguard to keep me alive until I could do that.

I made a three-point turn from the dead end, drove down the street, and turned down Centennial Ave toward the beach.

THIRTY-ONE

AT ONE TIME, REVERE Beach was the place to be. That time was 1908. Revere Beach was, as is usual for Boston, America's first public beach. It was established in 1896, and in ten years it became a hot tourist attraction. The beach thronged with people who came up from Boston to enjoy the Wonderland amusement park, dance at Ocean Pier Ballroom, and watch the thirty-foot-tall smoking volcano that had been built into the sand of the smooth, curving shoreline.

That was a long time ago. The amusement parks went out of business, and today "Wonderland" is the name of a train station. The beach still curves gracefully toward Nahant, but the only noted attraction is Kelly's Roast Beef, which is "World Famous," according to its sign. I'd once asked some folks from Budapest if they had heard of Kelly's Roast Beef in Revere and they had not. It was very disappointing.

I was standing on the sand, holding a Kelly's milkshake and wearing an orange Worcester Tornadoes hat, black polo shirt, and blue jeans. The hat was the only one on the beach, which was the idea. Wearing a Red Sox cap would have only blended me into the crowd.

The sun was setting. The beach crowd had dwindled with the onset of evening. I was alone on the warm sand looking out toward Graves Light, watching its blink-blink-pause pattern as the sun descended behind me.

"Enjoying the view, baby?"

Carol was standing next to me, looking out into the sea.

"This place reminds me of the Cape," I said.

"I loved the Cape," she said. "We decided to get married down there."

"Yeah, after that camping trip at the Audubon place. If there's one test for marriage, it has to be camping," I said.

"It rained for three days. We couldn't leave the tent."

"That was a good three days."

"Then we went to Coast Guard Beach and got sunburned. We couldn't touch each other for the rest of trip."

"I seem to remember that we could touch each other. Thank God for tan lines."

Carol blushed.

"Are you blushing?" I asked.

"No." It wasn't Carol.

Carol was gone, replaced by a woman with black hair, high cheekbones, and an olive complexion. She had a trim form, high breasts, and long legs. A pair of black sunglasses rested on a hawkish nose. She carried a black leather purse. I looked at her and followed Bobby's instructions to say nothing. She was supposed to make the first contact.

"Are you Mr. Tucker?" she asked.

"Yes," I said. "Can't you tell by the Worcester Tornadoes hat?"

She cocked her head and looked at me. She said, "The hat could be wrong. I have never heard of Worcester." She had an accent I couldn't place.

"You're not from around here, are you?"

"No."

I stuck out my hand. "Please, just call me Tucker. What's your name?"

The woman ignored my hand, and I put it back by my side. She asked, "Agent Miller didn't give you my name?"

"No. He said you had a thing about that."

The corner of the woman's mouth twitched up. A smile?

She said, "From what Agent Miller told me, I am not certain that I want to have my name involved with you."

"Because of my reputation?"

"Because you may be dead soon."

"Well, that's a cheery thought. What makes you think I'll be dead?"

"You are very bad at this sort of work."

"What? Detective work?"

"Dangerous work."

"How do you know?"

"Earlier today, an amateur tried to garrote you. One would expect you to be nervous. What do they say, 'Have your neck in a swivel?'"

"Head on a swivel," I corrected.

"Yet you are so distracted that I was able to surprise you on an open beach."

I could have blamed Carol, but that didn't seem like it would help my cause. I changed the subject.

"Why do you say he was an amateur?"

"Because if he were a professional, you would be dead. The garrote is very effective."

"I cut him with my Mr. Coffee."

"You should have been on the floor."

"Well, I fought him."

She stepped forward and pushed my chest. I was surprised and tried to step back, but her left foot was in my way. I fell on my ass in the sand.

She said, "You see how easy it should have been. He was an amateur."

I looked up and said, "All right, Mata Hari, I get your point."

The woman turned and started walking back up the beach.

I got up and ran after her.

I said, "Hey, wait." She kept walking.

If I lost her, I was doomed. I caught up with her. "Wait a second."

She walked on and I put my hand on her upper arm to get her attention. She stopped and looked at my hand, then into my eyes. A chill ran through me. I put up my hands in surrender.

I looked around the beach. The setting sun was still hot and the air smelled of fried food and seaweed. I felt the familiar feeling of helplessness that came just after I had spoken hastily and my words were still floating around doing damage.

I said, "I'm sorry. I spoke without thinking."

"It seems to me, Mr. Tucker, that you do many things without thinking."

"I know. Look, I really need your help."

"Why?"

"Well, you said it. That amateur is trying to kill me. He already killed Kevin."

"You should run away. The man who tried to kill you is a criminal and a bully. He is not an assassin. Once you are out of his sight, he will forget about you. His kind does not have the attention span for a long hunt. You would be safe if you went overseas for a year."

"Yeah, but here's the thing. I want to catch him."

"Why?"

Why? Why did I want to risk my life to catch some killer? I didn't know, but an image formed in my mind. It was a movie of Carol fighting for her life as this bastard cut her open in our kitchen. I thought about how frightened she must have been as she lay there, trying to stop the bleeding with her hand and thrashing.

I felt a burning in my throat, different from the pain from the garrote. It was a familiar knot that I usually washed away with Scotch. I looked at the woman in gray, and my lip quivered. This absolutely wouldn't do. I turned and walked back down the beach, toward the ocean. Sobs began worming their way past my chest, and my lower lip contorted. I didn't want to break down in front of her.

I walked into the water. My sneakers filled. Dead seaweed made the ocean into a broth. Brown waves slapped at my knees and I knelt, taking dirty seawater and splashing it onto my face. It worked. The cold water, wet shoes, and salty smell pulled me away from the abyss. I turned to go back up the beach and … dammit! There she was, standing in the water right behind me.

"Why?" she repeated.

I took a deep breath and talked past the subsiding constriction in my throat. It was time for the truth.

"You were able to sneak up on me today because I was talking to my wife."

"Your wife? Detective Miller told me that she is dead."

"She is."

"I see."

"She haunts me. She's haunted me ever since she died. She comes when I'm alone. We were talking when you arrived. Am I crazy?"

Her eyebrow notched up. I probably was crazy.

I had made a fool of myself. I stood, waiting for this hard woman to leave. She wouldn't. She just kept looking at me with her gray eyes as scummy water slapped around our legs.

"I miss my wife," I said. "I want to find out who killed her. I want revenge."

The woman put out her hand.

She said, "Mr. Tucker, I am Jael Navas. I will help you. We will get your revenge."

I shook her hand and said, "Please call me Tucker."

TUESDAY

THIRTY-TWO

My BlackBerry's ringer dragged me awake, its shrill voice creating a sparkle of lights across my closed eyelids. I sat bolt upright in a strange room. Then I lurched out of bed, tripped over my shoes, and landed heavily on my elbows at the desk. I fumbled for the BlackBerry as the dull pain from my garrote bruises reasserted itself.

"Yeah," I croaked, too tired to look at the caller ID.

Nate said, "What the hell did you do? Jack wants you fired."

"Huh?" It was too early for this.

"Jack wants me to dump you. He says you've been a loose cannon."

"Jesus, Nate, what time is it?"

"It's seven o'clock. Did I wake you?"

"Of course you woke me." I couldn't focus.

"Well, get down here. We need to talk."

I made a slow circle, looking at the room. That's when I remembered that I was in the Marriott in Newton. Jael had insisted that I sleep in a hotel and wait for her to return. I had no idea when she was coming back.

"I'll call you when I get there."

"When will that be?"

"I don't know. It's complicated."

"Really? What is it, a girl or something?"

I hung up and looked around the room, which was perfumed with French fries. The room service tray sat on the desk. The sheets were rumpled. I was lonely. I lay back in the bed and hoped that Carol would make an appearance. No such luck. The room remained quiet, and I fell back asleep until someone knocked at the door. It was Jael.

She held out a Whole Foods shopping bag and said, "I have brought you fresh clothes from your apartment."

I asked, "How did you get into my apartment?"

"You have a very poor lock. It is no wonder you were almost killed."

I took the bag of clothes into the bathroom, showered, dressed, and followed Jael downstairs to her car: an Acura MDX SUV.

The day was already humid and it was going to be hot. I plunked myself down in the front seat. Jael started the car and drove to the Mass Pike, where she accelerated though the Fast Lane. Jael drove with simple economy, her long legs resting on the leather seats.

She said, "There are three rules you must follow for us to work together."

"OK…"

"First, you must accept that I am not trained as a bodyguard. I will not stand beside you. I will not take a bullet for you. If this man means to kill you with a rifle from a distance, he will succeed. However, we have an advantage."

"What's that?"

"He has pushed you down a staircase and tried to kill you with a garrote. He seems to enjoy a personal connection. That will give us time to see him coming and to respond."

Running away was starting to look better and better.

"There are two other rules," said Jael. "The next rule is that you will carry your cell phone always. You will not see me, but I will be watching. If your cell phone rings, you will look at the caller ID. If it is I, you will answer it. I do not care what you are doing at the time. You will always answer the cell phone. If I call and you do not answer, we will not work together."

"Understood. Now, can I ask you something?" I said, "You said that you were not trained to be a bodyguard. Why should I trust you to do this?"

"You have no choice but to trust me. But your question about my training is fair. I am not trained as a bodyguard, but I am trained to defeat bodyguards. I am very good at this."

"Then why aren't you out doing it?"

"I am retired."

"Why?"

"It is none of your concern."

"Do you carry a gun?" I asked.

"Yes. I carry a Glock 17."

"Do you have it now? I don't see it."

"The day that you see my weapon will be a very bad day for you."

I looked out the window. Fenway Park slid past behind the wall of nightclubs that made up Lansdowne Street. I had season tickets to the Red Sox. I thought about how much more fun it would be to be at a ball game, where my biggest concern was the bullpen. It beat getting strangled. I turned back to Jael.

"You said there were three rules. What is the last one?"

"I am Jewish. I don't work Saturdays. It is the Sabbath."

"You observe the Sabbath and carry a Glock 17? What kind of Jew does that make you?"

Jael looked at me and smiled for the first time. "A dangerous one," she said.

THIRTY-THREE

"DAMN IT, TUCKER. I finally get you back into the company and the first thing you do is give Jack an excuse to fire you," Nate said, spearing a breakfast sausage as if it were trying to escape.

We were sitting in the lobby restaurant of the Boylston Suites Hotel. The atrium reflected the sounds of kids zooming around the place, hopped up on a combination of maple syrup and breakfast cereal. Parents sat wearily at their tables, wearing brand-new Boston T-shirts and telling their kids to stop throwing Cheerios at the koi. I was wearing one of my business shirts and a tie that Jael had brought me. The tie hid my garrote mark. Somewhere in the hotel, she was watching over me as I drank coffee and ate a bagel.

I sipped my coffee and asked, "What did Jack say?"

"He said that you were harassing Roland and that Roland wanted you gone."

"Roland can kiss my ass."

"That's not a helpful attitude."

"Well, it's the only one I've got." I took a bite of my bagel. It was a generic white-bread toroid covered in an inch of Philadelphia cream cheese. I scraped extra cream cheese off the bagel, made a model of the Matterhorn on my plate.

Nate said, "You're going to get yourself fired again. Roland has a lot of political juice."

I poked at my cream cheese sculpture, focusing my attention away from Nate. I asked, "Whose side are you on?"

"What? What do you mean 'whose side'?"

"I mean that there are sides in this thing. Not bullshit political sides. Not stupid power game sides. Real good and evil sides. People are getting murdered, and you're worried about Roland's political juice."

"Let's not be melodramatic," said Nate.

I pointed to my forehead and said, "You never even asked me about my stitches."

"I figured there was some embarrassing story behind them."

"The embarrassing story is that some guy pushed me down a glass staircase and told me to mind my own business."

Nate put down his fork and peered at my stitches. He said, "You're kidding."

"Yeah. I'm kidding, Nate. I'm also kidding about Carol, Alice, and Kevin being murdered. Do you still believe that Carol was killed in a random home invasion?"

"I hadn't thought about it."

"Well, she wasn't. I'm sure of it. She was murdered and all you're worried about is Roland's political juice."

"I don't know if she was murdered randomly or not, but getting yourself fired isn't going to help anything."

"So don't fire me."

"I need you to keep a lower profile."

"And I need you to grow a spine." I hadn't realized that I was still so angry at Nate.

"What's that supposed to mean?"

"It means that I'm tired of you rolling over and firing me every time there's a little pressure. Carol and Jack wanted me gone, and I was gone. Now Roland wants me gone, and you're making noises like I'll be gone. I'm risking my frigging life here and you don't have the balls to tell Roland, who works for you by the way, to shove his political juice up his ass."

"It's not that simple."

"Yes, Nate, it is exactly that simple. It's time for you to put up or shut up. If you're going to fire me, fire me now. If you're not going to fire me, then stand up for me."

I leaned back in my chair, drank some coffee, and took a nibble of bagel.

Nate sipped his coffee and looked up into the atrium balconies. He said, "You know, Jack can fire you without asking me."

I said, "That's true."

"This is what I mean about it not being as simple as me standing up for you. I can't protect you from the CEO, and Roland is Jack's golden boy. It doesn't matter if Roland works for me, and he knows it."

I sighed and pursed my lips. I hate office politics, perhaps because I suck at it.

Nate continued. "So, if we're going to save you, we need to force Jack to ignore Roland."

I said, "I'm fired, aren't I?"

Nate said, "No. Of course not. We just need a new strategy to keep you employed. It's good that you wore a tie today. It's the perfect outfit for where we're going."

"Were are we going?"

"You're going to attend your first board meeting."

THIRTY-FOUR

THE BOYLSTON SUITES HOTEL had spared no expense in ensuring that the denizens of the conference room named "The Board Room" felt that they were sitting in a boardroom and not in a hotel. The room contained a long mahogany table with leather writing pads, heavy goblets for water, and high-backed chairs. A large plasma display hung from the front wall, framing Jack's opening slide.

Nate and I walked to the back of the room to get coffee. A little sign on the coffee pot said that the Boylston Suites Hotel proudly served Starbucks Coffee. I was happy to see that they had taken a stand on such an important issue.

Nate said, "Jack is announcing the Bronte deal to the board today. He asked me to come and answer questions. I'm bringing you along as a technical resource."

I said, "Great. What do I do?"

"Nothing. Sit down, be quiet, let me do the talking. When I introduce you, just wave."

"You mean I'm like a figurehead?"

"More like a prop."

I looked around the room. The board members weren't what I had expected. Instead of bald men with stern expressions and sharp pencils, I saw a bunch of guys who looked like they were on vacation.

One of them, wearing short pants, a blue Hawaiian shirt, and Teva sandals, came over to pump Nate's hand. "Nate, how you doing? Did you come to watch Jack? He says he's dropping a bomb on us today."

Nate shook Hawaiian Shirt's hand. He said, "Carl Von Waters, this is Tucker, he's one of our top engineers. He's part of Jack's big announcement."

Carl pumped my hand and said, "Hi ya, Tucker. Haven't I heard of you?"

"Oh, I doubt that, Carl."

"Yeah. You're the Rosetta guy, right?"

Nate interrupted my response. "Here comes Jack."

"Oops. Gotta go!" said Carl.

Jack Kennings walked into the boardroom, trailed by Margaret Bronte and Roland. Margaret saw me and smiled. Roland looked at her smile, followed it with his eyes, saw me, and scowled. Jack looked at me, made eye contact, and looked at Nate. Nate shrugged.

Jack called out, "Let's get started." He emptied his pockets onto the conference table between two chairs near the head of the table. Obviously, he was claiming one for himself, but since he had not made it clear which he wanted, nobody sat in either. I had a glimmer of an idea and took one of the chairs, leaving Jack the one closer to the front of the room.

Jack stood, waiting for people to settle down. He picked up his BlackBerry and said, "Everyone, please mute your phones," as he muted his own. He placed the BlackBerry on the table next to me.

Jack had the same silver, company-issued BlackBerry as mine. The idea that had caused me to grab a seat next to Jack crystallized, and I emptied my pockets onto the table.

As Jack started his introductions, I took out my wallet, my key, and my silver, company-issued BlackBerry phone. I put mine next to Jack's, with mine a little closer to Jack's seat. I looked up at Jack.

Jack was focused on connecting with his audience and didn't notice the phones. He made a joke about SecureCon giving him a revolutionary headache. The board laughed politely as he brought up his first slide. It said, "Confidential" and had the MantaSoft logo.

As Jack talked, I reached over and pressed the space bar on his phone. The phone lit up. It was unlocked. Being a security-minded company, MantaSoft required that all its BlackBerries lock if they were unused for fifteen minutes. I had just reset the timer on Jack's.

Jack got into the meat of his presentation.

"We have been presented the opportunity to capture an insurmountable lead in security software."

That got my attention. We already had a pretty good lead in security software, and Rosetta would put us even further in the lead. Jack must have something big.

"Please allow me to introduce Margaret Bronte, the founder of Bronte Software."

Margaret Bronte smiled and nodded toward the assembled group of men. I wondered how she fit into a technological leap forward.

Jack put up a slide with the Bronte logo—which was the word BRONTE—and the MantaSoft logo side by side. The slide read, "Delivering the future." I was starting to get a bad feeling about this.

Jack continued. "Margaret Bronte has built a company of unparalleled technical power. Being a startup, her small group of engineers has advanced the technology of software surveillance. She has out-classed us, but we are ready to respond."

Bullshit! That was complete bullshit. No way did that idiot Kurt Monroe and his gang of lovable misfits over at Bronte outclass me, Huey, or any of the engineers on my team. I glanced at Roland to see if he was hearing this. He was watching Jack with the adoring eyes of a first lady.

I pressed the space bar on Jack's BlackBerry as he continued, "Margaret Bronte has agreed to sell her company to MantaSoft for fifty million dollars in cash. It is an investment that will pay off hand-somely as we upgrade Rosetta with Bronte technology."

I threw up in my mouth a little. Upgrade Rosetta? My Rosetta? I knew for a fact that Margaret's company had nothing new. Noth-ing that would upgrade Rosetta, and sure as hell, nothing that was worth fifty million. I glanced at Nate to get his reaction just as Jack said, "Nate Russo, our vice president of product development, is also part of our merger task force. Nate, say hello."

Jack seemed to expect Nate to nod as Margaret had done, and did a tiny double take as Nate said, "Thanks, Jack. Let me introduce Tucker." Nate gestured to me, and I remembered my role in this meeting. I smiled and waved.

"Tucker is consulting with us to provide technical due diligence on the Bronte software," Nate continued.

Carl said, "Good job, Nate. Given his track record on Rosetta, Tucker's the right guy for the job." Apparently, nobody had told Carl that I had been fired.

Jack's smile tightened. The corners of his mouth pulled taut against his high cheekbones, while his eyes relaxed into a dead man-nequin-like calm. He stood perfectly still, holding the presentation clicker out like a phaser. Margaret looked at me with an appraising eye, and Roland crossed his arms and sulked. Nate had cornered Jack into keeping me.

Jack reanimated and continued his presentation. "Let's get down to the financials." As he began talking about merging of assets, shares, cash, and other financial stuff, I pressed the spacebar on his Black-Berry. With each press, I moved Jack's BlackBerry a little closer to me.

Jack finished his presentation with a flourish that promised un-ending prosperity and growth as Bronte and MantaSoft forged a new future together. I stood, leaving my wallet and phone on the table, and walked over to Nate. I debated blowing the whistle on Bronte right there. It would save time. But this was a political mine-field. The strategy of keeping my mouth shut had rarely failed me.

I said into Nate's ear, "Well played, sir."

Nate didn't smile. He said, "You're locked in as long as you don't do anything rash. You just need to find out why that company is worth fifty million."

"Will do."

Nate patted my shoulder. I turned back to collect my things from the table. My plan had worked. Jack had refilled his pockets. Just as I hoped, he had taken his wallet, his room key, and *my* cell phone.

In a few minutes I'd be reading Jack's email.

THIRTY-FIVE

NOTHING SAYS *LUXURY* LIKE floor-to-ceiling bathroom stalls. I love these little oases of privacy. I was sitting in one with Jack's Black-Berry, trying to read as many emails as possible before Jack figured out his mistake. The results were disappointing. Jack was a bore. The emails were all business. They talked about planning, budgets, and conference calls to Wall Street. One from Jack's wife asked him to swing by Target and Ace Hardware when he got home from this trip. One was from a PTO committee Jack was heading; apparently his hometown was building a new playground. The battered women's shelter asked Jack if he'd chair their fundraising committee for another year. A forwarded joke said that studies showed that PMSing women were more attracted to certain types of men: specifically, men with tape over their mouths and a spear through their chest while they were on fire. I chuckled at that one.

"Laugh it up, baby." It was Carol. She was in the next stall.

"Well, that was a good joke," I said.

"When exactly do men grow up?"

"I think it's right after they stop laughing at farts."

"Then never."

"One can only hope," I said.

After a silence, Carol said, "What were you hoping to find on that thing?"

"I don't know. It seemed like a good idea at the time. A fish rots from the head, so I figured Jack would have all the secrets."

"What made you think that Jack, CEO of a company that writes email spying software, would write the secrets in email?" Carol asked.

"I hadn't thought of that."

"Of course not. You're not very good at this."

"That's what Jael said."

The red light on Jack's BlackBerry started blinking. He had a new email. It was from Roland.

```
To: Jack Kennings
From: Roland Baker
CC: Margaret Bronte
Subject: Tucker?
```

"Hah! This will be a good one," I said to Carol.

```
Jack, why was Tucker at the meeting today?
I thought you had taken care of that problem.
Roland
```

That problem? That's how he refers to me? Asshole.

I marked the email as unopened so that Jack wouldn't know I had read it. Another email popped into the BlackBerry. Margaret had replied-all:

```
To: Roland Baker
From: Margaret Bronte
CC: Jack Kennings
Subject: RE: Tucker?
Roland, you worry too much. Tucker is a
dear. I'll talk to him. He won't be a problem.
And Jack, please try to be careful to see
that our deal closes. It would be a disaster
for all of us if it were to fail.
M.
```

I marked the email as unread. The light blinked again. Roland had replied all.

```
To: Margaret Bronte
From: Roland Baker
CC: Jack Kennings
> a disaster for us all
For some of us more than others.
Roland
```

Carol said, "So, what did you learn?"

I said, "Nothing. Roland hates me and is even an asshole to Jack. Margaret likes me."

"Sure she does."

I ignored Carol. Another new email had come in:

From: Nate Russo
To: Jack Kennings
Subject: Tucker
Jack:
Thanks for your support in today's meeting. I know you have concerns about Tucker. Rest assured, if he gets out of line, I'll get rid of him immediately.
Nate

I said to Carol, "Friggin' Nate is still playing both sides of this. Is anybody not trying to get me fired?"

"I'm not, baby," Carol said.

"No. You already danced that dance."

"Fuck you."

"You had your chance."

"You are a self-centered jerk!"

"Whatever."

I scrolled through all of Jack's messages, looking for an interesting subject line or person. It was more garbage.

An email caught my eye. It was sent Sunday morning, about the time I was talking to the redhead in the Common about her squirrel-feeding problem.

From: Jack Kennings
To: Kevin Murphy, FBI Assistant Special Agent in Charge
Subject: Meeting

```
Agent Murphy:
Thank you for calling me to discuss Ro-
setta. Your information is disturbing. Let's
take the rest of this discussion offline.
I'll meet you tonight as planned.
Jack
```

So Kevin knew about Rosetta, at least as a project name, and he had disturbing information about it. What could be disturbing about Rosetta? The software was a powerful decryption tool, but the U.S. government already tracked who bought software like this and who sold it. What could Kevin have heard about?

The cell phone rang. I had wondered what Jack would use as a ring tone. I hoped for something clever or musical. I got neither. Jack's phone sounded like an old fashioned rotary phone with a metal bell and a clapper. I answered it.

"Tucker, this is Jack. I have to apologize. I took your cell phone."

"You did?" I said. "Oh shit, you're right, you did. This isn't my cell phone."

"That's what I'm saying. Meet me in the lobby in five minutes so we can swap."

"Sure, Jack."

"By the way, Dana called your phone. She says she'll be late to lunch and that you should let yourself into her room. I told her I'd give you the message."

I had forgotten about Dana. I said, "Thanks, Jack. See you in five minutes."

I opened the floor-to-ceiling door and left my little room. A guy stepped out of the stall to my left. He had wild eyebrows, gray hair, a paunch, and a business suit. We made eye contact, nodded, and walked to the sinks together to wash our hands.

The guy said, "Son, can I give you some advice?"

I said, "Sure."

"You talked nonstop in there."

"I know. It's a busy day."

"Son, you got to find yourself some quiet time. You're gonna have a heart attack at this rate."

I dried my hands and said, "You're right. I'll work on it."

"You gotta take the long view," he said and walked out.

I went to meet Jack, wondering if I'd live long enough to have a heart attack.

THIRTY-SIX

"Did you read my emails?" Jack asked.

I said, "Once I knew I had your phone, I tried to take a peek. But it was locked."

Jack clicked a button on his phone. The phone was locked because I had locked it on the way back from the bathroom.

He said, "You know I bitch about that locking timer all the time. I guess it works."

"The best security is automatic."

Jack turned to leave, but then turned back and looked at me. I felt like I was being scanned. He asked, "Do you think you could have guessed my password?"

"No."

"Why not? I thought you hackers were good at that."

I said, "Everybody knows about not using their name, or their kid's name or whatever for passwords. The best passwords are just strings of letters from a sentence."

"What's your password?"

"I switch it around, but recently I've been using IWWKMW."

"What does that stand for?"

"I Wonder Who Killed My Wife."

Jack pocketed his BlackBerry. His hands went to his hips. "Is that why you're doing this?"

"Doing what?" I asked.

"Wandering around like you're conducting due diligence for Nate."

"I thought I *was* conducting due diligence for Nate."

"You don't understand. That is a bullshit assignment Nate dreamed up for you. The Bronte deal is locked. We're buying her company. You're wasting your time and you're distracting Roland. We both know he's trying to deliver Rosetta. He's under a lot of pressure."

"Yes. I know. That was me once."

"Then you know that he can't have you poking around, talking to his engineers, and generally fucking the thing up."

"Well, what do you want me to do?"

"Here's what I want you to do. I'm going to authorize Nate to pay you $100,000 for your work on this project. To earn that $100,000, you are going to go home and create a boring PowerPoint presentation to deliver to the board on Thursday morning. That presentation will say that Bronte's software does exactly what it says it does."

"Does it?"

"Of course it does. Don't play games with me, Tucker. Margaret told me you saw a demo. It does everything in the demo. You just say that you viewed the product, which you did, and that it works, which is what it does. Then Nate pays you $100,000 and we part company. I'm not asking you to lie, just report what you already know."

I thought about getting a check for $100,000. It would come in handy. Carol and I hadn't saved much for retirement and didn't have much life insurance on each other. That fact alone had saved me months of wrangling with the Wellesley Police when they tried to blame me for her murder. I had no motive, other than the fighting—and what couple doesn't fight? I'd need to get a job soon, but the $100,000 could keep me free a while longer.

"Let me think about it."

Jack took a step toward me. He smiled a cold grin. "You're not going to think about it. You're going to take your $100,000 and create the presentation. That's what Nate's hiring you to do, because that's what I'm hiring you to do. I'm sorry about your wife. I'm sorry about your situation. But I'm not going to let you disrupt my business. Understand?"

I swallowed involuntarily. "Yeah."

"Now go have lunch with Dana. She's cute. You might get lucky."

Jack turned on his heel and left me standing in the lobby. My stomach churned. I felt like my dad had just yelled at me. Jack was right. Maybe I should just go upstairs and see if I could get lucky. There were worse ways to spend a Tuesday afternoon.

THIRTY-SEVEN

DANA'S ROOM WAS IMPOSSIBLY neat. It was beyond the tidiness of a recent maid visit; it looked like nobody had ever been here. Either Dana was a neat freak, or she wasn't really staying in the hotel.

The Boylston Suites Hotel earned its name because all its rooms were two-room suites. Each suite had a front room with a television, a couch, and a round table under a hanging ceiling light. A closed door connected the front room to the bedroom and bathroom. Dana's oversized laptop sat on a table in the front room. I decided to check out her bedroom and opened the door feeling like a naughty spy.

The bedroom had a sweeping view of the Charles River and MIT beyond it, MIT's green dome reminding me of simpler times. The sun was high overhead, and shone down on white triangles that scooted around the Charles. Kids in Boston could learn to sail for a buck, and they were out in force taking advantage of the weather.

I turned to Dana's chest-of-drawers. I opened the bottom drawer expecting to find it empty, but it wasn't. It had a rumpled pile of clothes, obviously the laundry pile. The next drawer up had a collection of T-shirts with jeans next to them. The T-shirts had the kind of nerdy sayings that Dana had been wearing all week. The top drawer taught me something new about Dana. She wasn't a Jockey girl.

Instead of the sports bras and practical panties I'd expected, my eyes landed on a frilly pink thong with strategically placed lace. I found a black one, a red one, and even a hot pink. Each thong had a matching lacy bra, with a generous cup. I guiltily ran my hand inside the cup of the hot-pink bra.

"Baby, you are such a pervert." It was Carol.

I threw the bra back into the drawer, slammed it shut, and spun around.

"How does checking to see if Dana really lives here make me a pervert?"

Carol pointed at my tented crotch. "Because Mr. Winky is still at attention."

"You leave Mr. Winky out of this. He's nobody you'd remember."

"For Christ's sake, will you give it a rest? You know our shitty sex life wasn't all my fault."

"Really? Mr. Winky disagrees."

"You would ignore me all day at work, miss supper, come home, and then want me to fuck you. The hell with that. I wasn't your hooker. I was your wife."

"You weren't my hooker or my wife. You were a roommate."

"I'm glad I got you fired."

My phone rang. I looked at the display. It was Jael. I answered and looked around the room. Carol was gone.

"There is a woman heading toward your location," said Jael.

"Thanks." I walked out of the bedroom, shut the door, and sat down at the computer holding the phone to my ear.

"How long will you be with her?" Jael asked.

"It's not what you think," I said.

"I don't think it is anything."

"She wants me to help her with her computer code. There's no telling how badly her code is screwed up, so I don't know how long I'll be here."

"Call me when you are about to leave the room."

"OK." I hung up just as I heard the card key.

Dana entered the room. She was stunning in an electric-blue dress that was conservative enough for a business meeting, but still showed off all her curves. I wondered if she was wearing a matching bra. A deep V in the front showed a hint of cleavage, and the dress stopped just above her knees. She was wearing a gold necklace, matching earrings, and blue shoes. I would never have guessed that Dana had blue shoes, or matching jewelry for that matter.

"Well, well, well," I said. "You clean up pretty good."

Dana rolled her eyes. "Roland had me in a meeting today with that Bronte woman to talk about sharing code. I am so screwed."

Only if I can get you out of that dress.

Dana kicked off the shoes and picked them up by the heels. She said, "They want to start merging engineering operations as soon as the deal is done. They want me to have all the code packaged up so that both teams can start working on it."

"What's it like now?" I asked.

Dana crossed the room and looked at the laptop. She said, "You haven't even logged in yet." Her voice had a tense whine to it.

"Don't worry," I said. "I can fix it."

"How do you know?" she asked.

"I always fix it."

I logged into Dana's computer using the password she had written on the pad of paper. *Who writes down their password in a security company?* It was becoming clear to me that she didn't know this business. I took my keys out of my pocket and attached my new USB drive to the computer.

"What's on that?" asked Dana.

"There are some programs on it that I like to use when I write code. You know, editors, search tools, that sort of thing."

I installed the programs, pulled out the USB drive, and tossed the keys onto the table.

Dana's files were like an archaeological dig. As I read them, I traveled back through time. I could see the foundation Carol had laid down—the orderly structures and efficient scripts that had held the software together.

Carol's work gave way to Alice's. Alice didn't have Carol's skill, so the file structures got messier. Huey and his teammates created new code, but they had no good place to put it. It was clear that the structure deteriorated as time passed.

When I reached Dana's code, the structure was gone. It was clear that Dana had no idea what she was doing. Different file types were mixed together. The programs that built the software didn't match the code. There was no way to build a working release. Dana was right: she was screwed.

Dana was looking over my shoulder. She said, "I was trying to refactor the code."

I said, "More like *de*factoring" and made a snorty nerd laugh.

Dana said, "I'm doomed" and stood behind me.

I puttered around a bit looking at files while Dana looked over my shoulder. She said something about getting comfortable and went into the bedroom. I focused on the screen, lost myself in her code.

I got into software programming because when I'm writing code, the world disappears and I enter the flow—a place where time has no meaning. It's just me and the machine, working together to create something that had never existed before.

Programming a computer is more addictive than a video game. Like the video game, you start out solving simple problems. These reveal other problems that you solve to reveal other, more intricate problems that teach you more about the problem at hand, leading you to find other side issues to solve and knock off, and then come back to the main problem, only to fork again onto another challenge, and another, and another—each a testament to your own prowess, each a tiny win that gives your ego the stroke that it desperately craves, demonstrating that while you may not have mastery over the world outside, in this world, the computer world, you are a god and nothing can stop you.

"I brought you a burrito," said Dana.

"Huh?" I looked up.

"You've been working on that code for five hours. I thought you'd like a break."

"Did you go out?"

"You didn't notice that I left? I told you I was going out."

I remembered that Dana had said something a while ago. I grunted. Ghosts of my marriage began seeping out of the walls. I'd been in this conversation before.

"Sorry," I said, "I was just fixing this." My eyes drifted back to the screen. My cursor blinked seductively at the end of a line. Only five or six more errors remained. I clicked at the key, finishing the code on the line. Only a few things. A couple of scripts, a program or two, moving some files, fixing some others, cleaning up some errors, just this one, just that one, I'd be done in a minute. Just one more thing, and another. Write a little documentation, and *voilà!*

I looked up. Dana was not in the room. I heard the television running in the bedroom with the door closed. My burrito sat in its foil. It was stone cold. I was thirsty, and my head was fuzzy from extended concentration. I knocked on the bedroom door.

Dana opened it and said, "Wow. Were you working the whole time?"

"Yeah, let me show you."

Now came my favorite part. All day, I had pictured showing Dana what I had done. I had looked forward to seeing her appreciation, her acknowledgement that I was a fantastic coder, a smart guy, and a programming stud. I had imagined walking Dana through the cleanliness of the new file system, the smoothness of the operation, and the elegance of the architecture. Now, I proudly gave her the grand tour.

Dana took it all in and said, "This is nice."

"What?" *Nice?*

"It's simple."

"It *looks* simple. There's a lot going on in there."

"I can imagine," said Dana. "It took you all afternoon."

"Yeah, well, it's hard to make things simple."

"Thank you, Tucker," said Dana. "You're a sweetie. You should get some rest." She reached up and pecked me on the cheek, picked up my burrito and handed it to me. *Don't let the door hit you on the way out.*

I said, "I wrote you some documentation."

Dana said, "I saw. I'll look at it tomorrow. It's late now."

"Late? It's only six o'clock."

"I'm bushed. Are you heading home?"

"I'm staying at a hotel. My kitchen flooded. Do you want to get a drink?"

"Oh no," said Dana. "I'm pooped."

"Well, OK. Good night."

"Good night."

With that I was standing in front of room 804 holding a cold burrito, but now I knew that Dana was not who she said she was.

THIRTY-EIGHT

I CALLED JAEL FROM the glass elevator as I headed down to the lobby. As I talked, I watched exhausted show attendees get free beers at the Boylston Suites' daily happy hour. Jael picked up on the first ring.

"I'm out of her room," I said.

"I know."

I looked around from the glass elevator trying to spot Jael. Where was she?

Jael said, "Stop that. Do not look for me."

"Sorry."

"And if you ever see me, look the other way."

"OK. OK. What should I do now?"

"You should go to the lobby bar and wait. Remain in a very public place, and be ready to leave. We are going to follow the woman."

"Follow Dana? She's not going anywhere. She said she's tired."

"She lied."

The phone went dead.

The lobby bar was bordered by a low wall of potted plants. I walked around the pots and entered the line for free happy-hour beer. The choices were limited to Bud and Miller Lite. Not such a happy hour after all. I flashed Dana's room key, and the bartender placed a blue metal bottle of beer in front of me. As I grasped the cold bottle by the neck, I felt a gentle hand snake around my waist.

I turned, expecting to see Dana, but instead saw Margaret. She was dressed for business and held a clear drink in a rocks glass.

I said, "Oh, hi!"

She said, "Tucker, you are such an eloquent young man."

I said, "Um…"

"Why of course dear, I would love to have a drink with you. Let's sit."

Margaret put her arm through mine, her breast pressing against me. She led us to a table where two broad-faced Russians were engaged in an animated, unintelligible conversation. They both wore Bronte shirts. When they saw Margaret, they stood, offered their seats, and left.

I said, "The Brothers Karamazov didn't want to join us?"

Margaret said, "They don't speak much English. But they are excellent engineers."

I said, "You're outsourcing your engineering?"

"Russians need to eat too, dear. Also, I can hire five of them for the price of one American."

I started to answer but was distracted by movement behind Margaret. It was Carol. This was new behavior for her. She usually appeared only when I was alone. I looked at Carol and she said, "Baby, why are you talking to this woman?"

Margaret noticed my eye movement and looked over her shoulder. Of course, she couldn't see Carol. She turned back at me, her eyebrows arcing in a question. She sipped her drink and asked, "Are you enjoying SecureCon?"

I said, "I'm not seeing much of the show. I've been to your booth and the MantaSoft booth, but that's it. I spent all day today coding."

Carol said, "Shut up. Why can't you shut up?"

Margaret leaned forward and patted my knee. "Nate is such a slave driver. He's got you working for Roland already?"

I said, "Shit no. I'd never work for Roland. I was helping Dana pull the source code together."

Carol was pacing behind Margaret, her thumb and forefinger pressing against the bridge of her nose. She said, "You are such a fucking moron."

Margaret left her hand on my knee and said, "What do you think of the MantaSoft code?"

I took a swig of beer and realized that I had stepped into a pile of shit. Jack had specifically told me not to mess up the deal with Bronte, and yet here I was discussing the quality of source code with Margaret. I sipped more beer, stalling.

Margaret continued. "I just ask because I want to know if I'm making the right decision selling to MantaSoft."

I said, "Absolutely. The code is in great shape."

Margaret took her hand off my knee and sipped her drink. "That's not what I heard."

"It definitely is because I fixed it today."

Carol spun and glared at me. She said, "Don't blame me when you get killed! This is not my fault!" She disappeared.

Margaret said, "You did? I heard it was beyond repair."

"Who told you that?"

"I have my sources."

My cell phone rang. It was Jael.

I said, "Sorry, I have to take this."

Jael said, "You can see me now at the front entrance to the hotel."

I stood up, and sure enough, there she was. A tall, trim figure in a gray cotton top and black jeans with a large black handbag. She wore a Borg-like Bluetooth headset, and I half-expected to see a red laser shooting out of it. I waved.

Jael said, "Don't wave. I am following Dana. You follow me." Then she hung up and left the hotel.

I said to Margaret, "I've got to go. See you soon."

Margaret didn't say anything. She was lost in thought as I left the lobby bar and followed Jael into the early-evening humidity.

THIRTY-NINE

By the time I got to the lobby, Jael was across the street and turning down Dalton. I timed my run and scooted through the traffic. No cars honked, nobody complained. I was in Boston, where pedestrians might not get the right of way but also didn't need to contend with jaywalking citations.

As I passed Bukowski Tavern, I wondered if Dana was retracing our walk back to the Mary Baker Eddy Library. I gave up on that idea when Jael, following Dana, took a left at the Sheraton Hotel and started working her way toward the shops at the Prudential Center. My phone rang as I was passing the huge concrete horses that guarded the entrance to P. F. Chang's, ready to attack if General Gau came back for his chicken.

It was Jael. She said, "Do not try to catch up to me. Dana will see you."

"Well, I'm not used to following people," I said.

"That is obvious," she said. "Keep your distance."

"Where is she going?" I asked. But Jael had hung up.

Jael stopped at Huntington Ave in a crowd of people waiting for the Walk signal. Dana was in the crowd, but she was ignoring Jael, who was hiding in plain sight. I ducked into a Cold Stone ice cream place, thinking about the ice cream I'd bought for Dana a hundred years ago, back when I thought she was just a cute programmer. What was she doing?

I peeked out of the store and saw Dana and Jael crossing the street. Dana was walking quickly, pulling ahead. She stopped at the corner, looked around as if expecting to see someone, and then continued down the street into the South End. I was getting an idea of where we'd end up.

I crossed the street and walked down West Newton to the corner of St. Botolph. I knew where we were going now, and I called Jael.

"I'm thinking that I should hang back," I said.

"That is unnecessary," said Jael. "Dana has entered your house."

"How did she do that? The front door is locked."

"She had a key."

"How did she get a key?"

"That is unimportant now."

I turned the corner at Follen Street. Jael was standing in front of my apartment with her back to the door. I took her cue and hugged the building to avoid being seen from my windows.

When I joined Jael on the front step, I said, "What's she doing?"

Jael said, "There is no use speculating. We will know soon."

I unlocked the street door and followed Jael up the stairs.

Jael was carrying only her large purse. I said, "Shouldn't you have a gun?"

"It is unnecessary."

We reached the top step, stopped in front of my door, and listened. My apartment was silent. I moved to the staircase that led to the roof and flattened myself against the wall. Jael stood in front of the door, her right hand resting on her handbag. She looked like she was waiting for a bus.

Jael motioned me closer and whispered in my ear. "I suspect an ambush," Jael said. "We need to go in now."

I whispered, "Wouldn't we want to avoid entering an ambush? Why don't we wait for her to come out?"

"If she is patient, we would be waiting for hours. If it were I, you might wait days. She has food, water, and a toilet. She can out-wait us. If we enter now, we will surprise her."

I shrugged. "You're the expert."

Jael said, "Unlock the front door normally, as if you are coming home. Let me enter first."

I took out my key, the only key on the USB drive keychain. It rattled as I pushed it into the lock and turned. I opened the door wide and Jael walked into the apartment, looking right and then left. I followed closely into the small hallway between the kitchenette and living room.

Dana came out of the office opposite my kitchen, the office where the amateur garrote assassin had hidden. She saw Jael. She gasped, and her right hand went behind her. She pulled out a small, boxy black gun, pointed it at Jael, and said, "Don't move!"

Jael and I had completely different responses to the gun. Mine was to raise my hands up in the air and say, "Oh Jesus!" Jael's was to step forward. The apartment was small and Jael covered the distance in two steps. When Jael was close enough, she grabbed Dana's wrist behind the gun, pivoted, and drove Dana toward the front of the apartment. I got out of the way, dodging into the hallway as the women hurtled past.

When I looked back inside, Jael had disarmed and pinned Dana. The gun lay on the floor and Dana's arm was bent back. Dana grunted and pulled on her arm, struggling to free it. She twisted her legs trying to get them under her, but Jael had a knee in Dana's back. Dana's left arm flailed back trying to get hold of Jael, but she only found air. Jael ground Dana's face into the rug. While Dana made angry grunting sounds, Jael was silent. The thought *This is so hot!* wormed its way into my head. I pushed it down as I shut the door to the apartment.

Jael twisted Dana's arm and said, "I will break it." Dana winced and lay still.

Jael reached into her big purse with her free hand and produced white plastic zip ties. She slipped one over Dana's wrist with a zipping sound. When Dana heard it, she tried to pull her hands under her and roll, but she was pinned. Jael grabbed the other wrist, with another zipping sound. With Dana's wrists bound, Jael used another twist tie on Dana's ankles, then a piece of tape over her mouth. What else did Jael have in that purse? It probably wasn't mints.

Jael pulled Dana to her feet and hopped her over to the galley kitchen. She sat her on one of the barstools and used zip ties to fasten Dana's hands to the chair behind her and Dana's ankles to the chair's footrest. Dana, resigned to this treatment, looked at me with cold eyes.

I said, "Well, what do we do now?"

Jael said, "We find out who this woman is working for. Where is your stove? I need to heat instruments."

At that, Dana began a new round of muffled sounds and tugging at the plastic ties. She pulled on her arms and flailed with her legs, rocking the tall chair. Jael watched her and said, "She will injure herself." Then she added another tie around Dana's knees, pinning her legs together. The chair stopped rocking despite Dana's struggles.

Jael went into the kitchen and turned on the stove. Then she rooted around in the drawers and came out with knives from the silverware tray.

"What are you going to do with those?" I asked.

"I'm going to heat them," Jael said.

"Why don't you just ask her what you want to know?"

Jael looked at me. "You may ask her. Find out who she is working for."

I went and stood in front of Dana. Her T-shirt, stretched tightly across her chest with her arms behind her back, read, "Silly boys. Trucks are for girls." I took the tape off Dana's mouth.

Dana said, "Aloysius Tucker, you are in so much trouble. You untie me right now!"

Aloysius? Dana knew my first name. I never told her my first name, for obvious reasons. This was getting scarier and scarier. Who was this woman?

I said, "What were you doing here? How did you know my name?"

Dana said, "I wanted to make sure I could trust you."

Jael emerged from the galley kitchen. She stood behind Dana and put another piece of tape over her mouth.

Jael said, "You are wasting time by allowing her to lie to you."

I said, "How do you know she's lying?"

"You spent the afternoon working on her computer, yes?"

"Yes."

"Would she have allowed that if she didn't trust you? She is lying. The instruments are almost ready. Ask her again who she is working for." Jael pulled the tape off again with a ripping sound and Dana winced. The skin around her mouth was red.

I said, "Who are you working for?"

Dana said, "MantaSoft. You know that."

"You broke in here for MantaSoft? You know, Jael's right, I'm tired of you lying to me. For example, what the hell do you really do for a living? Because I've seen your work, and you are not a programmer."

Dana pulled at her arms and said, "Of course I'm a programmer. Just because I'm not as good as you doesn't mean I'm not a programmer."

"You're beyond not being as good as me. Watching you trying to program is like watching a monkey work a backhoe. I wrote all that code for you and you didn't understand a line of it. Why did Roland bring you in? Who are you really working for?"

"Roland didn't bring me in. Alice brought me in. Roland signed off."

Jael came up and slapped the tape over Dana's mouth again. She handed me a purse and said, "I found this in your office. It is hers. Look for identification."

I took the purse into the front living room. Dana was trussed in the little hallway facing me. Behind her was the kitchenette where I had talked to Kevin, the office where someone had hidden to try to kill me, the bathroom, and the bedroom where I had slept with Margaret so long ago.

While I fumbled with the clasps on the purse, Jael began working. She waved a hot butter knife in front of Dana's face and said, "One last time. Who are you working for?"

Dana said "MantaSoft" through the tape and began struggling harder. She watched the hot knife go behind her.

Jael said, "I'm going to burn you, unless you tell me. Who are you working for?"

Dana bucked and pulled on her ties; tears squirted out of her eyes and down her face as she tried to say "MantaSoft" again through the tape. Jael brought the knife down. Dana's arms were pinned behind her. She screamed into the tape, her head thrown back.

I couldn't stand watching this. It was horrible. I dumped Dana's bag onto the floor and pawed through the pile. I found a brush, a little plastic box of Kleenex, Advil, a feminine product of some sort, a wad of receipts. Nothing that would stop this torture.

The bag felt heavy, so I felt around inside it and found a pocket. I opened it and pulled out Dana's wallet. The wallet contained a Maryland driver's license, some credit cards, a Starbucks card, and a picture of a fluffy dog that looked up at the camera with its head tilted to the right. I looked back at Dana, who wept and pulled at her ties.

"Jael, stop it!" I said.

"You still don't understand. This woman would have killed you."

Dana shook her head and looked at me with pleading eyes. She muffled, "No! No!" through her tape gag. Jael left her and went back into the kitchen. She came out with another hot butter knife.

"Again," Jael said, "who do you work for?"

Dana wailed and shook her head. The knife disappeared behind Dana, and she screamed into the gag. I began scraping through the purse. There had to be something. Something heavy clunked in another pocket. I opened it and pulled out a clip of bullets that must fit Dana's gun, and another small wallet.

The wallet contained an ID card with a picture of a younger Dana with cropped hair. She was looking grimly into the identification camera. I looked at the card and called to Jael.

"Stop it! Stop it! I know who she works for!"

I shoved the ID at Jael. Next to Dana's grim picture were three letters: F-B-I.

FORTY

JAEL LOOKED AT THE ID, said "Interesting," and went back into the kitchenette.

I pulled the tape off Dana's mouth as she wept softly in the chair, her bound arms held limply behind her. I wanted to comfort her, but didn't have the right.

Jael returned with a pair of scissors and cut the ties that held Dana's knees and ankles. When she cut the ties that held Dana's wrists, Dana whipped her arms forward to survey the burns. She stared at the sources of her pain in wonder. The skin was undamaged. She looked at Jael.

Jael said, "I used an ice cube. The body cannot tell the difference between extreme heat or extreme cold. It is a useful technique."

"You bitch!" Dana screeched. She launched herself at Jael, trying to land a punch.

Jael calmly parried Dana's blows. While this played itself out, I walked back into the dining room and picked up the gun off the floor. I turned the gun over in my hands until Jael said, "Put that down!"

Dana, who had switched to trying to kick Jael, stopped her attack and said, "Tucker, put it down!"

I said, "What?" I turned to Dana and Jael. They separated and pushed themselves against the hallway walls. The gun was pointing down the hallway.

Jael said, "Put the gun down. It's dangerous."

"I was just going to make sure the safety was on."

Dana said, "Oh for God's sake. It's a Glock, it doesn't have a safety. Put it down!"

"Take your finger off the trigger," said Jael, "unless you mean to shoot someone."

My finger had found the trigger, just like it did with toy guns. I put the Glock on the table. Jael strode over to the gun and picked it up. She removed the bullets by dropping the cartridge into her hand. Then she pulled back on the top of the gun with a click, and, to my surprise, another bullet flew out. She picked the stray bullet off the floor, and put it into the cartridge. Then she gave the cartridge and the gun to Dana who put them into her purse.

Dana said, "I ought to arrest the two of you."

I said, "For what?"

"You assaulted a federal agent."

I said, "And you broke into my house. You're lucky you didn't get shot. I'm pretty sure I'm allowed to shoot someone who breaks into my house. What were you doing here?"

"The same thing you were doing when you broke into Roland's office."

"Trying to catch a scumbag? Thanks."

"I was trying to get a—"

A loud knock rapped at the door. "Boston Police Department. Open up."

Dana and Jael waited in the living room as I opened the door. A police officer stood before me in a blue uniform. FBI Agent Bobby Miller stood behind him.

Bobby said to the officer, "Yup. This is the guy. I'll take it from here."

The cop said to me, "So this isn't a domestic disturbance?"

"Nope," I said, "it's more of an international disturbance."

"Mind if I look around?" asked the cop.

"Have at it," I said and stepped aside.

The cop walked into the room and saw two sweaty women in the living room. Then he looked at the chair, the cut plastic restraints on the floor, and me. He said to Jael and Dana, "Are you ladies OK? Would you like to come with me?"

Dana said, "We're fine, officer." She grasped Jael around the waist in a friendly hug.

Jael stiffened at the contact, not returning the hug. She said, "Yes. Fine."

The cop looked at Bobby, who gave him a wink. The cop smiled a *whatever turns you on* smile. He said to me, "Thank you, sir," and left.

When I closed the door, all hell broke loose.

Dana and I said simultaneously, "Bobby, thank God you're here." Then we looked at each other in horror as we realized that Bobby had been playing us both.

Dana pointed at me and said, "You know him?"

I pointed at Dana and said, "You could have told me."

Bobby said, "I only reveal undercover operations on a need-to-know basis. And I didn't think either of you needed to know."

"You thought wrong, you cocksucker!" I had never heard Dana swear. Dana the cute programmer was gone. This was Dana the FBI agent.

Bobby said, "Calm down and just tell me what happened."

"This happened!" Dana thrust out her arm, displaying an angry red line where the ties had bound Dana's wrists.

Bobby looked at her wrists and turned to me. "Do you mind telling me about this?" he asked.

"It was a misunderstanding," I said. "She broke into my apartment, and Jael thought—"

Bobby turned back to Dana, "You broke into his apartment? Why would you break into his apartment?"

Dana said, "Don't you tell me how to do my job. I needed a techie guy to keep my cover, and I wanted to make sure Tucker wasn't working for the people stealing Rosetta."

I said, "How did you get a key?"

Jael said, "She made a copy while you were in her hotel room. I followed her."

I remembered Dana going out to get me a burrito while I was coding. My keys, with my thumb drive, had been on the table in front of me. I couldn't remember if they were in the same place when I had come out of my coding zone.

I was going to start in on Dana about copying my key, but she was already going at it with Bobby about protocols, and whether she followed them, and what did he know anyway, and how he had screwed up her cover. Jael watched them, her eyes flicking back and forth like a cat watching mice play tennis.

It was time for Scotch.

I went into the kitchen and got four on-the-rocks glasses. I threw ice cubes into each and grabbed my bottle of Lagavulin out of the cabinet. Then I cupped the four glasses in my hands and put the bottle under my arm. Dana and Bobby were still yelling at each other as I walked back out into the living room.

"Team player? Team player?" shouted Dana. "I get dropped into a company as bait for a serial killer and you want me to follow the rules?"

Bobby said, "Just be a fucking professional."

"Like you're the poster boy for professionalism." She pointed at Jael. "You brought *her* into this? How fucking professional was that?"

I put the glasses on the coffee table and poured the smoky liquor onto the ice, which cracked and popped. Jael took a glass and said, "Thank you." I took the other drinks to where Bobby and Dana had squared off.

I said, "Enough," and handed each of them a Scotch. They stopped arguing and looked at me.

I raised my glass and said, "I propose a toast to the idea that we stop screwing up and start acting like a team."

Bobby said, "Hear, hear," and drank.

Jael said, "L'chaim," and sipped her Scotch.

Dana looked into her drink, then downed it. She walked over to the bottle and poured another, covering her ice cubes with Lagavulin. A leather couch sat under the bay window that overlooked Follen Street. Dana sat heavily on the couch and held the cool glass to her forehead. We arrayed ourselves in a semicircle around her. I sipped my whiskey and focused on its peaty flavor.

Bobby looked at Jael and asked, "Have you and Tucker accomplished anything?"

Jael nodded to Dana and said, "We thought that we had caught an assassin. We were mistaken." As Jael told Bobby what had happened tonight, Dana sipped her drink and stared into space, shaking her head in small quick arcs. I saw her eyes start to glisten. She looked at the red lines on her wrists, and then she took a drink. She seemed small and alone.

I sat next to Dana. Our hips touched as the couch sagged. Dana ignored me, but didn't move away. I could feel her body heat through her jeans. She gave off a faint whiff of sweat that mingled with the fragrance of the Scotch.

I slid away from her. It wasn't right to be so close after what I had done. The image of Dana pulling at her arms while Jael tortured her wheeled around in my head like a bat in a living room. I saw myself doing nothing to help her but fish through her purse and look at a picture of her dog. I downed my Scotch and got up to pour myself another.

Dana looked at Jael and said, "I was sure you were going to kill me."

Jael said, "I am sorry."

I said, "I'm sorry too."

Dana ignored us. "I mean, somebody killed Kevin. I never thought it was Tucker, but—in the chair—I was sure I was going to die, and I started thinking about Alice. Now I know how she felt when that bastard killed her with the duct tape. Tied up, afraid, helpless, alone." She drank and said, "It worked out for me, but it didn't work out for Alice."

Dana finished her Scotch and motioned her glass at me. I walked over and poured a little bit more into her glass. She slid to the right, making room for me. I sat and Dana stretched out her legs. Now her hip and knee touched mine. I maintained my composure. Dana sipped Scotch, looked around the room, and said, "Why did we stop trying to find out who murdered Alice?" Then to Bobby, "You and I got her killed, you know."

Bobby said, "That's bullshit."

"It's true."

I asked, "What do you mean?"

Dana said, "Alice Barton was a whistleblower. She told us that someone was stealing Rosetta's source code, and she asked for our help. She wanted to quit and go into protective custody, but we told her to stay and bring me up to speed. Once I was in place, we'd move her to a safe house."

I said, "Stealing Rosetta. That's what Kevin said. He said that someone was offering to sell the source code."

Jael asked, "Who is selling this source code?"

Bobby said, "We don't fucking know. We're wandering blind. That's what happens when they kill the guy driving the investigation. Kevin had pieced it together the day they machine-gunned him."

I said, "If that source code gets out, they'd get control of the Nappy Time code I wrote. Hackers could get the Rosetta onto millions of computers and use them as a giant decryption machine. They could read anything."

Dana said, "We know." She finished her drink and clinked my bottle. I covered the bottom of her glass. She took the bottle away from me and covered her cubes. She put the bottle on the floor between us. Her shoulder touched mine. "We know what's at stake and so did Alice. She was definitely murdered by the same people who killed Kevin."

I said, "I thought Alice was murdered by a serial killer."

"She *was*. The serial killer is also stealing Rosetta."

"So that's why Kevin knew the guy worked at MantaSoft. It wasn't just based on the fact that the duct tape guy had changed his pattern."

Bobby said, "I think Kevin had the whole thing figured out. Now I don't know where to start."

I said, "I do. Dana's right. We go back and find out who killed Alice, then the whole thing will unravel."

"How do we do that?" asked Bobby, draining his glass.

I said, "Let me think about it."

The party was over. Jael finished her drink and brought the glass into the kitchen. She rinsed her glass and put it upside down on the counter. Then she picked up the zip ties from under the chair and put them into her handbag of horrors. Finally, she slid the chair back into place as if nothing had happened. Apparently, neatness counts among assassins. I appreciated that.

Bobby walked with Jael to the front door, pointed at me, and asked, "What do we do with him?"

Jael said, "He will be safe as long as he stays in this apartment."

Bobby said, "You heard the lady, Tucker. You stay here tonight. No going out until Jael comes for you."

Dana stretched out on the couch, tucking a leather pillow under her head. She said, "I'll stay with him. Keep him safe until morning."

"You got it," said Bobby. He left with Jael. I locked the door behind them.

The room was silent. Dana closed her eyes, and her mouth fell open. The Scotch had knocked her out. I rinsed the glasses and put them away. It was good to engage in something simple and domestic. I knew that the simple action of rinsing these glasses could not erupt in some unexpected way and cause damage. Dana getting tortured, Kevin getting killed, and Rosetta getting into the hands of the highest bidder were all tributes to my inability to look around corners and see the havoc I was about to wreak. I sprinkled some food onto Click and Clack's sponge, contemplating ways I could screw up this simple task. "You guys aren't going to grow into giant mutants who eat the Back Bay, are you?"

So much had fallen into place, and I was still processing it. Clouds of fact swirled in my mind, forming themselves into theories, then dissolving back into vapor. Kevin must have needed help on this Rosetta thing. Dana was undercover, but knew that she wouldn't be able to maintain the ruse. He must have planned to introduce us: why else would he have mentioned "older women" to Dana?

A theory formed around that fact. Dana let the "older women" comment slip because she thought I was already on board. When she realized that I wasn't, she went back into undercover mode. It took her breaking into my house to put Kevin's plan into place. She didn't know that I had stormed out of his office and never given him a chance to explain. Then he was dead, and nobody knew who to trust.

I yawned. The Scotch had done its job. I went back into my bedroom. It was neat and tidy. The bed was made, courtesy of a habit instilled by my mother. I reached into the closet and pulled out a spare blanket for Dana.

I turned and she was standing behind me. I said, "I got you a blanket for the couch."

Dana said, "I don't want to sleep on the couch." She reached down and untucked her T-shirt. Then she crossed her arms, grabbed the edge of the shirt and pulled it straight up over her head. She was wearing an electric-blue bra. The color complemented her tanned ribs.

I babbled, "Look, you've had a tough day. Lots of adrenaline. You know, they've shown that people can confuse an adrenaline high for lust. The heart rate elevates, palms sweat, breathing increases. It's indistinguishable. Plus the alcohol. You had too much Scotch. I wouldn't want to take advantage."

Dana said nothing. She reached up behind her back with both hands and did whatever magic it is that women do to make their bras unhook. She shivered and her bra fell away, freeing her breasts. The pink nipples were erect.

I stared and put up my hands. *Look-I-don't-want-any-trouble.* "There's really no need. You can sleep in the bed if you want. I can take the couch. Chivalry would—"

Still, Dana said nothing. She was beautiful, shirtless, in her jeans, with her blond hair cascading over her shoulders. She stepped forward, grasped my right hand, and placed it on her breast with my thumb over her nipple. We both gasped. She reached up, put her hand behind my neck, and pulled my head toward her. Her lips tasted of smoky Scotch. My left hand found the small of her back and caressed it. She moaned. Her tongue found my lips, as her other hand slipped beneath my belt and seized its prize.

Chivalry never stood a chance.

WEDNESDAY

FORTY-ONE

MY EYES FLUTTERED OPEN. I saw Dana sleeping next to me and remembered last night's clothes-ripping melee. We had needed to feel close and safe and loved, to tell death to keep its clammy hands to itself.

Dana lay on her side facing me, her arms covering her breasts, her fists pressed into her throat. She snored through parted lips. She looked cold. I reached out and pulled the blanket up over her shoulder.

Dana's eyes popped open at my touch. She said, "Oh no," jumped out of bed naked, and bolted into the bathroom. I heard retching.

"Do all your girls throw up in the morning, baby?" Carol said from over my shoulder.

I groaned. "Must we do this?" Dana's retching continued in the other room.

Carol said, "Poor thing. I know how she feels."

"Don't you have a mansion to haunt?"

"Don't be so sensitive."

I climbed out of bed.

Carol said, "My goodness. You still have a great ass."

I put on some boxers and said, "How about a little privacy." Carol disappeared.

I put on jeans and a "Yankees Suck" T-shirt, and headed into the galley kitchen. The bathroom was quiet for a moment, followed by a little more retching. Dana had definitely drunk too much. I doubted that she wanted me to hold her hair while she threw up, so I left her alone.

I filled the electric kettle with water and turned it on. I hadn't replaced the coffee maker, so we would be having tea. I got out a box of Celestial Seasoning's Morning Thunder and put it on the counter as I heard Dana come out of the bathroom and stand, blinking, in the hallway. Her hair stuck out and she swayed. She looked as if she had been struck by lightning.

She was still a knockout, but it seemed impolitic to compliment her when she had just been sick. Instead, I said, "There are towels in the bathroom." Dana mumbled something about "mouth tastes like Raid," and stumbled back into the bathroom. I heard the shower running.

I fished through the fridge and pulled out four eggs, some shredded mozzarella cheese, and a tomato from the Haymarket farmer's market. As I preheated my cast iron skillet with some olive oil, I pulled out a cutting board and the Cutco kitchen knife that Carol and I had bought from a friend of hers who'd had a brief fling in knife sales. The friend gave up sales after a week; the knife remained, another reminder of Carol.

I beat up the eggs and poured them into the oil. Then I diced the tomato and threw it in. Finally I sprinkled some mozzarella on the whole thing and added a pinch of oregano. While it cooked, I put toast in the toaster and tweeted.

`Tucker's patented pizza omelet. Breakfast of Champions!`

The water in the kettle was boiling. I took a tea bag out of the box, put it into a mug, and poured water onto it. Morning Thunder's distinctive maté smell filled the air. I hadn't smelled it in months.

Carol said, "Baby, you kept my tea." She was sitting in the chair in front of me.

I said, "It reminds me of you."

"You're sweet. I miss being married to you."

"Really? I don't remember you having much fun."

"The end wasn't so good, but our first year was incredible. Remember how we traveled all over? The Cape. London. San Francisco."

Carol was right. We were young, we were in love, and we had a little cash. We backpacked all over, slept in cheap motels, and screwed like bunnies. She was my soulmate. At that time, I could look far into the future and see Carol standing beside me as we grew old together.

I said, "And then I got promoted."

Carol's lips twisted with annoyance. "Yup," she said. "It was the beginning of the end."

"And now it's the end of the end."

"Don't be so glum. You've got a bright future," said Carol, "assuming you don't get killed."

"What future?"

"The future you'll start living once you figure out why I died."

"And who killed you."

Carol leaned forward. "You know who killed me."

220

I rubbed my neck where the garrote mark was fading and said, "I guess I do."

"And you know he wasn't the guy who killed Alice."

"Yeah, but the two are linked, aren't they?"

"You know that too," said Carol.

The bathroom door opened. Dana stepped out, wearing a long blue Wellfleet sleep shirt that had once belonged to Carol. She sat where Carol had been a second ago. An upgrade over Carol? A downgrade? An upgrade. Dana was alive. Big advantage.

Dana crinkled her nose at my tea and said, "What's that smell?"

I said, "It's maté."

"Does it have caffeine?"

"Yup."

"Fill me up."

I put a tea bag into a Linux-penguin mug and poured hot water on it. The bag floated to the top like a Portuguese man-o'-war and steeped. I focused on the tea bag to avoid staring at Dana's nipples as they poked through her shirt. She was obviously going commando.

I grabbed the frying pan and flipped the omelet onto a plate. Then I put it on the counter between us and gave Dana a fork.

"*Mangia!*" I said.

Dana said, "You're Italian?"

"On my mother's side."

She breathed in the steam from the maté, took a sip, then dug into her side of the omelet. The toast was done. I served it dry with butter on the side. Too bad I didn't have scones. The thought of scones made me think of England, Roland, MantaSoft, and Kevin.

I said, "It was a code, wasn't it?"

Dana nibbled some omelet. "What was a code?"

"When you told me that I liked older women. You and Kevin had set up a code so you'd know I was helping you. But he never got a chance to tell me."

"It was a code. I felt it was kind of mean, but Kevin thought it was funny."

I asked, "So what now?"

Dana said, "There is no 'what now.' I have to go back to work. Maybe tonight."

"No, not that kind of 'what now.' I meant what about figuring out who killed Alice?"

Dana looked disappointed. She said, "You mean last night was just a one-night stand?"

"Well. No. What I mean to say is …"

Dana's eyes developed a pixie-like glint.

I asked, "Are you screwing with me?"

"Maybe." Then a laugh.

"Well, quit it."

"I just like seeing you get all worked up," she said. "It's cute."

I drank some tea and said, "You know, we don't have much time. Tomorrow Jack announces the merger, the show ends, and everybody scatters. After that, we'll never figure out what happened."

Dana shifted back into being serious. She said, "Don't forget the serial killer. He's still going to need his Thursday-afternoon kill."

"That's true. But I still don't see how he fits into this. Or why he was the one to kill Alice. Why didn't they just cut her throat?"

Dana forked some omelet and said, "I think it was an opportunity killing. They thought Alice needed killing and this guy was horny. He just took on the job." Dana drank her tea and continued, "I read Kevin's report on Alice."

"The one where Roland said that I did it?"

Dana cocked her head, gave me a *How did you know that?* look.

I said, "Bobby told me it was Roland. He wanted me to watch my back."

"Bobby was right. You do need to watch your back," she said. "Roland told Kevin that your wife was sleeping with Alice and that you were probably out for revenge."

"Roland is a fucking asshole."

"Is it true?"

"That Roland is a fucking asshole? Absolutely. Hand to God."

"Is it true that your wife was sleeping with Alice?"

"I don't know. It doesn't make sense. It was a rumor around the office."

Dana hopped off the stool and said, "We need to figure out how that rumor started." She walked back to the bedroom.

I called after her, "I have just the guy." Then I started texting.

Two breakfasts in one day. Bonus!

FORTY-TWO

Huey, the programming man-child, dug into a pancake the size of a laptop and considered my question. We were in the cafeteria in the Waltham building, an airy expanse where you could get a bite to eat and listen to the water rushing in the fountain. Huey was making short work of his pancake, and I tweeted his success while I let the silence build:

Man vs. Food. @hueybigdog 1, Pancake 0.

Huey asked, "What did you tweet?"

"I gave you props for showing your pancake who's boss."

"Thanks."

"But you still haven't answered my question. Where did people get this idea that Alice and Carol were lovers?"

"I don't know," said Huey. "Suddenly it just seemed that guys were talking about Alice and Carol."

"Come on, dude. That kind of thing doesn't just start up. There must have been a trigger. Did you guys go out drinking or something?"

Huey shifted his girth in the small aluminum chair. If I had ever had doubts about the tensile strength of aluminum, they were gone. Still, the chair seemed burdened. He shifted back. Huey was uncomfortable, and it wasn't just the chair. He wolfed some more pancake. Somewhere above us, Jael was watching.

"You've got some on your mouth," I said, and pointed to the corner of my own mouth. Huey's tongue flicked out and nabbed a syrup-soaked crumb.

Huey looked at the floor and said, "Sorry, man, I can't help you."

"Bullshit. You're a crappy liar. That's why they don't let you in front of customers."

"I'm not lying," he whined.

"It's all over your face."

"I got that piece."

"Not the crumb. The lying. You should never play poker. Now tell me who started the rumors about Carol."

Huey shifted in his seat again. He tore at his pancake, gulped a chunk of it, drank some Diet Coke, and rubbed his hand down his face. Then he leaned close and said conspiratorially, "All right. I think I started it."

"What? How? Why?"

"Look, I just want you to know that I don't look at porn all the time."

I said, "OK."

"But you know, while I'm waiting for the computer to do something and have nothing else to do ..."

"You don't do it on company computers, do you?"

Huey looked at me like I had just suggested that he wore his pants inside out.

"Of course not. I have an Android tablet. I steal WiFi from the office next door. They use WEP, so it's easy to hack."

Huey was right. Using WEP security was like hiding your house key above the doorframe. I said, "So you've got your own little porn thing going? What's that got to do with anything?"

Huey shifted again, creaking his seat. He stopped making eye contact.

He said, "I'm not proud of it. I just like certain things. You know. Specific things."

"What? Whipped cream or something?"

"No," he said softly, poking at his food.

I thought of the pictures of Alice and guessed, "Bondage?"

Huey's face went red under his beard. He looked miserable.

I chucked him on the shoulder and said, "Don't sweat it, man. Everybody's got something." Something occurred to me. "It's just porn, right? You don't do anything, do you? Like with Alice?"

Huey's eyes shot up and locked on to mine. "You mean about killing her with duct tape? No! Of course not. It's just porn."

"Then what's this got to with anything?"

"It's got to do with those rumors about Alice and Carol. There's this—" Huey's eyes flicked up and over my shoulder, and widened.

"They weren't rumors." The British accent cut through the room. "Your wife was a lesbian, and a hot one at that."

I knew that voice. Roland was standing over us. I stood and faced him. He was wearing a black MantaSoft-logo shirt and black pants.

I said, "Roland, you stylish devil. You matched your colors today. Was it for me?"

Roland took a step closer and said, "Laugh it up, wanker. Your wife had given up on you. You put her off the entire male sex."

The people around us stopped talking. Roland and I were standing in the middle of the cafeteria, nose to nose. It was breakfast time, and the place was full. The clanking of glasses and chatting died away.

"How the fuck would you know?" I asked.

Roland said, "I know because there were three of us in that room. It was incredible."

"You're full of shit."

"Am I? I suppose I should offer proof."

"I suppose you should shut your mouth."

Roland leaned in close and whispered in my ear, "When did Carol get that lovely tattoo on her ass? What was it? A lizard?"

It had been a gecko. Carol had gotten it just after we were engaged. She said it would be our "saucy little secret."

Roland continued in a septic whisper, "She had an amazing set of tits. Real ones. You would have been a lucky man if you had been getting any. It's a shame your work interfered."

Then I left my body as something else took over. I watched, like a spectator, as I shoved Roland in the chest with both hands. He took a step back to regain his balance. The people around us stood and formed a circle. It was like a fight at the ball game.

"Shut the fuck up," I said. "You don't know what you're talking about."

"Truth hurts, doesn't it? It just burns you that someone else was seeing her naked. Touching her tits."

I stepped close and said quietly, "Did you fuck her?"

Roland smiled, his bad teeth jutting like tombstones.

He said through rank breath, "I did much worse."

That's when I hit him. I'd never hit anyone in my life, but I balled up my fist and took a swing. It landed on his cheek, and his head snapped sideways. He looked at me with pure hatred and grabbed at me. I grabbed him back, leaned my weight to the right, and then when he resisted, I pushed to the left and threw him into the fountain like a sack of shit.

The crowd surged in. People bumped and jostled me as they went to help Roland out of the fountain. Then Huey was next to me. He said, "Get out! Get out before they call the cops."

I took his advice, turned, and left. I walked straight out of the cafeteria, took a right, and walked down the hallway. The commotion in the cafeteria faded away, and I was walking past offices. My cell phone rang. It was Jael.

"Meet me in front. I am in the car," she said. *God, she's fast.*

I walked out through the front doors feeling light and elated. I was coming to the end of a long dream, and better days lay ahead. I floated down the front steps of the office building toward her Acura MDX, which idled in the visitor lot.

Jael jumped out of her car and rushed around to embrace me. She pressed her left hand into my back and her right hand into my side. I raised my arms to hug her back. She said, "You are bleeding."

I looked down. Blood trailed down my side, soaking my T-shirt and smearing my jeans.

I said, "Holy shit. I'm bleeding."

FORTY-THREE

I LAY ON THE floor in Jael's bathroom and winced as she applied antiseptic to my cut. We were in her apartment in Brookline.

"Maybe I should go to the doctor," I said.

"I would be happy to take you to the doctor. Are you willing to lose half the day?" asked Jael. She poured some liquid on the cut.

I gasped and said, "No."

"Then be still. I will close the cut with butterfly bandages."

Jael patted the wound dry. Then she began applying the bandages.

"How did I get cut? I didn't even feel it."

"There was a man in the crowd. He was 175 centimeters tall. He was wearing a blue striped shirt, black suit pants, and good shoes. He had short, dark hair. He was a little bit fat."

"You saw all that?"

"Yes, but I noticed him too late. I did not have time to help you."

"Don't feel bad."

Jael stopped applying bandages. "I do not feel bad."

"You don't?"

"No."

"Oh."

Jael started applying the butterfly bandages again.

"How did he cut me?" I asked.

"After you threw Roland into the fountain, the man brushed past you in the crowd. He cut you with a switchblade. Obviously, it was very sharp. I saw him walk away from the fountain, closing the blade."

Jael poured more liquid onto the cut.

"Son of a bitch!" I swore as I pounded the floor.

She ignored me and continued to close the cut with butterfly bandages. "We are lucky in a way."

"How are we—Jesus, that hurts! How are we lucky?"

"The man is a sadist. He could have killed you just as easily as cut you, but he likes to torture his victims. It is unprofessional."

"By God, you're right. I am lucky."

Jael poured some more liquid into my cut and I gritted my teeth. *Was that a smile?* It seemed an excessive punishment for sarcasm. She said, "He is not a killer. He is one who kills. I am worried for you."

"Well, that's not very comforting coming from my bodyguard."

"It is the truth. I am not sure I can defend you."

"Maybe if you walked next to me."

"It would not help. He would know about me and plan his attack with me in mind."

Jael went back to applying bandages. I lay on my side as she worked. Then I turned to talk to her again. Carol was standing over Jael and crying.

"Baby, quit! Please quit. It's too late. You can't save me, and she's right. He'll kill you just like he killed me."

I looked at Carol and said, "I'm not quitting."

Jael said, "I did not suggest it. I believe you need to find this killer of your wife."

I said, "And if he kills me?"

"Then he will die. I will make sure of it."

So I had that going for me. I looked at Carol who was still standing over Jael, her hands folded against her mouth as she sniffled.

I asked Carol, "How did Roland see that tattoo?"

Jael responded, "Which tattoo?"

I glanced at Jael and Carol was gone. It was just the two of us again.

"Carol had a tattoo of a gecko on her left butt cheek. Roland told me that he had seen it. That's when I hit him."

"There are only two ways that Roland could have seen the tattoo you describe."

"They are?"

"He either saw it himself, or saw a picture of it."

That brought me back to Huey and his laptop. Alice and porn. What was he driving at? As soon as Jael was finished, I grabbed my phone to call Huey's cell.

It went immediately to voicemail. Why would he shut off his phone?

I left Huey a message" "Call me." Then I sent him an email and a text. All with "Call me." When I was done, my phone rang, but it wasn't Huey. It was Nate.

Nate said, "Tucker, you're fired."

FORTY-FOUR

The Boylston Suites lobby was resting in mid-morning silence. The conventioneers were across the street pitching each other, and the tourists had all gotten in line for the duck boats. Nate said he'd meet me here, but he was late. Another commitment shot to hell. A koi bobbed to the surface. I snapped his picture and tweeted it:
`Sushi on the hoof`
The elevator doors opened and Nate entered the lobby. He saw me and pointed to a pair of overstuffed lobby chairs. He sat in a chair and I took the other one.

"Hi, Tucker," Nate said and put out his hand to shake.

I ignored his hand and said, "This is bullshit!"

"Will you keep your voice down?" said Nate.

"It's the middle of the morning. Who's going to hear? The fish?"

"There's no need for a scene," said Nate.

"A scene? You think this is a scene?"

"Let's be adults here," said Nate.

"Oh, screw that," I said. "You fucked me over again. Again! And you want to have a quiet chat?"

"I fucked you over? How did I fuck you over?"

I had never heard Nate drop the F-bomb.

Nate continued. "You're the one who punched the Rosetta project lead in the face and threw him into a fountain. If anyone is fucked over, it's me. Jack told me not to hire you, but I did it anyway and then you assault a manager? Not just a manager, but his pet? What the hell is wrong with you?"

"Whose side are you on?"

"Side? What side? I'm on the side of not punching people because you don't like them. I'm on the side of getting my job done."

"And all that bullshit about me being like a son to you? What was that about?"

"That wasn't bullshit. That's a fact. You are like a son to me. A pain-in-the-ass son who thinks he's smarter than his father."

"I saw your email, you know."

"What email?"

"The one to Jack. 'Rest assured. If he gets out of line, I'll fire him immediately.' You were true to your word there."

"How did you read that?"

"I have mad skills."

"Yes, I know."

"I mean, that was why you hired me. Because of my mad skills. That is, until my wife cried in your office and the political wind started blowing. Then you called me into the office and ripped my life away."

"Don't blame me for that, Tucker. I'm not the one who killed Carol."

"And yet it happened just as I was in your office. Nice alibi."

Oh shit. My shields were down and everything that ran through my head was running out of my mouth. I'd never had that go well for me. Not once.

Nate leaned in and asked, "What are you saying?"

"Nothing. Nothing. I was—"

"Are you saying that I had something to do with Carol's murder?"

"I wasn't saying anything. I'm sorry. I'm upset."

"Why would you say something like that? To me, of all people."

"I'm sorry. I didn't mean it. It just slipped out."

"What the hell is wrong with you?"

The cut in my side burned. I put my head in my hand, and my thumb brushed the stitches. I squeezed my other hand into a tight fist that blanched to white as I forced the blood out of it.

Nate grabbed my fist and held it. "Tucker. What is going on with you? Talk to me."

I was about to do it. I was about to tell Nate everything about Rosetta and the FBI and the Russian and my garrote mark and the knife cut in my side. I opened my mouth to tell him and then closed it again because I saw someone leave the elevator, walk to the center of the lobby, and make eye contact with me. He crooked his finger at me. *Come here.*

He was 175 centimeters tall. He was wearing a blue striped shirt, black suit pants, and good shoes. He had short, dark hair. He was a little bit fat. It was the guy who had pushed me down the staircase. He smiled when he saw that he had caught my attention.

I stood up. I was going to end this.

FORTY-FIVE

WHEN YOU CONFRONT A bloodthirsty killer, it's important to have a plan.

I know that now.

I left Nate at the table and stalked across the empty Boylston Suites Lobby. There was no direct path. I had to wind my way around koi ponds and over bridges. The Russian also began working his way through the lobby. We met on a little bridge in the middle, far away from everyone. The Russian had a bemused this-should-be-good expression as he approached me.

"What are you doing here?" I asked, poking him in the chest. He ignored my poke.

He said, "I want to talk to you. I thought I would have to chase you because you would hide like a rabbit from a wolf. But now I see you are a very stupid rabbit." His accent was so thick that it was like talking to Boris Badenov. *Moose picks up bomb, bomb explodes, moose is dead. Then we shoot squirrel.*

"Fuck you, Boris."

The Russian looked puzzled. "Boris? I am Dmitri. Who is Boris?"

"Your mother. What do you want?"

Dmitri reached into his left pocket and pulled out a black package of cigarettes and a gold lighter. He flipped the package open, took out a cigarette with a gold filter, and lit it, holding the cigarette between his first two fingers. Then he put the cigarettes and lighter in his pocket and took a deep drag.

I said, "There's no smoking in here."

Dmitri blew a cloud of smoke into my face. I coughed. He said, "Go home, Mr. Tucker."

"What?"

"Go home. Go back to your little house and stay there. On Friday I will be gone and you will be safe."

"I am safe."

"You think so? Then you are stupid or naive." Dmitri appraised me as he took another drag on his cigarette. Then he said, "Naive. You are naive. But now I have warned you. So now you are stupid. Soon you will be dead."

I said, "You could have killed me today, but you chickened out. Got a case of conscience?"

Dmitri laughed and said, "My partner thinks you may be useful."

"Partner? What partner? Who?"

"You would like to know, eh? Stop interfering, Mr. Tucker."

"Interfering with what? What are you doing?"

Dmitri took a step closer and said in a quiet voice, "I am making money. I am making more money than I ever made before, and my partner thinks you could help." Dmitri took another drag on the cigarette and threw it into the koi pond. A fish inhaled it, then spit it out.

I took a step closer to Dmitri, got in his face. I loomed over him. He did not step back. My looming didn't seem to be a problem for him. I said, "I'm never helping you make a fucking dime."

He looked into my eyes and nodded slowly. "I know. You are an idiot."

"And you are a sick fuck."

I could barely hear the next words as they hissed out of Dmitri's tobacco-stained lips. He said, "You are right. I am, as you say, a sick fuck. If you are lucky, I will shoot you. If you are not lucky, I will tie you to a tree and skin you like a deer." He smiled and said, "Why don't you just go away."

I whispered, "Because you killed my wife."

Dmitri glanced over my shoulder, then looked me in the eye. He plucked the front of my black T-shirt, pulled me even closer, and breathed, "Do you know what I liked about your wife, Mr. Tucker?"

Liked about my wife? I shook my head as Dmitri spoke. I could smell the stink of the cigarette as his warm breath puffed against my face.

Dmitri said, "Her tits were real."

The demons in the back of my mind sprang out of their cages. I pushed Dmitri away and tried to punch his ugly Russian face. I missed. He had moved.

He was holding a switchblade. He snicked it open.

"Gentlemen, gentlemen! There's no need for this." Nate interposed himself between Dmitri and me. Nate said, "I'm sure this is all just a misunderstanding."

Dmitri sneered at me. His lip curled in an ugly crescent. Nate stood between us. Dmitri showed us the knife and said, "Listen to my warning, Mr. Tucker, or I will skin you with your wife's favorite knife."

"I'll kill you, you bastard!" I launched myself at Dmitri again, but Nate was in the way. He was old, but he was in good shape. He grabbed me and stood his ground. Dmitri laughed, folded the knife, and walked out of the hotel.

Nate watched Dmitri leave. He let go and said, "Who—?"

My cell phone rang. It was Jael, and she wanted to see me.

Great.

FORTY-SIX

LEIF ERIKSON'S NIPPLES GLINTED in the afternoon sun as his shapely thighs poked out from under a flowing skirt. I stood at the base of his statue and looked up his skirt while waiting for Jael. She had wanted to meet somewhere far away from the convention center, and no place was better than the base of Leif Erikson's statue on Commonwealth Ave.

The monument was the brainchild of Henry Wadsworth Longfellow who, along with Protestant Brahmin society, preferred to believe that a Norseman had discovered the new world rather than an Italian. They built the statue because the immigrant Catholics were growing in power, and Boston's elite wanted to give the Irish immigrants a poke in the eye.

Leif Erikson had to be rolling in his grave. The statue made him look like a hairdresser trying to find his partner at a costume party. It was so gaudy that it was a useful landmark. I had told Jael, "Go to the end of the Commonwealth Ave mall and meet me under the brown statue of a guy with pointy nipples and great legs." She had found it easily.

Jael crossed her arms and said, "I need to know if you intend to commit suicide."

"Suicide?" I said. "Absolutely not."

"It would be possible. You are very upset about the loss of your wife."

"What? No! I'm not going to commit suicide over losing my wife."

Jael leaned against the flower garden at the base of the statue with her long legs straight out in front of her and her handbag over her shoulder. She wore black sunglasses. I could see the empty sky over the Charles River reflected in them.

She said, "So you are like David? You expect God to save you?"

"What?"

"David stripped off his armor and faced Goliath alone because he expected God to bring him victory. I imagine you expect the same."

I was stunned. I said, "God never crossed my mind."

"Then," asked Jael, "what were you planning when you walked up to a killer and presented your neck?"

I didn't answer. I was starting to feel like a little kid getting scolded. My hands shook. That bastard had killed Carol, cut her throat in her own kitchen, and stood in the middle of a hotel lobby as if he were the fucking mayor.

"I see," Jael continued. "You didn't have a plan."

I knew then why I didn't have a plan. The right plan would have involved putting a bullet into Dmitri's twisted brain. I wanted to kill him, but I had been impotent. My lower lip started taking on a life of its own. I couldn't believe this was happening.

Jael said, "You simply wanted to see what would happen."

"That bastard killed my wife!" I cried. Hot tears fell down my face. "I couldn't just let him stand there."

Jael grabbed me by the upper arm and said, "Walk." She led me down Charlesgate toward the river, then pulled me into a little stand of trees next to the road. Nobody came to this park. Even the homeless had deserted it. Once she had me hidden by the trees, she slapped me across the face. Hard. My lip rammed into my teeth and began to bleed.

"Ow! Jesus, what are you doing?" I said.

"Jesus has nothing to do with this."

"I didn't mean to make you angry."

Jael said, "You are interfering with the business of a mobster who has killed an FBI agent."

"I know."

"This is not therapy, and I am not a therapist. You cannot do stupid things. If you must be stupid, then I will not work with you. I do not want to die because of your emotions."

I said nothing. I was ashamed of myself. I looked at the ground where city grass struggled to grow through the packed earth.

Jael put her hand on my shoulder and said, "There will come a time, soon, when you will be in danger, and where you will have to do brave things. I will help you as I can, but I cannot help you if you are suicidal."

"Why are you helping me at all?" I asked. "You said yourself this is dangerous. It's not your fight."

Jael took her hand off my shoulder and said, "It is an obligation."

"To who?"

"To God. You are trying to mend the world. I must help."

"What?"

Jael took off her mirrored sunglasses. She looked at me with her gray eyes, as if she wanted to see me clearly before speaking again.

"The world is a broken place," she said. "You are trying to mend it, to put the pieces back together, to create justice. That is why I am helping you."

I had nothing to say to that. I didn't think of myself as fixing the world, but I was grateful nonetheless. I wanted to hug Jael, but that was a bad idea. I put out my hand and said, "Thank you."

Jael shook it awkwardly, a concession to my Americanism, and said, "You are welcome."

We stood that way for a moment, looking at each other. I had never trusted anyone as deeply as I trusted this strange friend of Bobby Miller's. She was hard, and she was unyielding, but she would do what she promised. I felt at peace.

My cell phone beeped. It was a text message from a strange phone number. I read the message and said, "Shit."

The text message was from Huey. He needed my help.

FORTY-SEVEN

THE MANTASOFT MARKETING PEOPLE had crammed Huey into the largest pair of eighteenth-century breeches they could find, but it was no good. While the pants covered most of his backside, they weren't up to the job, and Huey looked like a Revolutionary plumber. He slouched in front of a computer, in a triangle hat, trying to give a demo.

Jael was hidden somewhere again, but she was worried that Dmitri would strike now that I had uncovered him. She had made me call Bobby Miller before she'd let me enter the hall. Bobby and I were standing behind Huey's customer, listening to Huey's slick sales pitch.

"Well, this menu here is called *Reports*, and it makes reports. You can pull down on it with the mouse and see the different reports…"

The customer yawned, pretended that he had gotten a cell call, thanked Huey, and fled.

I clapped Huey on the back, pointed at his backside, and said, "Hey, buddy. Just say no to crack."

Huey jumped. "Oh God, Tucker, it's awful. Roland was so mad at me for talking to you that he threw my phone in the fountain and then told me come down here to work the booth. They weren't going to put me in a uniform, but Roland made them. I had to borrow a phone to text you."

A customer came by, tapped Huey on the shoulder, and said, "Can you give me a demo?"

Bobby said, "He's with us." He made it sound like as if the guy had asked to dance with our dates. The guy shrank back and left.

Huey pointed at Bobby and asked me, "Who's that?"

Bobby flipped open his badge. "Special Agent Bobby Miller, FBI."

Huey blanched.

I said to Huey, "It's OK, dude, he's trying to figure out who killed Alice."

Huey pulled me close and whispered in my ear, "But that's what I was going to talk to you about before, you know, the fight."

I answered in a normal voice. "Well, tell Bobby too. He needs to hear it."

Huey whispered in my ear again, "But he might arrest me."

I whispered back, "Did you kill Alice?"

"No…"

"Then don't worry about it."

Bobby said, "Are you girls done whispering?"

"Huey has something to tell us about Alice," I said.

Huey's face went from white to red. Something was definitely wrong. He said, "It's on the Internet."

"Can you bring it up on this machine?" said Bobby, pointing to the demo PC.

"Oh no, we can't use this one. We need my tablet."

Huey led us to the back of the MantaSoft booth. The booth had a desk in front of a large sign that said *MantaSoft*. Behind the desk and sign was a cubby that served as storage for the booth workers. Huey squeezed himself into this cubby. We followed. He fished through the computer bags, his plumber-like pants causing me to avert my eyes, and pulled out a black Android tablet.

He turned and squatted among the backpacks, looking like a bear in a den. After fiddling around and bringing up a webpage, he pointed at Bobby and said, "Does he have to be here? I'd like to just show this to you."

"Why?"

Huey looked at his computer screen, then back toward me. He wouldn't make eye contact. I could hardly hear him when he said, "It's embarrassing."

Bobby said, "Look …" He prompted me for help with the name. I said, "Huey."

"Look, Huey, Alice Barton died alone and afraid because of some douchebag. That guy's gonna kill someone else, probably at this show. It's probably going to be one of your friends. So cut the crap and show me what you got."

Huey cringed and shrank inward.

I looked at Bobby and shook my head. *Nice going.* Like many engineers, Huey would rather die than engage in open conflict. When the going gets tough, they close like clams. Bobby had just made this much harder.

I squatted in front of Huey, who looked at his tablet and slid his finger around it aimlessly. A background picture of Captain Picard from *Star Trek* looked out at us. Picard was pointing his finger in his classic "Make it so" pose.

I said, "Bobby can be an asshole, but he's right. You've got to know that nobody's judging you here. We just need to figure out who killed Alice and Carol."

Huey said, "But Carol wasn't killed … that way."

"No. But they're connected somehow."

"I liked Carol," said Huey.

"I loved her."

"Really? You never said that. You guys were always fighting."

"Oh shit, dude, we were married, you know? I sucked at being a husband, and I'd give anything to go back and do it right."

"It stank, what happened to you guys. I always felt bad for you both."

"Thanks. Now all I want to do is catch the guy who killed her."

"You think this will help?"

"Yeah."

Huey tapped the browser icon and started to type in an address. "You've gotta keep this a secret. I don't want anyone to know that I go to this site."

"We'll keep it a secret, right, Bobby?"

Bobby said nothing, and Huey and I turned to look at him and Bobby said, "Right. Right. Secret."

Huey gave him a look and then typed the address into the browser. It was a long address that ended in the extension .ru. The webpage came up. Big white letters on a black background promised, "The girl next door, forced to fuck for you." It had a picture of a girl tied to a table, her arms above her head, her legs spread, a strategically placed star covering her crotch.

Bobby said, "Fucking Russians."

I said, "Or Russians fucking."

"What's wrong with you?"

Good question.

Huey took a deep breath and tapped in a username and password. He was a subscriber. His hands shook. He mistyped his password several times. This was costing him. Huey was exposing a side of himself nobody could have suspected. The shame came off him in waves.

Huey said, his voice barely audible, "I'm doing this for Carol. I liked her."

"I know, pal."

"I always thought this was a cool site because they didn't use models. They have hidden cameras, you know?"

The webpage had pictures to indicate the different types of hidden cameras. One picture showed young girls climbing out of their field hockey skirts. It was called *LockerCam.* Another showed a naked woman yawning on a bed, waiting for a fat guy in a business suit to get his pants off. It was *PimpCam.* Finally came a picture of a girl tied to a cross, face down. It was called *DungeonCam.* Huey clicked on DungeonCam. No wonder he was embarrassed.

"I found this," Huey said in a tiny whisper.

Huey clicked around the DungeonCam area and then found what he was looking for.

The camera focused on a bed, a twin-sized box spring and mattress on a cheap frame. The mattress had no sheets, no blankets, no pillow. Four ropes ran off the mattress and down to the bed's legs. The ropes connected to a woman's arms and legs. She was spread-eagle on the bed, struggling to get comfortable. The woman was Alice Barton.

Bobby said, "Son of a bitch."

A naked man entered the picture. Alice looked at him with wide eyes. She tugged at her wrists as he ran his hands over her breasts and spoke to her in Russian. He forced her to kiss him as he climbed between her legs. She stiffened as if being examined.

Huey said, "When I saw this, I thought that Alice must be doing porn, you know, for kicks. But she's not. She doesn't like it. You can see it."

Bobby said, "It's a kind of sexual slavery the Russians came up with. They get their hooks into drug addicts and force them to make movies like this. They make more money from the movies than they would by turning them into prostitutes. This makes sense."

I said, "Makes sense? What makes sense about Russians having their hooks into Alice?"

"Tell you later."

Drugs? Oh, Alice.

The movie had kept running on the tablet; the guy had started humping Alice. She was crying. I felt sick. Then the door to the cubby opened and Dana looked in. Huey reacted like he'd been hit with a Taser. He held the tablet behind him and cowered. Crying and moaning sounds slipped from video.

Dana said, "What's up, boys? Porn party?"

Huey said, "No! No! Why would you say that?"

I stood up and shielded Huey. I said, "Can we help you?"

"I need to talk to you. The people at the desk said you were in here with Huey." She ignored Bobby, who ignored her in turn.

"Is it important?"

Dana said, "Yeah, it's important. Meet me at that Starbucks on Newbury Street in a half hour."

Dana shut the door, and I turned to Huey. I patted him on the shoulder and said, "Thanks, man."

"That's OK," said Huey.

"You should get out of that costume and go home."

"What about Roland? He told me to come here."

I said, "Tell him to fuck himself."

Bobby agreed. "Yeah. Tell Roland to fuck himself. That's a direct order from the FBI."

Huey grinned. He was feeling better, but there was no way he'd go home. He was a wimp. He'd be here for the rest of the show in his ass-crack breeches, poor guy.

Bobby continued. "And, Huey, I don't care what you look at on the Internet, but stop paying these guys. It's blood money."

Huey's grin faded. "I will."

Bobby and I left the cubby. I shut the door and said to Bobby, "Alice was a drug addict? How did I not notice?"

Bobby pointed back toward the cubby with his thumb and said, "People are real good at hiding their dirty laundry."

"Huey was a mess."

Bobby started walking and I followed. "You know, they teach us in school that there are two primary motives for murder: money and sex."

"Yeah, I've heard that."

"But there's a third one."

"Drugs?"

"Shame. People will do anything to avoid shame. Including..."

"Killing someone?"

Bobby tapped me on the chest and said, "Exactly." He gave me a little shove toward the exit and said, "Go find out what Dana wants. She wouldn't have come near me if it wasn't important."

FORTY-EIGHT

WATER DRIPPED DOWN THE sides of my Frappuccino, a result of the humidity that had overwhelmed the air-conditioning system in Starbucks. I was sitting at the table where I had first met Dana, dorking around on my Twitter account.

Hot, sweaty Frappuccino. Oh yeahhh!

I flipped through the messages that mentioned me, and saw a recent one from @rubabemaster:

@tuckerinboston I am following you.

I tweeted back:

@rubabemaster Thanks for the follow. And I am not a babe master.

"Oh, baby, you're so cute when you're geeking out." Carol had appeared.

I took out my cell headset and put it in my ear while Carol watched with amusement.

I said, "Hello," into my fake phone call.

Carol said in a nasal voice, "Mr. Tucker, we have a collect call from beyond the grave. Do you accept the charges?"

"Do I have a choice?" I said. Then, "Did you know that Alice was a drug addict?"

Carol slipped out of her nasal voice. "I suspected."

"Why didn't you say something?"

"You mean you don't remember that time I said, 'I think there's something wrong with Alice?'"

"No."

"How about when I said that Alice seemed to get sick a lot?"

"No."

"Or the time I said, 'I think Alice has a drug problem'?"

"Nope."

"That was the problem, baby. You just didn't want to hear it. You didn't care."

"Of course I cared."

Carol evaporated as Dana sat in her seat holding a red iced tea, shaken not stirred. She was wearing a pink polo shirt with the MantaSoft logo over the left breast. Dana put her thumb and forefinger up to her ear, pantomiming a phone, and mouthed, "Who are you talking to?"

I pocketed my headset and asked, "Did you know that Alice did cocaine?"

Dana paused, looking at me and sipping her red drink. Then she said, "Her addiction is how I got here."

I stared. I had missed something again. I couldn't get my bearings on this problem. My debugging skills usually got me through life's puzzles, though I have to admit they were useless when it came to understanding Carol and they were failing me again now. I was out of my depth.

Dana moved over to my side of the table and sat next to me, snuggling in as if we were on a date. She smelled of the shampoo from my shower. She crowded my mind. "Local cops arrested Alice for possession, and the narcotics guys wanted to roll up her dealer network. So they squeezed her. Instead of giving up the network, she gave up MantaSoft." She gave my ear a little bite. I shuddered.

I would have returned the ear bite, but Dana's lobes were guarded by spiky earrings and I didn't want my lip pierced. I whispered back, "What did Alice tell them?"

"That someone in MantaSoft was selling Rosetta. That's when Kevin and I got involved. We forced Alice to get one of us hired. Alice said that Roland liked cute girls, and, well—" Dana made a Vanna White gesture down her body. She got up, sat back on her side of the table, and sipped her red tea.

I leaned forward and whispered, "I'll give you a hint about that. Did you know that Alice was being forced to make porn?"

"What are you talking about?"

"I just saw a video of Alice, tied to a bed, getting screwed by some Russian asshole. She didn't look happy about it."

"Sexual slavery."

"Yeah, at least that's what Bobby said."

"She never told me. Dammit. I would have put her into the protection program faster if she had told me." Dana paused and clicked her nail against her plastic cup. Her lips tightened; she closed her eyes and shook her head. "It was bad enough she was killed because of me, but now I hear she was tortured too."

"It wasn't your fault. You didn't kill her or torture her."

"If I threw Alice in a lion's den, I wouldn't be the one who killed her, but I'd be responsible. Just like I'm responsible now. These people are killers. It was just that I needed her help with the code. Like you said, I'm not a real engineer."

"That didn't work out, either."

"You mean because she's dead?"

"I mean because she wasn't a real engineer either. She's the one who broke that code, not you. Alice was randomly making changes trying to figure out what worked. It was a disaster."

"Well, it's not broken anymore, thanks to you," Dana said. "I think maybe you did too good a job."

"Why?"

"I saved your changes into the central server last night. Roland called about an hour later. He was happy as hell, telling me I did a great job, and I was an asset to the team."

"Sounds good."

"It was, except that I just saw Roland talking to Margaret Bronte at her booth, and neither one of them was happy. Then they looked at me and looked away again. Something was up, so I went over to see what was going on. That's when Roland said to Margaret, 'Here's little Miss Fix-It.'"

"What did Margaret say?"

"Nothing, she just turned and left. Didn't even acknowledge me."

My phone rang. I looked at the caller ID and said, "Speak of the devil."

Margaret was on the line. She said, "Tucker, do you have a suit?"

I said, "Of course I have a suit."

I didn't have a suit.

Margaret said, "Well, wear one, dear. I'm taking you out to dinner at Mooo tonight. We need to talk."

"About what?"

"Your future. Meet me there at seven." She hung up. The phone switched back to the Twitter app. I saw another mention of my name. I clicked on it automatically. It was from @rubabemaster, replying to our thread.

@tuckerinboston Enjoy your milkshake. It is your last.

I frowned at my phone.

Dana said, "What is it?"

"Some asshole just tweeted me. He mentioned my drink. He's watching us."

We looked out through the big Starbucks plate-glass window. A large black car parked across the street pulled into traffic. It drove off to my left toward Mass Ave. Dmitri was driving.

Dana said, "Shit. He's seen us together. That's not good. How did he know you were here? Did he follow you?"

"I'm pretty sure Jael would have warned me."

Dana crossed her arms and looked around. "It's almost like he planted a GPS on you."

Then it hit me. I looked at the Twitter app on my BlackBerry and realized that I had just committed the worst kind of engineering error: the failure of imagination. The deadly fire on *Apollo 1*, the *Challenger* explosion, and the *Columbia* disintegration were all caused by failures of imagination. Whether it was oxygenated Velcro, cold O-rings, or Styrofoam punching a hole in the spaceship, all three disasters were caused by things that looked obvious in hindsight. In my case, it was the location finder on my Twitter app.

In all these cases, somebody was shouting a warning before the disaster, a person who was ignored until later being considered a prophet. In my case, that was Kevin. He had warned me about the "creepy" feature, and that feature had gotten him killed.

I said, "It's my fault."

Dana asked, "How is it your fault?"

"My tweets all had my location on them. Dmitri's been following me on Twitter."

"Oh for God's sake, Tucker, how could you be so stupid?"

Definitely a failure of imagination. Dmitri had found me at the Apple Store, on the bridge, and in the hotel all because I had tweeted my location to him. No wonder he was a step ahead of me. I was my own spy.

I said, "I'm sorry."

"Sorry's not going to help when he machine-guns you."

"I mean I'm sorry that he's seen us together. It's going to expose you."

"No it won't. As far as he or anyone else knows, I'm just the programmer who fixed Rosetta and screwed up the deal. Whatever that means."

"You should quit," I said.

"This from the guy with the stitches on his forehead and the garrote mark on his neck."

I pulled up my shirt, exposing my seeping butterfly bandages. "You forgot the knifing."

"When did that happen?"

"This morning."

"You have got to leave town."

I fiddled with my phone and deleted the Twitter app. I was tired of being stupid.

Dana reached out and touched the cut. I winced.

"Seriously," she said. "Run."

I gave her a quick kiss on the lips and then stood up.

Dana asked, "Where are you going?"

"To buy a suit," I said. "I hear Mooo is a pretty classy joint."

FORTY-NINE

I HAD ALWAYS WANTED to buy an expensive suit. I stood in a three-way mirror in a men's clothing store on Newbury Street that was so trendy it didn't have a sign. Instead it had suits displayed in a second-story window. A gray Belvest jacket draped over my shoulders. Its sleeves reached that perfect spot just below my wrist and above my thumb, and its collar ran into my back as smoothly as a seal's pelt.

"Baby, it's perfect," said Carol. She was standing next to me in the changing area.

"Thanks," I said.

"You look hot."

"Wow. You haven't said that in years. I should have bought a suit earlier."

"You would never have worn it. Still, you do look hot."

Carol's plum funeral dress hugged her hips. My hands wanted to cradle those hips, and my fingers wanted to rest on the small of her back. Instead I said, "I always loved that dress."

Carol plucked at the purple fabric and said, "What, this old thing? I only wear it when I don't care how I look."

"*It's a Wonderful Life*," I said. Memories of popcorn and snuggling crowded into my mind.

Carol asked, "Remember how we'd watch that movie every year?"

"It always made you cry."

"It always made *you* cry, you big softie."

I smiled and Carol sniffed, wiping a tear from her cheek. I can look at the most complex software in the world and tease out the one thing that breaks it, but I was never able to debug my marriage. Carol and I had birthed a fiery relationship, then watched in horror as it took on a life of its own, grabbed us by the throats, and dragged us down into unhappiness.

I went back to adjusting the blue-and-gray striped tie.

Carol said, "I'm sorry."

"For what?" I had decided to go with a four-in-hand knot.

Carol paused, looking at me in my suit. In the mirror, she reached up to touch me on my shoulder, but withdrew.

"I'm sorry that you're wasting your life over me."

I turned. "I'm not wasting my life. We need to know what happened. You deserve it."

"No, I don't deserve it. Nobody does. I'd give anything to be with you again. I love you. But we can't be together again, even when you die."

"I'm not going to die," I said.

"You're going to have dinner with Margaret Bronte, aren't you?"

"Yeah."

"Then you're going to die."

FIFTY

THE SOMMELIER'S NOSE WAS long, hooked, and tucked deeply into
a snifter of thirty-year-old Glenlivet Scotch. He breathed deeply,
sucking in the essence of the drink. Margaret had bought the
Scotch and had asked him to analyze it as after-dinner entertainment.

We had just finished our meal in Mooo, a fancy steakhouse next
to the golden dome on Boston's Beacon Hill. Margaret and I sat in
plush seats in the corner of a plush room. The restaurant was quiet,
as if the mundane sounds of clanking silverware would not be tol-
erated within its rarified environment. Square columns held up a
high ceiling, and I kept looking for John Kerry to come in with
Teresa Heinz on his arm.

"Complex sherry. I'm getting spice and ginger, some fruit in
there, fresh fruit, and some wood—oh, and there is a hint of dried
fruit as well. Peach?"

I sniffed my own thirty-year-old Glenlivet. It smelled like
Scotch.

He sipped his drink and pronounced, "Light mouth feel. Vanilla hints."

I sipped mine. It tasted exactly like Scotch. A little lighter than I liked.

The sommelier knocked the whole drink back as if he was doing a shot, but he didn't swallow. The Scotch sat in his mouth as he closed his eyes and put his head back, then breathed out through that nose. Finally, he swallowed it and proclaimed his verdict.

"An explosion of spices, fresh fruit, and oak. Well crafted."

I knocked mine back. It tasted like more Scotch, and now my glass was empty.

"Would you like another, dear?" Margaret asked. She motioned to the server, who was standing by and refilled my glass.

"Try the next one with an ice cube, sir," said the sommelier. "It will fully expose the complexity."

"Thanks," I said. If I didn't know better, I'd think that Margaret Bronte was trying to get me drunk—again.

"This is the life that wealth affords us," said Margaret, as the sommelier and server dissolved into the background.

"It's good to be the king," I said.

"Yes. Or queen."

"And how did you get to be queen?"

Margaret was drinking port wine from a tulip-shaped glass. She sipped it now as she considered the question. "It's very hard. Have you ever founded a company?"

"No," I admitted. "I've thought of getting some venture capital money and starting one."

"Ha!" Margaret's laugh was sharp and unpleasant.

"What's so funny?"

"People like you. The ones who think that VCs will line up to fulfill their dreams."

"Well, I'd have a business plan."

"A business plan? For God's sake, everybody has a business plan. There are thousands of business plans. The key is to get those vultures to invest in *your* plan."

"Did you get funded by VCs?"

"Of course not. Oh, I tried at first. I sent out hundreds of copies of my precious plan, which generated dozens of breakfast meetings. The breakfasts led to ten presentations, and I had two deals go all the way to where they turned over every rock in my life. But nobody funded me."

"Why not?"

"Who knows? Each rejection had its own reason. In the end, I guess they just didn't believe in my business. But one man did."

"Who?"

"Roland Baker."

"Roland? Roland's an idiot. What did he have to do with your business?"

Margaret sipped some port and tipped the glass toward me. "You know, you keep saying that Roland is an idiot. But from what I see, Roland has been a step ahead of you at every turn." She slurred a couple of her *S*s.

"He's an asshole."

"He's a sweet man. He saved my company."

"How?"

Margaret gazed into her wine, recounting her story. "We met at a networking breakfast. I was desperately poor. I was down to one suit; my refrigerator was empty, and my cupboards were full of ramen noodles. I had paid my last fifty dollars to attend this breakfast, and I realized that everybody there had already rejected me."

"You mean your plan."

"Me, my plan, whatever. Getting your plan rejected means people are saying you don't have what it takes to succeed. That seems personal to me." Margaret sloshed her port a little. "Then Roland walked in."

"Love at first sight?"

Margaret smiled with sad eyes. "I wish. I walked up to him, introduced myself, and started bawling. It was horrible."

"What did Roland do?"

"He took me across the street for a cup of coffee. He listened as I told him about my business, and then he promised to help. The first thing he did was get me cheaper engineers."

"How?"

"He had contacts in Russia. I got five Russian engineers there for the price of one American."

"And look at you now. Drinking port in Mooo on the backs of cheap engineers."

"No. That wasn't what did it. I was still going out of business. I had no cash."

"How did Roland help with that?"

"He got me some creative financing." Margaret finished her port and ordered another, along with more Scotch.

I said, "Margaret Bronte, I do believe you are trying to get me drunk."

She said, "All the better to proposition you."

"An indecent proposition?"

Margaret smiled. "We'll see how indecent you think it is. It all depends on how far you are willing to go."

"After this much Scotch? Pretty far." I sipped again. My worries were starting to dissolve into the alcohol. I settled into my plush seat and had a disturbing thought. "Does sleeping with a rich older woman make me a gigolo? Because if it does, I'll need to update my résumé."

Margaret's smile vanished. "What makes you say I'm rich?"

"The fifty million dollars you're getting for your company."

Margaret sat back in her chair and took a deep drink. "That deal is dead."

The news couldn't get through my fuzzy brain. "What?" I said.

"The deal is dead. I'm not getting the fifty million dollars. And it's your fault."

"My fault? How is it my fault?" I asked as I drank some more Scotch.

"You fixed the code for Dana, didn't you?"

Deep in my mind, a warning bell went off, but it was muffled and I ignored it.

"How did that screw up your deal?"

Margaret shifted gears. "What do you think of my software? Be honest."

I was drunk enough to be honest. "I think your software is un-original and derivative. It looks exactly like the stuff I was working on at MantaSoft a year ago."

Margaret arched an eyebrow.

I said, "I'm sorry, but that's how I feel."

Margaret smiled. "You are just so cute, I could eat you up."

"What?"

Margaret shifted gears again. "Do you think that MantaSoft's code was worth anything before you fixed it?"

I had no idea where she was going with this. "No. It was a mess."

262

"What do you think it's worth now that you've fixed it?"

"You mean software that can decrypt almost anything? I have no idea. The government doesn't let MantaSoft sell it to most people, or even most countries, so the market is tiny. Maybe ten million?"

"No. I mean what if you could sell it to anyone—internationally. Without government interference."

"Twenty million?"

Margaret sat back and took a deep drink of her wine. She muttered, "This is like talking to a child."

"What?" I said.

"What do you think a country like, oh I don't know, Russia, would pay to be able to decrypt any file? The Russians are incredibly paranoid. It kills them not to be able to read encrypted files."

"MantaSoft can't sell Rosetta to Russia," I said.

Margaret drained her glass and waved the empty at the server, who jumped to get her another. She said, "You are right. A big public company like MantaSoft can't get away with it. But a little company like Bronte Software can. Who pays any attention to us? How much do you think Russia would pay for Rosetta?"

"But it's not legal, even for Bronte."

"How much money do you think it's worth?" asked Margaret, ignoring my point.

"Thirty million?"

"A billion!" Margaret said loudly. She caught herself and continued, "They will pay a billion dollars—that is a billion with a *b*—for Rosetta."

"Oh my God," I said. "You're selling the Rosetta source code to the Russians?"

Margaret spread her hands. *There you go.* This was horrible.

My Scotch had been refilled. I hadn't even seen it happen. I drank it too fast. It burned my throat. "But you can't sell it. It belongs to MantaSoft."

"It belongs to whomever has the source code. The working source code."

I knew I should get up and leave, run, right now. But I couldn't. This was it. This was the conspiracy that Kevin had found.

I said, "I don't get it. What's this got to do with MantaSoft buying your company? How could fixing the code have screwed up that deal?"

Margaret leaned in and said, "Remember when we were discussing financing? VCs want a return on their investment. They like to see five times their investment back in five years."

"You said the VCs wouldn't back you."

"I'm not backed by VCs. When I couldn't get funding from them, I had to turn to other financing. These people wanted to make more than five times their investment."

"How much financing did you get?"

"Ten million dollars." Margaret slurped her port.

"You borrowed ten million dollars from them?" I asked.

"Him. I borrowed the money from a man. A Russian. I was desperate," said Margaret.

Even with Scotch gumming up the gears of my mind, I could still generate a flash of horrific insight.

I said, "You borrowed the money from Dmitri? Oh my God."

Margaret said, "I took the loan a year ago. Originally it was only for a month. I thought I had a deal in the works that would pay him back. But the deal fell through."

"He'll kill you."

"He'll do worse. He'd already started. Then he came up with this plan to get Rosetta's source code. We were to sell the software to Russia and split the money. Five hundred million was fifty times his investment."

I emptied my drink as a big chunk of the puzzle fell into place.

"You were selling your company because the source code was useless."

"Exactly."

"You never wanted the fifty million dollars for your company because you weren't going to see a dime. Dmitri was going to get it all."

Margaret tipped her nearly empty port glass at me. "Very perceptive. I wasn't going to see a dime, but I would be free. Dmitri would get his money. He said that would be enough to avoid continued consequences."

I wondered if Huey's porn site had a CougarCam.

Margaret continued. "But now that you fixed the code, Dmitri has gotten greedy. He won't let me sell the company. He wants his five hundred million."

My Scotch was empty. The server came over to pour more, but I covered the glass and shook my head. "Why are you telling me this?"

"Because now I need you to maintain the code. You're the only one who has managed it."

"You want me to work for you?"

"Yes. Keeping the code ready for shipment. Easy work."

"Is this why you slept with me? To get me to work for you?"

Margaret leaned forward and placed her soft hand over mine. A chill of remembered pleasure slunk up my spine.

"No, Tucker. I met you at the Thinking Cup because I wanted to partner with you once I was free of Dmitri. I slept with you because you have a great body."

"How did you find me?"

"I've been following your Twitter feed for months."

Failure of imagination.

I asked, "Why would I help you sell Rosetta?"

"The money, dear. One hundred million dollars. Just for you."

"I don't need a hundred million dollars."

Margaret leaned forward and hissed, "Everybody needs a hundred million dollars! You could put it in the bank and live off millions a year in interest. Imagine the women you'd attract. Take it from me, money is even a better aphrodisiac than your fantastic ass."

I stood up. "I won't do it."

Margaret said, "Sit down, you fool. Don't be so dramatic."

I sat and repeated, "I won't do it. I'm going to turn you in."

"You're going to turn me in? And what will you say?"

"I'll just tell"—I almost said Dana—"them about this conversation."

"What conversation? You are obviously drunk." Margaret indicated the empty Scotch glass. "I don't remember anything about this conversation. I think the staff of Mooo will vouch for our being very, very drunk."

I stood up again and said, "We're done here."

Margaret sat back in her chair and crossed her legs at the knee. She said, "Just like your foolish wife." She reached into her bag and pulled out her BlackBerry. She started checking her messages.

I said, "What about my wife?"

Margaret ignored me and continued typing. The maître d' walked to our table.

"Is there a problem?" he asked.

Margaret looked up. "No. Mr. Tucker was just leaving. Please show him out."

The maître d' made a little Nazi bow. "But of course, right this way, sir." His light touch on my elbow steered me toward the door. I let him steer, but called over my shoulder, "We're not done, Margaret."

She looked up and said, "Yes we are. Goodbye."

I was standing on Beacon Street in front of Mooo. The humidity had finally broken, and hard rain drove down on me and my expensive suit. Thunder boomed as I crossed the street and started walking down Beacon Hill toward my apartment.

The best way to handle being caught in the rain is to ignore it. You get just as wet, but you don't look like an idiot trying to duck raindrops.

The alcohol swirled my brain. I needed to walk carefully. The sidewalk receded down a long tunnel of forced attention. It tilted, like a boat's deck, and the uneven bricks tugged at my ankles. My hair was plastered against my skull. Lightning flashed and lit the statue of Mary Dyer, a Quaker woman who had been hanged by the good people of Boston for teaching them that they could talk directly to God. What would she have said about talking directly to one's dead wife? Her statue inscription read, "My life not availeth me in comparison to the liberty of the truth."

The liberty of truth wasn't doing me much good. I had the truth. I knew who killed Carol, and I knew why. I just didn't know what to do with the information.

I imagined Carol getting the same treatment when they tried to recruit her: the drinks, the flattery, and the proposition. Or maybe it was simpler. Maybe Dmitri just showed up at our house, stood in our kitchen, and made her an offer that she couldn't, but did, refuse. He must have killed her then.

As I crossed Park Street, I considered taking a left and walking down to the T stop, but the thoughts of going underground and of being publicly drunk in such a small space kept me on Beacon Street. The entrance to the Boston Common passed. I ignored it because I didn't want to fall down the shallow stairs. Kept walking forward, along the wrought-iron fence that bordered the park.

My stomach churned, not from drinking but from realization and self-loathing. I had missed clue after clue. I got Kevin killed, Dana tortured, and I had helped them steal my software. Mr. Coding Genius had been played. My phone rang. I leaned against the iron fence, my back digging into the metal, and looked at the caller ID. It was Jael.

I said, "Hey."

Jael said, "Run!"

A black car roared out of Park Street and squealed toward me, the rear window lowering.

FIFTY-ONE

I RAN, TRIPPING AND skittering on the uneven pavement. The car's engine roared as I heard the same quiet popping sound that had killed Kevin. The air behind me whistled with bullets that clanged off the iron fence. I glanced at the street. The hood of the car blocked me in. I ran on down Beacon Street.

My toe caught on a brick and I lunged forward, falling down the street with long, loping steps. More popping, more whistling bullets. The nose of the car pulled next to me. The tinted driver's window was black and reflected the streetlights. Over the rain, I heard Dmitri's voice: "Goodbye, Mr. Tucker!"

Then came the gunfire, loud, and earsplitting. I winced and ducked as the car's windshield fractured in spiderwebs of glass. More gunfire and the windshield was gone, the exploding safety glass splashing into the car. Thank God for Jael.

I reached the entrance to the Boston Common and turned into the park. The car stopped behind me, and the car door opened. I heard some yelling in Russian and another burst of sound from the machine gun. I ran toward the Frog Pond as bullets plowed geysers out of the shallow water.

I risked a glance over my shoulder through the pelting rain and saw Dmitri slip to one knee on the wet grass and mud. He raised the gun to his shoulder. I turned away and ran as pain ripped across the skin on my upper arm. The force of it knocked me off balance. I sprawled across the grass.

I scrambled to my feet and ran, dodging among the trees. Bullets splintered wood around me. Warm blood slicked my arm as I darted among the uneven roots. I paused as the Common opened into a broad expanse in front of me.

The empty black lawn spread before me, offering me nothing in the way of a hiding place or help. The only break in the grass was a stone shed that led down to the underground parking garage. I ran for the shed, a plan forming in my mind. I looked over my shoulder and saw that Dmitri was getting closer. He had tucked the gun under his arm and was running full tilt, following me over the grass and paths as I cut across the open space.

I reached the entrance and pulled one of the doors open. Inside were a payment machine, an elevator, and a door leading to the staircase. I pulled on the staircase door. It was locked. A sign said something about using a parking ticket for entrance. I had screwed myself. I looked outside the kiosk. Dmitri was standing in the rain, his gun level with his gut. I flinched away from him and opened the other door. He fired, and the kiosk glass shattered. Bullets ricocheted, and something tore at my scalp as I ran back out into the rain. There was another burst of sound, but the kiosk was between me and Dmitri.

I lowered my head and ran down the concrete path, head down, arms pumping. I flew through the Common exit, and across the slick, empty street and into the Public Garden. I kept running straight and fast, no dodging, no hiding. But when I reached the bridge across the Swan Boat pond, drunkenness and exhaustion took me down.

I tripped, my foot hooking across the back of my calf, and sprawled across the rough concrete. By the time I had climbed to my feet, Dmitri was standing on the bridge, his machine gun swinging into position. He smiled and pulled the trigger as I bolted toward the low green fence that framed the bridge.

I heard bullets hit concrete and Russian swearing. I vaulted at the fence, kicked off of it with my foot, and threw myself into a long belly flop into the hard water. Water punched through my nose into my brain. I tried to gasp, filled my lungs with water, coughed, and dove. Bullets splashed around me as I swam along the bottom of the pond. Something cracked at the back of my head as a water slowed slug hit me and bounced off. Then I swam up into darkness.

My shoulder grazed a pontoon. I was under a raft of Swan Boats that had been stored in the middle of the pond overnight. Gunfire burst from the bridge, chipping at the benches on the boats. Then silence and swearing. Dmitri was out of bullets.

Dmitri called out, "You are a dead man, Mr. Tucker!"

FIFTY-TWO

I SQUATTED IN THE filthy water under the Swan Boats, trying to hear Dmitri over the rush of the rain. I peeked from between the pontoons, but the Public Garden was empty.

"Are you OK, baby?" asked Carol.

"My arm hurts," I said. I could feel blood on my triceps and my side. I was struck with an irrational fear of sharks being attracted to blood in the water. It passed. I closed my eyes and listened, holding on to the boat.

"You were very brave," Carol said.

"I was very stupid."

"That too."

"I can quit now," I said. "I know what happened to you."

"No," Carol's voice faded. "You don't."

"Tucker!" It was Nate.

I looked out between the boats. Nate Russo was standing on the shore with three uniformed cops and Bobby Miller. Rain splashed off Nate's umbrella. He called again, "Tucker? Are you in there?"

I swam out from under the boats and waded ashore. When I reached the grass, I fell to my knees and puked. My expensive dinner splashed across the grass. I was about to pitch into the puddle when Bobby's strong hands caught me by the shoulders and pulled me upright. He walked me over to a police car that was flashing next to the pond and put me in the back seat.

"Where's Jael?" I croaked.

Miller said, "She called me and told me where to find you. I called Nate."

"She saved me," I said. The scene dimmed, and I heard a distant order: "Get him to Mass General!"

FIFTY-THREE

From the taste in my mouth, I expected to find myself in the gutter. My lips were stuck together, and my tongue felt as if I had dragged it through a pigpen. I opened my eyes and saw a blurry head. The head moved and I heard a voice.

I sat up, feeling like crap. I said, "Errrgh."

Bobby's bald head reflected the hospital lights. He said, "You lost a lot of blood. But the doc said that was a good thing. All the bleeding kept the duck shit out of your system."

I wasn't wearing a shirt, and my left arm was bandaged. It burned where the bullet had grazed me.

"Where's my suit?"

"You mean the one with the bullet holes? They cut it off you. It looked expensive."

Bobby surveyed me in the bed. In addition to the bandage around my biceps, I had another bandage on my ear where the bullet had nicked me, and real stitches in my side. I reached up and felt the stitches in my forehead. They were unchanged. My hands were scraped and I had skinned my knee.

Bobby said, "Jesus, you're a fucking mess. What the hell happened?"

"Your plan worked. They tried to kill me, just like you said, and Jael saved me just like you said. You can arrest them now."

"Who?"

"Roland, Margaret, and Dmitri—that Russian guy with the machine gun."

"What are you talking about? Start at the beginning."

So I did. I told them Roland had turned Margaret's company into a sales channel for my code. How Margaret had recruited me to help her, and how the Russian guy not only made porn with Alice, but also loaned Margaret the money to save her business, and was planning to sell Rosetta to the Russians.

"It's convergence," I said.

Bobby said, "What?"

"Convergence. When different businesses get fused together." I ticked businesses off on my fingers. "Dmitri has fused drug dealing, pornography, loan sharking, and prostitution into one big business. Then he put a legitimate front on it with programming services. The engineers who make his website probably also work in his consulting business."

"So how do they get the code out of MantaSoft?" asked Bobby.

"Hell, the whole project fits on a single thumb drive. That's all it takes to get the code out. The hard part was writing it so that other engineers could work on it. Usually, we have the designer around and we can ask questions. Otherwise the code needs to be very clear."

"And you say it was all messed up?"

"Yeah, but Dana got me to fix it."

"That's why Margaret offered you a job?"

I said, "Yeah."

Bobby crossed his arms. He breathed in through his nose, then blew it out through pursed lips. He seemed to be getting himself under control. He said, "But you fucked up."

"How did I fuck up?"

"You should have taken the job."

"I wasn't going to help them. I told Margaret to go to hell."

"Yeah, noble of you," said Bobby. He pointed at my bandaged arm. "How did that work out? If you'd taken the job, they wouldn't have tried to kill you. You could have gotten us some evidence. Now all we've got is he-said/she-said. I can't arrest anybody based on that."

Bobby stalked to the hospital window and looked out into the night. I sulked. He was right. If I'd just told Margaret that I'd take the job, Dmitri wouldn't have tried to kill me. I'd have been able to package up the code to send to Bronte and then tipped off the FBI. He could have arrested them all even if the show had ended. I would have been in the inner circle.

There comes a time in the debug process where you give up on solving the puzzle intellectually. You've tried examining the problem; you've tried gathering data; you've tried theory after theory and had none of them work. When that time comes, you get desperate and start randomly making changes based on the barest of hunches. *I wonder what this will do?* I had reached that point. It was time to do something rash.

I told Bobby, "Get me out of here. Drive me back to my apartment."

"What are you going to do?"

I told him. He wasn't happy.

FIFTY-FOUR

IT WAS TWO IN the morning when I got home. Jael was waiting for me in my apartment. She sat on one of the tall chairs in front of the galley kitchen drinking Lagavulin. Apparently, she had developed a taste for it.

I had been expecting a hug when I saw her again. I would have settled for a handshake. I was disappointed on both counts. Jael looked at me as I walked into the door. She said, "I have checked the apartment. It is safe. No one has attempted to enter."

I said, "Did you pick the lock again?"

Jael said nothing.

"Dumb question," I said, eyeing Jael's handbag. "Thank you for saving me."

"You had put yourself into a dangerous position."

"I know." As I talked, I dismantled my pond-soaked BlackBerry. I took out the battery and checked the moisture indicator. It had turned black. The swim in the Public Garden Lagoon had voided its warranty.

"You were drunk."

"I was."

"Do you have a drinking problem?" she asked.

Drinking problem? I had always thought of it more as a drinking solution. Alcohol took the sharp edge out of life. It helped me focus on the present, and in a world where I'd lost Carol in the past and was facing a future without her, the present looked pretty good.

I said, "No, I don't have a drinking problem. I'm just stupid."

"That is too bad. They do not have meetings for stupidity."

Jael had just made a joke. I smiled and said, "Hello, my name is Tucker and I'm an idiot."

Jael said, "Yes."

"You're not supposed to say 'Yes.' You're supposed to say 'Hello, Tucker.'"

Jael sipped her drink and said, "They have made their first attempt. They will not give up now. I will take you to a hotel tonight."

"Let me take a shower first. My hair feels like it's full of duck shit."

I stood in the shower, being careful not to soak my arm. The bullet had just grazed me, but the cut still hurt like hell. I dried off, and wrapping the towel around my waist, went into the bedroom to get dressed. I put on a collared blue shirt and black chinos. Then I called the Hilton, got a room for the night, put my toothbrush in my pocket, and was ready to go.

We walked downstairs to where Bobby was watching Jael's car. As we got in, he nodded and drove away.

The Back Bay Hilton shares the parking garage with Bukowski Tavern. It was next to the convention center, MantaSoft, Margaret, Roland, and Dmitri. It was a risk to stay so close, but I wanted to be able to get to the Boylston Suites early in the morning. As Jael drove me to the hotel, I told her my plan. She hated it as much as Bobby did.

I didn't care. I needed closure, and I didn't want Margaret to get away with stealing my code. I didn't want the people who killed Carol to live happily ever after. I wanted Roland's ass to be traded for cigarettes in a federal prison, and I wanted Margaret's next dinner to be in a cell with an open toilet.

"I'll do it on my own," I said. "You don't need to be involved."

"I cannot leave you now. Still, this plan is too dangerous."

"I don't care."

"That is what makes it especially dangerous. I can see it in your eyes. Something changed in you tonight."

I had nothing to say.

Jael continued. "A man tried to kill you. It distorts one's attitude."

I looked at Jael, and it was clear that she spoke from experience.

"Yes. It did change my attitude. Now I'm angry."

"Anger will get you killed."

THURSDAY

FIFTY-FIVE

THE HOTEL NAME TAG on Jael's blouse read *Raphael*. I didn't ask her where she had gotten it. If Margaret read it closely, there would be a problem. That was unlikely, so we were ready to go.

This was the only part that I couldn't do alone. I needed to know Margaret's room number, and the hotel wouldn't give that information out at the front desk. We had to improvise. We waited, tucked into a corner of the lobby where we could watch the glass elevators.

"There is still time to leave," said Jael.

"No," I said, watching the elevator fill with businesspeople coming down to the lobby for breakfast.

"I cannot protect you if I am watching the Bronte woman."

"If you are watching Margaret, I won't need protection." I pointed at a glass elevator. Margaret was standing in it, surveying the lobby as she descended. I hid behind a plant and said, "It's showtime."

Margaret exited the elevator and headed over to the restaurant. I moved to the stairwell I'd be using to climb to Margaret's floor. I couldn't use the glass elevators, because the Boylston Suites lobby was a huge atrium. The rooms were tucked into the atrium's walls, and the hallways were really long balconies that ran around the building. If I tried to take the glass elevator, Margaret would see me.

I sat in the stairwell and waited for Jael. My phone was drying at my apartment, so Jael wouldn't be able to text me the information I needed. I sat on the third step from the bottom. I closed my eyes and relaxed on the step.

"You don't need to do this, baby."

I opened my eyes. Carol was sitting next to me. "Yes, I do," I said.

"For what?"

"I know they killed you. I can't let them get away with it."

Carol got up and stood in front of me. Her black hair framed her pretty face. It brushed against her funeral dress. She said, "So this is all for revenge? You're going to get yourself killed to avenge me?"

"I'm not going to get killed," I said.

The stairwell door opened. Carol was gone, and Jael was standing in her spot. She handed me Margaret's breakfast check and went back into the lobby to track Margaret. The room's number was written on the check: 1411. I needed to get climbing. It was on the top floor.

Lightning flashed in the hotel's skylight above me as I left the stairwell, puffing only slightly, thankful for the running I had done along the Charles. I stationed myself away from the edge of the balcony. Just as I had expected, the housekeepers were at work. I watched one as she worked her way down the hallway toward Margaret's room.

The maid was just finishing up with 1412. I started walking as she moved to 1411. She opened the door and placed her cart in front of it. When she was out of sight, I jogged the last few feet and slipped between her cart and the doorjamb, surprising her.

"*Ay, Dios mío!*" she said, putting her hand to her throat.

"Oh hell, I'm sorry. I didn't mean to scare you," I said. "Would you come back later? I need to get some work done."

The woman looked hesitant. I made an ushering movement with my hands.

I said, "Please."

She recovered herself and moved to the door. "Yes sir. Sorry, sir."

"No problem."

She hustled out of the room, and I closed the door.

Like Dana's room, this was a two-room suite with a front living room and a bedroom in the back. Margaret apparently considered closets to be optional, and had flung her dress onto the couch. The room was bare. I looked through the bedroom door and saw a laptop sitting on the desk. I'd get to it in a minute.

I looked around. Now that I was in her room, I didn't know how to search it. Did I start with the computer, or did I paw through Margaret's underwear drawer as I did Dana's? Where would the evidence be, and what would it look like?

"I don't like it here, baby," said Carol.

"You don't have to be here," I said.

"Neither do you."

"I'm not letting them get away with it."

"With what? Killing me? I told you to leave that alone. Why can't you listen to me? You never listen to me!"

"I do nothing but listen to you. You're dead and I still have to listen to you."

"You hear me, but you don't listen."

"Oh God, here we go. The 'You never listen to me' fight."

"Fuck you. It's true. I talk and talk, but you're always off doing your own thing."

"I'm trying to make things better for us."

"Better? Better how? I'm dead."

I started walking toward the bedroom. "I mean I was trying to make things better when we were married."

Carol followed, her voice rising. "No you weren't. You were trying to prove yourself. You've always had to show that you're just a little better than everyone else around you. Well, congratulations, you are better. Where did that get you?"

"It got me designing software worth a billion dollars."

"You're not designing software now. You're a bum. Haven't you noticed that you're unemployed?"

"Shut up."

"You let that fucking job take over your life and ruin our marriage. I told you to stop. I told you to quit and run away with me, but no, you couldn't do it. You just had to prove that you were the smartest asshole in the world."

"You could have supported me."

"Supported you? I cleaned up your goddamn code, I worked on your project. You'd think that would've gotten me a little love. A kind word. A dinner out. Maybe a present now and then. Instead, I got nothing. I got less than everyone else on that fucking project."

"Look, you're hysterical."

"Don't you go all hyperlogical on me, you bastard. You always do this. You get me so angry and upset, and you act like you're so fucking cool. You treated me like shit! You ignored me. Hell, you spent more time playing Ping-Pong with Huey than talking to me."

Carol was sobbing. I reached for her.

"Don't you fucking touch me! That's all it ever was to you. Sex. Sex. Sex. If you were horny, then I got your attention. Take off my top, prance around a bit, and suddenly I was more important to you than that fat idiot Huey. A little T&A and you were mine, until you came, passed out, and then went back to work!"

I looked around the room. I needed to search it.

"Look, I don't have time for this. I have to search the room."

"Go! Go then, you fuck. Go! Go to work! Isn't that what you were always good at? Isn't that how I lost you?"

I squeezed my eyes shut. "Just leave me alone!"

I opened my eyes. She was gone. My heart was racing, and my stomach felt like a fist. She had never gotten it, never realized how important my job was. She had never seen how happy I was at work. I loved her, but dammit, I needed to lead a life. My breath was coming in shallow rasps. I took a deep breath and got to work searching Margaret's room.

My fight with Carol had shaken me. I needed to do something familiar, so I broke out my Ophcrack USB drive and flipped open the lid on her laptop. It would be password-protected, but if she were running Windows XP, I'd be in there in a couple of minutes.

Then things became very wrong.

The first thing was that the PC didn't need a password. It came up directly to the desktop. Its background popped into place. Icons ran down the right side of the screen. There were three pictures under the Windows recycling can. No password?

The second thing was the background itself. The computer's desktop featured a pouty young girl in a knit halter top. Her long, red hair cascaded over her shoulders and between her small breasts. She posed with her flat belly, exposing a virgin, unpierced navel. The screen showed some Greek letters and a red, white, and blue rendition of the Windows icon.

This made no sense. Why would Margaret have a girl on her computer? And why the Greek? As I looked more closely, I realized that the icons also had Greek lettering. I double-clicked on one. It was a picture of another girl, tied to a pole, her arms stretched over her head and nipple clamps affixed to her breasts. *Oh, shit!* This wasn't Margaret's room.

I scrambled away from the laptop and opened the closet. Three striped shirts hung alongside three dresses. I glanced into the bathroom and saw shaving implements, aftershave, and deodorant with foreign lettering. But now I knew it wasn't Greek lettering. It was Cyrillic. The guy in this room was Russian.

It was the worst kind of programming mistake, the hidden assumption. You take your assumption as fact and don't question it until it bites you in the ass. I had assumed that Margaret would have her own hotel room. After all, what CEO shared a room? But it was clear now that Dmitri had been extracting his payments from her all along. No wonder she'd been so eager to spend Saturday night with me.

I walked back into the front part of the suite, to the couch near the front door. The dress on the couch told the story. I picked it up. It was the dress Margaret had worn at Mooo. The zipper was torn where Dmitri had fumbled with it last night. Dmitri must have made Margaret help him work off his frustration about my escape.

I had to get out of there. Jael was following Margaret, not watching me, and Margaret wasn't going to come back to this room. If Dmitri came back, I'd be alone with a man who had promised to skin me alive.

I reached for the door handle and remembered the laptop. It contained the evidence I needed. My plan had worked.

I ran back into the bedroom and flipped the laptop shut. I started for the front door, but the computer was almost ripped from my hands. The power cord was still attached to its European adapter. I pulled the power cord from the wall, wrapped it around the laptop, and headed back to the front door.

As I reached the door, I heard the electronic lock cycle. I stepped back as the door opened. Dmitri.

He was wearing a button-down shirt with vertical blue and yellow stripes. Blood spattered the shoulder of the shirt. He blinked in surprise, stepped into the room, then smiled.

Dmitri said, "Your protector is dead."

Something smashed across my jaw, and the room swam into blackness.

FIFTY-SIX

Hangover. THIS WAS THE first thought that wafted through my brain. My head was pounding, my mouth tasted of copper, it was dark. It had to be a hangover. I raised my hand to rub my face, but it was caught on the sheets. I flopped it around to free it, but it was still stuck. The other was stuck as well.

I felt my wrists and realized that the "sheets" were ropes.

I turned my head and felt rough cloth on my cheek. I tried to call out, but my mouth was taped shut. I stopped moving and took inventory.

My hands were tied. My ankles were tied. I had a bag on my head, and my mouth was taped. I was lying on a hard surface that smelled of gasoline and rubber. I felt a slight vibration, and my world bumped.

I was moving. I was in a car trunk, lying on my side, stuck between the front of the trunk ... and a body that had been crammed behind me.

What had Dmitri said just before he hit me? "Your protector is dead?" Jael. Just add her to the list. Carol, Alice, Kevin, and now Jael. I started to breathe quickly and thrash at my ropes in panic. A lump formed in my throat as my rage and sorrow overtook me. I pushed it down. If I cried now, with my mouth taped, I'd suffocate.

I considered suffocation as an option. If I suffocated, it would certainly piss off Dmitri. He had told me his plans. He was going to skin me. It would be a long, slow death. Suffocation would be quick and easy.

I couldn't make myself follow that path. As long as I was alive, I might be able to talk my way out of the worst. Perhaps I'd get him angry enough to fight me. That would give me a chance to run.

I searched the trunk for the sound of Carol's voice. I'd even have welcomed her telling me that she told me so, but she was gone. I was alone and scared. I lay still and listened to the vibration of the tires on the road. My shoulder was wet. I knew what caused the wetness. I had smelled it before.

When I'd found Carol in our house, she was sprawled across the kitchen floor. Dmitri had cut her throat, severing both carotid arteries and her larynx. The room smelled of blood, and that same smell flooded my small world in the trunk of a moving car.

My time in the trunk allowed me to collect my thoughts and focus. The terror I'd felt faded as I accepted my situation and made a plan for the future. In the trunk jostling against Jael's corpse and re-membering Carol's, I decided that one of us, Dmitri or I, would die today. *I'll get him for you, honey. I'll try.*

I tried to flip onto my back, but my hands were tied to ropes that led out of the trunk. They must be swinging outside, looking like an innocent packing mistake. The car bounced again, and its bouncing became constant. It was leaving the main road and driving over ruts and potholes.

The car stopped. The engine died, and I was left listening to the rain pelting on the roof. The trunk popped open. I turned toward the sound.

"Ah, Mr. Tucker," said Dmitri's voice. "You are awake." He grabbed me by my right arm and leg, pulled me out of the trunk, and dropped me. The bag over my head scraped my cheek as I fell to the ground. My shoulder crunched, and I grunted from the impact. I scrabbled around and felt wet pine needles between my fingers.

Dmitri hooked a hand in my armpit and dragged me across the forest floor. The rain in the trees sounded like meat frying. Thunder rumbled. Wherever these woods were, Dmitri and I would be alone on a day like today.

Dmitri dropped me at the base of a tree. My tailbone hit the root, sending tingles down my legs. He worked at my hands and I realized that, while my wrists were still tied, they were not tied to my waist anymore. I blindly flung my fists up, hoping to catch Dmitri on the chin.

He laughed. "You still have some fight left, yes? I will enjoy this." Dmitri grabbed my wrists, tied them to a rope, and started hauling. He must have rigged a pulley overhead, because my arms were yanked straight up.

Dmitri said, "Stand now or I will break your shoulders."

I got my tied ankles under me, and Dmitri pulled the rope until I was stretched along the tree. I heard the ripping of duct tape, and he ran tape around the tree, trapping my knees against the trunk. Another rip, and my elbows were pinned as well.

Dmitri pulled the bag off my head. "Asshole," I grunted into the tape on my mouth.

"What's that? You would like to speak? Yes, I think you would. You like to talk, talk, talk. But you shall wear the tape. We are away from people, but not so far away that your screams would not be heard." Dmitri tested the ropes and the tape that held me against the tree.

"Very good," he said in his Russian accent. "It is good to get back to my roots. I once did only this. Killing idiots. That was a long time ago. Now, I am mostly counting money. Drug money, engineering money, video money, Internet money. I have counted a lot of money, but selling your software, that will make all my other money nothing."

Dmitri reached into his back pocket and pulled out a long, black folding knife. He opened it, revealing a blade with a sharp tapering point, like the tip of a bat's wing. He touched the tip of the blade to my forearm, which was held between the tape on the tree and the ropes on my wrists. The blade parted the cloth of my shirt easily, and I felt a pinch. I tensed as if I were in the dentist's chair.

Lightning flashed and rain ran into my eyes and nose where I snorted it out in a mist. I was breathing hard, and skirting around the edge of panic. Adrenaline ran through my hands in twitchy waves.

"I am surprised you are here, Mr. Tucker. I know many engineers. They are smart, practical men. They would have left after the garrote." He traced the sharp knife along the faint line that still marred my throat. I pulled back.

"I will not cut your throat, Mr. Tucker. This will not be that fast," said Dmitri as he pulled a pair of latex gloves out of his pocket and put them on. "The skinning will take some time. Your body would normally be left as a warning to others, but of course there is no one left to warn. I have already killed the FBI man, your friend, and your wife." He paused. "Your wife was much smarter than you. I squeezed her real tits and told her what she must do. She did all that I asked."

I screamed into the tape and pulled at the ropes. If had been possible for me to break them, I would have done it in that moment. I would have given anything to break free and shove Dmitri's sharp knife into his eye. At that moment I realized that I was helpless and weak, a foolish man who would not be able to fulfill his promise to his dead wife. I slumped against the ropes, and Dmitri laughed at me.

He used the knife to cut away my shirt below my elbow, ripping it away, leaving my chest exposed to the cold rain. The storms that had been rumbling past the woods moved overhead. Lightning and thunder smashed together in crackling waves. Dmitri leaned close, his hand on my chest, the index finger over my nipple. He breathed, "You are ready, yes?" into my face with his cigarette breath.

The Russian leaned the sharp knife at an angle against the inner skin of my elbow. He pushed harder into my chest with his free hand to maintain his balance. I panicked, pulling spasmodically at my arms and legs flailing my head.

Something caught my eye in the woods. I couldn't be sure I had seen it, but I didn't risk a second look. That would ruin it. I did as I had been trained to do. I avoided looking at it. I looked away, peering into the trees as if I saw something among them.

Dmitri caught my stare and followed my eyes, looking deep into the empty woods. "What do you see there, Mr. Tucker? Maybe it is an angel, eh?" He looked through the rain. Then he said, "Such a pity. It is nothing."

Dmitri laughed again and his temple exploded. Shards of blood and bone splashed across my face. The knife nicked my arm and fell away as his body spasmed and pushed itself into my chest. I heard a rattle escape his throat as he fell on me. He slid to the ground as blood spurted onto my chest and down my pants.

I looked back to my right. Walking out of the rain, her hair plastered across her face, was Jael Navas, her gun glinting and smoking.

FIFTY-SEVEN

JAEL RIPPED THE TAPE from my mouth. I gasped and sagged against the ropes.

"He said you were dead," I babbled.

Jael picked something off my cheek. It was a bit of bone that had hit my face when she had shot Dmitri. She looked at it, grimaced, and flicked it onto the forest floor.

"He was wrong," she said. She picked up Dmitri's knife and cut the rope from my ankles and the tape from my legs. I was still on tiptoe. She cut the tape from my arms and finally she freed my wrists. I staggered away from the tree.

"He told me that my protector was dead," I said.

"He could not have known that I was your protector. I had not allowed it. He was an amateur and a sadist. Perhaps he was trying to frighten you."

"Then who's in the car's trunk?"

Jael looked down at Dmitri's body and nudged it with her toe. Then she went through his pockets. He had no wallet. No ID. Only car keys and the card that unlocked his hotel room. A thumb drive was attached to the keys, probably full of my software. Jael opened the key chain and removed the thumb drive. She handed it to me and said, "This is your expertise." I put the thumb drive in my pocket.

She turned and walked back down the path through the woods. I stumbled behind her in the hissing rain, walking over marks that showed where Dmitri had dragged me. I said, "How did you find me?"

"Margaret Bronte ate breakfast and left the hotel. Since she was not going to her room, I decided to watch over you. But I was too late. I saw the gangster come out of the room with Roland and a laundry hamper. It was clear there was something heavy in the hamper, and you had not come back to me. They took the service elevator. I followed them down to the back of the hotel and saw them put you into the trunk."

"Why didn't you stop them?" I asked.

Jael walked on through the wet pine needles past an old fire. The air smelled of charcoal. She said, "It was unclear that I could do it safely before you were in the trunk, and after I had no way to stop his car. So I followed. He never suspected."

"Because he thought my protector was dead."

"Exactly."

We had reached the car. It was the same black car that had chased me on Beacon Street and killed Kevin on the bridge. It sported a new windshield, the tags still stuck to the glass. The car looked squat and evil, as if it had been corrupted. We stood by the hood as Jael worked the key fob. The trunk unlocked at the other end with a clunking sound, but the trunk lid did not swing up. It rested against the car as if unwilling to give up its secret.

"You are sure there was someone in the trunk with you?" asked Jael.

"Yeah."

"Dead?"

I looked at my shoulder and down at my body. I was covered in blood. Half of it was Dmitri's. But I also had blood on my shoulder, older blood that had started to form a crust at its edges.

I pointed at my shoulder and said, "I think this came from the bottom of the trunk."

"Let us look."

I hesitated. Jael walked around the back of the car and threw open the lid. She didn't react. Her gray eyes scanned back and forth as I stood by the car's hood and examined my shoes.

"I recognize this person," she said, "but I do not know the name."

I closed my eyes and sighed. I focused on the first step that would bring me to the back of the car. The first step was the only one I'd need to get moving again. Images of Carol, lying in our Wellesley kitchen, flashed into my mind as I took that step. Moving, I walked quickly and looked into the trunk.

My mind snapped shut as I caught the emotions that filled me and stuffed them into a dark place. I breathed deeply and pulled my shit together.

Six months ago, Carol's neck had been cut from ear to ear, leaving a gaping second mouth. This killing had been done the same way. It was bloody and brutal, efficient and cruel.

I said, "His name was Nate Russo."

FIFTY-EIGHT

"How?" I ASKED. I was sitting in the wet pine needles, my shirt cut, my arm bleeding, my knife wound throbbing. "How could he have thought that Nate was my protector?"

Jael stood behind the car, looking at the body. Her arms were crossed, and the rain bounced off her black cotton T-shirt as if she were made of stone. Her gun was gone, hidden away in her black leather handbag. She said, "Nate came to you in the park."

"What?"

"He came to you in the park last night and the gangster was watching. The gangster assumed that the person who shot the windshield would come to check on your health, so he watched to learn who shot at his car. I knew the gangster would be watching, so I remained hidden. I called Detective Miller instead."

"And Bobby called Nate?"

"Yes. It was a mistake."

"A mistake. Nate is dead because Bobby Miller made a mistake?"

"No," Jael said. "Nate is dead because the gangster killed him."

I got up, stood next to Jael, and looked at Nate. He had been haphazardly thrown in the trunk. One arm was twisted behind him and the other had been flopped out of the way. Rage built in my gut, but it had no place to go. It banged against my throat, churned my stomach, and finally settled for squeezing my heart against my ribs. I had nothing to do. Jael had already exacted the ultimate revenge for this atrocity.

I sighed. "What now?"

"Go home," said Jael. "You are safe now. The others pose no threat. They think you are dead. If you go home, you will have your normal life tomorrow."

That couldn't be it. This couldn't just be over.

"What about that bastard Roland?" I asked. "What about Margaret? Shouldn't I do something about them?"

Jael looked at me, her impassive eyes softening around the edges. She said, "You have done enough. The FBI knows about the scheme. They have an undercover agent. They will collect the evidence they need, and then they will arrest Margaret and Roland. It is inevitable."

Jael produced a set of car keys and said, "Please, take my car. Go home and wash. Let others finish the job. This has been a very bad day for you. You have earned a rest. I will wait here and answer questions from the police."

I said, "Thank you." The keys were warm in my hand as I walked back to Jael's black Acura MDX. I took off my bloody shirt and threw it on the ground. I started the car. The GPS sprang to life. It told me that I was in North Andover. Dmitri hadn't gone that far after all.

I drove Jael's car down Route 93 to Boston and parked the car in the Prudential Center. I walked home shirtless. The rain continued to fall, but the wind was gone and the water was warm and cleansing.

Follen Street's brick sidewalks shimmered in the rain as the sun began to break through the clouds. I entered my building, climbed the steps back to my apartment, and opened the door. I stepped inside and stood in the doorway. It seemed wrong that the apartment should be unchanged from the time that Jael was sitting at my kitchenette drinking Scotch. I had nearly died, and I had lost a father—again. I somehow expected that the apartment would reflect the changes inside me.

Though the rooms were unchanged, memories wandered them like ghosts. I looked to my right and remembered Jael and Dana struggling on the floor. I looked to my left and thought about Kevin's visit and how Margaret had flashed from bedroom to bathroom. The broken Mr. Coffee carafe was still in the trash, and my BlackBerry lay on the counter.

I emptied my pockets onto the counter and put the battery back into the BlackBerry. The windows in my apartment glistened with emerging sunlight. I opened them all, inviting the world back into my fortress. The rain's slowing patter provided background noise in my silent home. New air moved through the house. I returned to the kitchenette.

Dmitri's thumb drive sat next to the BlackBerry and Jael's keys. The BlackBerry continued to boot, its little hourglass telling me that it was working hard at coming to life.

I stripped, made a wad of my pants, and put them into a plastic bag. Perhaps the police would want them; otherwise, I'd throw them away. I enjoyed the illicit pleasure of walking around my house naked and alone.

The BlackBerry's red light blinked. Email. I reached for the Black-Berry and stopped myself. I knew how this would go. I would read the email, feel obliged to reply, spend time crafting a response, and be right back in the maelstrom of my life. I needed five minutes of bliss before I started that again. I needed a shower.

I glanced at the email's subject. It was from Dana and said "WTF?" Five minutes wouldn't make a difference.

I started my shower. I ran my hand under the water and fiddled with the knobs until the water was hot enough to deliver a cleansing pain on the edge of burning. I wanted to scrub myself clean. I took a step into the shower and pulled my foot out.

The subject was WTF? What could that mean? That didn't seem like a relationship email. This early in a relationship, that subject would have been something like How's it going? or Miss you. WTF was something that Carol would have written. Dana's email called to me, and I wouldn't be able to enjoy the shower until I read it. I walked into the hallway with one wet foot and picked up the BlackBerry. Clicked on WTF?

Tucker,
Jack found me in the booth today. He's coming to my room after the show to discuss the changes you made to the code.
WTF? How did he know that you made those changes? I thought it was our little secret.
Get back to me before 2. I need to have my story straight.
Dana

"Dammit," I swore in the empty room. I had no idea how Jack knew about those changes. I didn't tell him. Maybe I'd told Nate. Images of Nate flooded my mind, but I crammed them back into their hole and called Dana's cell. No answer. I left a message and climbed back into the shower. The hot water reached into my pores and pulled out the blood, sweat, and fear-stink. They circled the drain and disappeared.

I got out of the shower and toweled dry. I saw a small blood stain from the nick on my arm. I found a Band-Aid in the medicine cabinet and covered the cut. I went back into my bedroom and got dressed in shorts, a Boston Beerworks T-shirt, and sneakers. I looked at the time. It was two o'clock. Dana would be meeting with Jack now. I was sure she'd come up with something to say.

Dmitri's thumb drive was on the counter. I picked it up, went into my office, and stuck the drive into my computer to look at my source code, all neatly packed courtesy of my ego. I opened the thumb drive, expecting to find compressed archive file full of text. Instead, I found a movie.

The file was called `pimpcam.wmv`. I double-clicked on it, and the movie opened. It was at an odd angle, as if it had been taken from somewhere on the wall. The movie showed a cute girl with large breasts, brown nipples, and muscular legs. She looked familiar.

The girl looked like she might have been an athlete, but she wasn't doing anything athletic at the moment because she was struggling in duct tape. The tape held her ankles and knees. Her arms were behind her back, and when she rolled over in her struggles, I could see her wrists and elbows were taped. Just like Alice and just like someone else I had seen. Some other girl who had been killed with duct tape. I'd seen pictures of women killed with duct tape, but only looked closely at two. They were Alice Barton and … Courtney Acres! The girl in the movie was from the pictures Kevin had showed me in the FBI conference room.

Courtney struggled in the tape. She rolled back and forth, and she tugged at her arms. Then she seemed to get tired and lay still.

A male voice spoke. "Done struggling?"

I saw him walk into the frame: the Duct Tape Killer. He tucked himself in behind Courtney, spooning her. He tickled her, nuzzling her neck as she screeched and twitched. Then he stripped another length of tape off the roll. I saw the whites of Courtney's eyes as she tried to see what he was doing. He wrapped the tape around her face, and Courtney kicked and twitched. Tears ran from her eyes as she stopped moving. The killer raped her as she died.

Nothing beats the giddy, mind-altering experience of cracking a tough bug. You feel revelation pulse through your brain as every scrap of evidence you had gathered snaps into place. Every question has an answer. Every fact makes sense. Everything works together in a beautiful model that ticks along in your brain, explaining the bug and how to fix it. That revelation flowed through me as I watched the man in the video climb off the bed, put on his clothes, squeeze Courtney's dead breast, and leave the room. It all made perfect sense.

My hands were shaking as I put the thumb drive in my pocket. The guy in the video was a bastard, a sadist, and a monster. He was an animal who used physical power over women to get his rocks off. He was also a business executive, family man, and community leader who helped out at the battered woman's shelter. He was MantaSoft's CEO Jack Kennings, and he was alone with Dana Parker on a Thursday afternoon.

FIFTY-NINE

I GRABBED MY PHONE and ran down the stairs. *Dana might be dead already.* Hitting the bricks in front of my house, I ran up Follen Street. Ahead of me, a pair of young women pushed baby carriages down the bumpy brick sidewalk. I dodged left and right trying to get around them, gave up, and ran into the street.

A car buzzed past me. I tried to pace myself, but adrenaline kept pushing me from a fast trot to a sprint. After sprinting a bit, I'd go back to a trot, knowing I'd be no good to Dana after sprinting a half-mile.

When I had to stop for traffic at Huntington Avenue, I finally began using my head. I dialed Bobby Miller. If Bobby was already at the hotel, he could save Dana.

Bobby answered on the first ring. "Miller."

"Bobby, listen. Jack Kennings is the Duct Tape Killer. He's with Dana in her hotel room."

"Miller."

"Bobby!"

"Tucker, I can read a caller ID. I know it's you, so stop fucking around."

"Kennings is killing Dana!" I shouted.

The line went dead just as the light changed. I ran across the street pressing redial.

"Miller," answered Bobby.

"Bobby, it's Tucker."

"This is Detective Miller. Who is this?"

"Shit!" I swore as I killed the call. My phone hadn't survived its dunk in the Swan Boat pond. The microphone was dead. I ran on. The uneven bricks of the South End gave way to the smooth concrete of the Prudential shopping mall. I ran up the sidewalk in front of the mall, dodging meandering idiots.

The concrete guardians of P. F. Chang's sprang up on my right as I slowed to a trot. My legs hadn't recovered from last night's chase. They burned. I sucked air and pushed myself up the street. I was tired—tired of being late, tired of being sore, tired of losing people to Jack Kennings.

I ran on. A group of little kids clogged the sidewalk. I shifted to running in the street. I ran up Dalton, past Bukowski Tavern. The convention center loomed up on my right side. I was almost to the hotel.

Then I had a revelation. I didn't need my microphone to get help. I could still text. Standing with my back to a gray loading door of the convention center, I typed a message to Bobby Miller with trembling fingers.

"Kennings is the DTK. He's got Dana. Rm 804"

"Tucker!" I jumped at the sound. Roland Baker blocked my way, trapping me against the loading door. Behind him, a car idled, the passenger door still open. Roland said, "Bloody hell, what are you doing here?"

I put the phone away and went to push past Roland. "Out of my way."

He pushed me back.

I said, "I don't have time for this. Jack is going to kill Dana."

Roland smiled. "Of course he is."

Roland knew? The pieces kept falling into place.

"Get out of my way, you asshole," I said as I pushed away from the wall.

Roland stepped back and produced the same gun he'd had in the office. He said, "Get in the car. Dmitri was supposed to take care of you, but now I'll have to do it. Jack will finish off your girlfriend. You just keep losing women to me, don't you?" Roland's finger tightened on the trigger.

Three days ago I had trembled at the sight of Roland's gun. Two days ago, I had thrown my hands in the air and surrendered when I saw Dana's gun. Now I was done being afraid of guns. I knew what to do.

I stepped forward. My forward motion surprised Roland and gave me a chance to grab his wrist. I pivoted so that I stood next to Roland with the gun pointing at empty space. Roland gripped the pistol harder and tried to pull his wrist free. I drove Roland forward and slipped my foot in front of his ankle. We fell. When we hit the ground, the gun fired. Blood sprayed across the yellow stones of the convention center wall. It wasn't mine.

I heard a scream. "Roland!"

It was Margaret. She had been driving the car. She ran around the car, knelt beside Roland, and screamed again. I bolted toward the Boylston Suites Hotel. Images of Dana in police photos flashed through my head.

I reached Boylston Street and heard a commanding male voice behind me. "You! Stop! Police!"

I looked over my shoulder. A cop stood next to Margaret. She was pointing at me. I ran on. No time for this. Cars honked and twisted in the traffic lanes as I ran straight across the street.

I burst into the Boylston Suites lobby. People looked up from their drinks and newspapers. I ran over the bridges and around the ponds to get to the elevators. I pressed the *UP* button and waited, hiding behind a big plant, staring at the shiny elevator door.

The elevator was on the fourth floor. Captain and Tennille Muzak played throughout the lobby. It enraged me. The elevator was on the third floor, then the second. It stopped. I looked into the mirrored elevator door. The stitches in my forehead were wavy in the uneven surface. The cut on my ear was crusted with blood and a sheen of sweat shone off my face.

I said, "C'mon. C'mon," and was catapulted sideways as the cop tackled me. He put a knee in my back and grabbed my wrist.

I screamed, "Let go of me. She'll die!"

He said, "You're under arrest."

I struggled and he put pressure on my arm, wrenching the shoulder. I roared my frustration. I wasn't going to save her. The cop said, "Just calm down," and I heard him pulling out his handcuffs. Once he put them on, Dana was dead, and my last fuck-up would be over. I battered my head on the ground and wrenched my arm trying to get loose. But the cop's grip was unbreakable.

Huey walked out of the elevator reading his BlackBerry and wearing a triangle hat. I shouted, "Huey, help!" and he didn't hesitate. He shouted, "Get off!" and four hundred pounds of angry nerd pounded down on the cop.

The cop didn't have time to react to the new threat. He let go of my arm and was squashed across the elevator-lobby floor as Huey bowled him over and pinned him beneath a mountain of manflesh.

I said, "Thanks, buddy!" and ran into the open elevator. As the door closed, I shouted, "Tell him I'm in room 804!" I jammed the *Close Door* button five or six times. Nothing happened. I pressed the *8* button again and the doors began to close. They slid shut and the elevator began to climb. It stopped on the second floor, and a guy in workout clothes tried to get on. I didn't need any more delays. I looked him square in the eye, stepped in front of the door, and said, "Elevator's full." He started to step forward, stopped, looked me up and down, and let the doors close.

My breath was slowing, but adrenaline snaked through my body, making it twitch. The numbers lit in sequence over the door. Each number seemed to take twice as long as the one before it. The numbers flickered to life as their bulbs engaged at each level. The elevator's whirring dropped in pitch as the elevator slowed on the eighth floor. It jostled up and down, lining itself up perfectly with the outside door. The elevator door creaked open, slowly creating enough room for me to slide through and out.

Dana's room was around the atrium from the elevators. I sprinted down the hallway and came to a stop in front of 804.

I pulled out my wallet. Dana's room key was still nestled next to my credit card and my driver's license. I slid the room key into the slot on the front of the door.

The door blinked back red. I was locked out.

SIXTY

"FUCK."

How could I be locked out? Maybe she switched rooms. Maybe she had checked out. I looked at her email again on my BlackBerry. It said, "He's coming to my room." What room?

The lock stopped blinking. I hammered the card-key in and out. Another red light. I peeked into the window next to the door, squinting to see through the gauzy curtain. Something was wrong. The light was on, the bedroom door was closed. Clothes were strewn on the furniture.

It was time for deep breaths. The key had to work. I must just be rushing it. I inserted the card again, this time slowly. My hand shook. I breathed deeply, then pulled the card out in a smooth motion. The light blinked green and I heard the lock cycle.

Dana's immaculate hotel room was a mess. Her "Math Is Hard" T-shirt was thrown across the television, where it was tented over the remote. Her hot-pink bra was hanging from a lamp. One chair was thrown backwards. A man's suit jacket was folded neatly on the couch.

I ran to the bedroom and opened the door. I didn't knock or shout. If I was wrong and they were screwing, it would be embarrassing, but nobody dies of embarrassment. If I was right, Dana needed me. I stepped through the door, and walked into Hell.

The smell hit me first. The room stank of sweat and sex. I saw Dana's ankles on the bed. They were tied with duct tape and kicking feebly. Jack was naked, lying on his right side, pulling her close to him as his hips thrust. He grunted with each thrust.

I stepped between the wall and the bed and grabbed Jack, wrapping my arm around his throat to get a handle on the naked man. Surprised, he flailed out. The momentum pulled him off the bed and away from Dana. He fell into the space between the bed and the wall.

Dana's arms and legs were tied with duct tape. Her nose and mouth were blocked, just like Alice and all those others. She was convulsing. I climbed over Jack and onto the bed to get the tape off her face. I tried to slide the tape off, but it was stuck. He had wrapped it several times and I couldn't find the end. As I searched, my head snapped sideways from a blow and I fell from the bed.

I was trapped on my back between the bed and the wall. Jack stomped on my chest and my ribs cracked. I yelped. He came at me with the phone, smashing it down with an overhead motion, like he was killing a rat.

With the naked Jack standing over me, my next move was clear. I drove my heel up and crushed Jack's balls.

He staggered away toward the back of the room. When the pain hit him, he dropped to his knees and vomited on the carpet.

I went back to Dana, searching for the end of the tape. She had stopped moving. I found the tip of the duct tape and unwrapped. The tape was endless. He must have used five feet of the stuff. I pulled the last bit of tape off and looked for Dana to take a deep shuddering breath. She didn't. Her mouth lay open and slack. I tapped her face, and caught motion out the corner of my eye. Jack was on his feet. I stood, blocking his exit.

I said, "She's gone."

Jack said, "Step aside and I'll let you live." He stared at me with flat, dead eyes.

I said, "Don't you get it? You killed her!"

"Accidents happen. Get out of my way."

The dark things I kept locked in my mind had slept after Carol's funeral. They had stirred when Kevin died, and started howling when I saw Alice fucked on a table. They began to pound their prison door when Dmitri tied me to a tree, and they had cracked the door when I saw Nate in the trunk. Now they blew the door off the hinges. The dark avatars of rage escaped their cell. Their malevolence overtook me. The demons were loose, and I didn't give a shit.

Jack ran at me. He was big and strong, but the things in me would not be denied. I stepped forward, dropped my shoulder, and drove it into his gut. He stumbled backwards, slipped on his puke, caught himself, and threw a punch at me. It hit me square on the mouth. Pain flared through my lips as they were driven into my teeth.

I spit blood on the floor, looked at Jack, and grinned a bloody grin. I punched him in the stomach and, as he doubled over, I kneed him in the face. Jack fell backwards into the puke puddle on the floor. I dropped onto Jack, driving my knee into his gut. He gasped as the breath was driven from his body. I hissed, "People trusted you. We all trusted you."

310

I straddled him and started punching. I said, "Nate trusted you most of all." The image of Nate, discarded in the trunk, drove me to greater fury.

All the dead floated into my vision: Alice, Kevin, Nate, Dana, and most of all Carol. I punched Jack in the face. His face held the hint of a smile. I punched him again. I remembered Carol. I saw her laughing on the Cape, cuddling with me in our little tent as it rained outside. I remembered our first date, and our honeymoon. I remembered making love to her and then I remembered the blood that covered the kitchen floor.

I punched and punched, but I felt weak, impotent. My punches were nothing. They didn't smash Jack's bones. My hand hurt from hitting his head. Jack was impassive. His calm unnerved me.

Jack lay beneath me and said, "Get off me. Because I'm leaving now. I'm going to bury you."

"What are you talking about?"

"Your word against mine, right?"

"What?"

"First your wife, then Alice, then all the others, and now Dana. Tucker, you're a monster."

I needed a tool. I looked to my right, but saw nothing that would help. I looked to my left. Dana's laptop was on her briefcase, next to me. I grabbed it and held it by the edge, like a hammer.

"What do you even care about me?" asked Jack. "I didn't kill Carol. She killed herself."

The final tumbler clicked into place. It was time to end Jack.

I heard myself say, "You're gonna die." The demons within me laughed and danced.

I cracked Jack's head with the laptop. It caught his temple. He bucked beneath me as his scalp split and he started to bleed. My vision narrowed. I pounded away. I saw Jack's face mixed with my ghosts. Carol, rolling over in bed and ignoring me. Nate, looking sorrowful as he fired me and then surprised, with his throat slit from ear to ear. Roland, taking my job and selling my project. Dmitri, slicing my arm. And then Carol again, her hand clutching her slit throat.

I smashed Jack's other temple. Tears flew off my face and mixed with the blood running down Jack's cheeks. His eyes closed, and I started smashing his face with the laptop flat on the bridge of his nose. I sobbed and gasped. I couldn't catch my breath.

My arms burned as I brought the laptop down. Jack coughed and spurted blood in an aerosol across my shirt. I remembered Carol hearing that I had another late meeting. She said, "No, Tucker. No, not again." I remembered leaving. I could hear her standing in the door as I focused on Jack and cracked the laptop across his mouth. Teeth flew onto the carpet.

Carol said, "Tucker! Tucker! No, Tucker!"

I aimed the corner of the laptop for the center of Jack's head. Time for the kill shot.

Carol said, "No!"

I said, "I'm sorry."

It wasn't Carol talking. "Stop! You're killing him!" Dana screamed from the bed.

I looked up and my vision cleared. Jack lay below me. He was unconscious. His teeth lay on the rug. The orbit of one eye was smashed. His face hung crookedly. Flecks of blood blew out of his lips as he breathed heavily. Dana was struggling on the bed.

"Tucker. Tucker, please don't kill him. Help me."

I climbed onto the bed next to Dana and unwrapped the tape from her arms. She grabbed me and pulled me close, her sobs shaking us both. I held her and said, "Shhh."

Bobby Miller walked into the room. "Jesus, what happened here?"

SIXTY-ONE

BOBBY AND I STOOD in the front room of Dana's hotel suite. My shirt was ripped. My head was bleeding from where Jack had hit me with the phone. My knuckles were sore and made a new popping sound when I closed my fist. It hurt to breathe, and I was covered in blood. Again.

Dana was gone. A Boston cop had taken her to Mass General. Meanwhile, the paramedics had reassembled Jack and strapped him into a gurney. They were rolling him past us when Bobby stopped them.

"Just one thing, guys," he said. He snapped a handcuff over Jack's wrist and attached the other end to the gurney.

I looked into Jack's shattered face, cradled in a neck brace. He was unconscious, and a clot of blood flicked back and forth under his broken nose. I thought about what it would be like for him to wake up, his face destroyed and a handcuff on his wrist. I considered the shame he would feel when he learned that his secret was out. I remembered that Kevin's wake was tonight, and spit in Jack's face.

"Hey! Hey! Cut that shit out," said one of the paramedics. He wiped at the spittle with a latex-gloved hand.

Bobby touched my shoulder. He said, "C'mon, let's get you to the doctor." As he turned me away from Jack, he whispered into my ear, "Good shot."

We walked onto Boylston Street. SecureCon conventioneers were everywhere. Some of them climbed into cabs to fly home, while others were heading out for dinner and drinks and would fly home tomorrow. They were all exhausted after the tough week. Now it was clear why Jack picked this time to kill. It was his way of blowing off convention stress.

Bobby's car was parked on Hereford Street. We climbed in, and he drove toward the Charles River. We turned right on Back Street, an alley that ran between Storrow Drive and the brownstones. Bobby drove slowly on the narrow street.

"Your buddy Roland's going to live," said Bobby.

"Imagine my relief." I looked at a bum picking through a trashcan.

"Of course, the same can't be said of Dmitri Petracovich."

"So that's his name."

"Jael called me and said she'd popped him."

"She actually said *popped him*?"

"Oh no, she said something like 'I have killed the gangster who was threatening Tucker.' But she meant that she popped him. He was a bastard. She made the world a better place."

I settled deeper into my seat, wishing that we could just get to the hospital. Each breath was painful. I definitely had a broken rib. Bobby bumped along, stopping at each alphabetized street to look for traffic: Hereford, Gloucester, Fairfield.

He said, "So, did you ever find it?"

"Find what?"

"That single key that opens all the locks."

"Yeah, I found it." I dug into my pocket and pulled out Dmitri's thumb drive. Handed it to Bobby. "Here you go."

"What's this?"

"It's the key. A video of Jack killing Courtney Acres. It started the whole thing."

"How?"

"Dmitri had a porn site called PimpCam. He used a secret camera to video guys screwing hookers. Then he sold the videos online. The cameras usually caught normal stuff. You know, some fat marketing exec humping a teenager."

Bobby interrupted. "Then he caught Jack killing Courtney."

"Yeah. Dmitri recognized Jack because he and Roland had been exploiting high-tech startup CEOs for years. They'd sell them cheap engineering services, and then loan money to the promising companies at ridiculous rates. Dmitri and Roland must have taken this video to Jack and demanded that he give them something huge."

"And Jack promised them Rosetta?"

I said, "Right. Dmitri made Jack hire Roland to keep an eye on things, and Roland hired Alice to package the code."

Bobby said, "They fired you and killed Carol to make room for Roland and Alice."

Bobby was close to the last piece. But I didn't want to give it to him. Instead I said, "They got suspicious of Alice, and decided to kill her. Jack must have jumped up and down and said, 'Ooh ooh. Let me do it.'"

Bobby said, "But why did they kill Carol? Why not just fire the two of you?"

I said, "Damn, it really hurts to breathe."

"Almost there, buddy. We'll have a doc fix you up."

Bobby was true to his word. The doc gave me a pill for the pain and popped the rib back into place. He stitched my lip and told me to ice my hand. He said I should go home and rest. I was glad to get out of there. I needed to get onto the Internet.

I went home and fired up my computer. A little poking around showed me the movie I had expected to find. I watched it a couple of times. When I was done, tears had run down my face. I wiped my eyes, blew my nose, and got dressed. I was heading to Revere. I was going to say goodbye to Kevin. I hoped Charlene wouldn't mind.

SIXTY-TWO

KEVIN DIDN'T LOOK LIKE himself. He didn't look peaceful. He didn't look like he was in a better place. He just looked dead.

He was wearing the Boston Bruins tie that Charlene had bought for him when the Bruins won the Cup for the first time in forty years. He never liked that tie, but it was a gift from Charlene so he had praised it and worn it regularly.

"He always loved that tie," said Charlene, who had materialized next to me.

"Yes," I said. "He did." I turned to leave. "I'll get out of here."

Charlene touched my arm and said, "No. Please stay."

"You're OK with me?"

"Of course. I'm sorry, Tucker. I was a mess. I never meant those things."

"No need to apologize. Poor Kevin."

"You were his best friend. He loved you. I'm glad you're here."

Charlene started to weep, and that set me off. My eyes filled and my throat burned. Charlene handed me a tissue from the wad she was carrying, and I dabbed my eyes.

She said, "He loved her, you know."

I said, "Who?"

"Carol. Not in a bad way. But his eyes would light up when he'd see her."

"I never noticed that."

"You're a man." Apparently that explained it. She continued, "It was an innocent thing, but it bothered me. Then he came home Saturday night all excited about solving her murder, and the next day they killed him."

I opened and closed my mouth several times, trying out things to say. I had nothing to offer but sorrow. I was lost in my silence when Dana appeared.

"Charlene, I'm so sorry," Dana said. And Charlene bent at the waist to hug the much shorter woman. Dana's mascara had been mixed with tears and smudged against her eyes. Her small arms wrapped around Charlene's shoulders. I could see red patches on her wrists where I had torn the tape away. It amazed me that she was here.

I let the women commiserate and knelt in front of Kevin.

"I thought I'd let the girls have their moment," I told him. I waited, half-expecting to see him standing over my shoulder.

Kevin's lips were glued together, and I could see the edges of the foundation where the mortician had given him color. His eyes were shut, and a little crucifix was intertwined with his fingers. "You're really not coming back, are you?"

Kevin's dead mouth remained motionless.

"Because, you know, if you ever want to do some haunting, I'd be up for that."

The fingernails were drained of color. The crucifix caught the light, but didn't twinkle. It was a static symbol. I reached out and covered it with my hand. Kevin's fingers were dead. I remembered Kevin using his fingers to measure his Scotch. "Two fingers, then ice." That's what he used to say. Now his fingers might have been made of wax.

I said, "So long, buddy."

I stood and turned to see Charlene and Dana watching me. I hugged Charlene and pecked her on the cheek. "I'll see you tomorrow morning."

"Thank you for coming, Tucker," she said.

Dana followed me into the parking lot.

"How are you doing?" I asked.

Dana said, "Not so good. If it were anyone but Kevin, I wouldn't be here. I'm going home to my parents for a few weeks."

"Are you coming back to Boston?"

"Eventually."

"Can I call you?"

"You had better. Otherwise I'll break into your apartment again."

We hugged and kissed a goodbye. I got in my car.

"Heading home?" Dana asked.

"Going over to the beach," I said. "I've got to see someone."

SIXTY-THREE

I SAT IN THE dark on Revere Beach and watched Graves Light blinking in the darkness. The night air was chilly. The sand was damp, and the surf pounded onto the shore, still agitated by the recent storms. I was alone on the beach, which curved away in a big arc that eventually formed Nahant.

"Aren't you cold, baby?" asked Carol. She sat next to me, her plum funeral dress shimmering slightly in the night. The ocean breeze waved strands of her black hair. Her dress outlined her thighs as she got comfortable.

"Yeah, I'm a little cold." I looked back at the ocean. It had been a long day. It would be a tough night. "I figured it out, you know."

"I know," said Carol. "Congratulations."

"I just have to wonder why."

"Why I was killed?"

"No. Why you betrayed me."

Carol was silent. She looked out toward the sea. Her eyes filled. She had been appearing to me for months, taunting, helping, guiding, but also hiding something I hadn't wanted to see.

She asked, "How did you know?"

"It was the timing."

She nodded, her lip trembling.

I continued. "I saw Margaret's demo in her booth. Her software was a year-old version of our project."

Tears were rolling down Carol's cheeks.

I said, "Alice couldn't have given Rosetta to her, because you hired Alice nine months ago. You gave Margaret our source code."

Carol blew air out between her lips. She wiped at her nose with her hand.

"Was it the money?" I asked.

The dam burst and Carol sobbed. She didn't cover her face. Her arms lay at her sides, palms up as the tears spilled. She tried to speak, but couldn't get the words out. Her sobs twisted my gut, and I wished I could trade places with her. Take her pain away. But I couldn't even hold her, so I stared straight ahead and focused on the blinking lighthouse.

Carol's tears slowed. "The money? You know I never cared about the money."

"Then why?"

"To get you back from that horrible project. I hated Rosetta, and Nate, and Huey, and the whole company, because they took you away from me. I loved you, baby, and I lost you to them."

"I was right there," I said. "I was there the whole time."

"You know what I mean. You were mentally gone. Emotionally gone. You weren't there for me anymore. You lived for that horrible project. It was all you talked about."

Carol's tears had stopped and her breathing slowed as she spoke. "One day I caught Jack trying to make a copy of the code. He told me he was debugging it, but that was ridiculous. I could see what he was doing. He asked me what it would take for me to keep quiet about it. I told him that I'd make the copy for him if he'd fire you. I missed you so much. It just slipped out. It was stupid."

I nodded. Kevin had been right. If I had known the real reason Nate fired me, the whole thing would have fallen into place.

"Then I was trapped and it all went bad," Carol continued.

"The movies," I said.

"That bastard Dmitri saw me. He actually walked up to me in Jack's office and grabbed my boob, then he turned to Jack and Roland said, 'Real ones. Wery nice' in that fucking accent. He said that if I didn't make movies, Jack would tell the police that I was selling your software. I'd get arrested and I'd lose you."

"Whose idea was it to do lesbian scenes?"

"Mine. I told them I wouldn't do it with guys. I didn't want to cheat on you. So they made me do things with Alice while that bastard Roland watched."

"I know. I found your movie on that website."

Carol looked at the sand. "What did you think?"

"It was the first time porn made me cry."

Carol stared into the sand. I peeked under her chin, and she was smiling her little "that's not supposed to be funny" smile. She looked up at me, her blue eyes glistening.

She asked, "Why did Dmitri kill me? I did everything he wanted."

I sighed and said, "You set yourself up."

"What?"

"Jack finally got Nate to fire me. With me gone, they lost their hold over you. You became a loose end."

"And Dmitri cleaned up the loose end."

"Yeah."

Carol stood and I followed her lead. We looked out over the water. We were silent, breathing the salty air and listening to the rushing surf.

Carol said, "We were good together, weren't we?"

"We were great."

"Remember that time we did this on the Cape, in Wellfleet? Looked out at the ocean? That was the night we built a bonfire, and stayed by it and drank tequila until the beach was empty."

I said, "I remember. It was the first time I'd made love on a beach."

"The first time for me too, you know."

"Yeah, and the last."

Carol laughed. "Oh my God! Wasn't it horrible? We got all gross and sandy and then we passed out and almost got caught sleeping there. What a hangover. I still hate tequila."

I could feel a change coming. Carol's dress was shimmering more brightly. The string of lights from Nahant began to appear through her, like stars in the evening. She looked down at herself, then back at me. She smiled.

Carol said, "I have to go."

"I know."

"You'll be all right now." She looked at the lighthouse and back at me. "Can you forgive me?"

"Of course, you silly girl. I love you."

"Goodbye, baby."

I closed my eyes. A breeze came in off the water, and I felt Carol's lips brush mine as her hand traced across my neck. I caught a whiff of her perfume. Then she was gone.

I opened my eyes. Graves Light winked in the distance. I turned and walked up the beach.